KNOT IN

"Go home and look at your new quilt," Lucy said. "Maybe working on it will help you make sense out of all those pieces floating around in your head."

I drove back home, determined to follow Lucy's advice. The thermometer on my dashboard put the outside temperature in the nineties. I rushed from the air-conditioning of my car to the cool interior of my house. I cleaned up the coffee cups and donut crumbs, put in a load of laundry and made my bed.

As I worked, I kept wondering about Dax Martin the loving husband, father and beloved coach and Dax Martin the pompous jerk and bully.

A savage beating indicated his killing was personal, an act of rage. Who was Dax Martin really, and who did he piss off so fatally?

Also by Mary Marks

FORGET ME KNOT

Published by Kensington Publishing Corporation

KNOT IN MY BACKYARD

WITHDRAWN

MARY MARKS

KENSINGTON PUBLISHING CORP.

http://www.kensingtonbooks.com

KENSINGTON BOOKS are published by

Kensington Publishing Corp.
119 West 40th Street
New York, NY 10018

All Kensington Titles, Imprints, and Distributed Lines are available at special quantity discounts for bulk purchases for sales promotions, premiums, fund-raising, and educational or institutional use. Special book excerpts or customized printings can also be created to fit specific needs. For details, write or phone the office of the Kensington special sales manager: Kensington Publishing Corp., 119 West 40th Street, New York, NY 10018, attn: Special Sales Department, Phone: 1-800-221-2647.

Kensington and the K logo Reg. U.S. Pat & TM Off.

ISBN-13: 978-0-7582-9207-0
ISBN-10: 0-7582-9207-4
First Kensington Mass Market Edition: November 2014

eISBN-13: 978-0-7582-9208-7
eISBN-10: 0-7582-9208-2
First Kensington Electronic Edition: November 2014

10 9 8 7 6 5 4 3 2 1

Printed in the United States of America

This book is dedicated to
the source of my *nachas*:
Olivia & Chloe, Genevieve, Makayla,
Lilliana, Danielle, Oliver & Camille,
and Chyanne & Chelsea.
Nine girls, one boy, three sets of twins. *Oy!*

ACKNOWLEDGMENTS

Heartfelt gratitude goes to my mentor, Jerrilyn Farmer, and my critique partners, Cyndra Gernet and Lori Dillman. Along with Dawn Dowdle, from Blue Ridge Literary Agency, you all made me so much better than I started out to be.

For technical help I'm indebted, as always, to Linda Greenberg Loper, retired Deputy DA, LA County—my source for all things legal. Also invaluable was the expertise of the very observant and somewhat legendary David Ham, Senior Lead Officer, LAPD West Valley Division.

And, finally, a big thank-you to John Scognamiglio and all the wonderful folks at Kensington, who work so hard to help this cozy-mystery author.

Writing this book was particularly satisfying for me because, although purely fictional, it was inspired by true events perpetrated by the US Army Corps of Engineers. If you want to know more, Google "Sepulveda Basin Wildlife Reserve Devastation."

CHAPTER 1

Yesterday I joined Weight Watchers for the eighth time. The lecturer, Charlissa, told me to get rid of all the bad food in my house and take a walk every day. So I did what she said, confident *this time* I'd work the program successfully.

After a breakfast of egg whites scrambled in one teaspoon of olive oil, I bent over to put on my new white athletic shoes. The top of my size-sixteen Liz Claiborne stretch denim jeans dug into my waistline. No doubt about it. At the age of fifty-five, I, Martha Rose, was outgrowing the largest clothes in my closet. I didn't think I could feel any worse today, but I was dead wrong.

I lived with my orange cat, Bumper, in a friendly residential area of the San Fernando Valley. Directly behind my house stood a fenced-off baseball field. A ritzy private school, whose nearby campus ran out of room, had muscled their way in and built a large new stadium on park land right behind our quiet street.

On the far side of the field, less than two hundred yards away, the Los Angeles River flowed east through the San Fernando Valley, crossing Glendale to Downtown LA, and out to sea at Long Beach. I planned to walk around the perimeter of the field to the bank of the river and back again. What a mistake.

In the summertime, the air can sizzle by noon. At eight this morning in late August, the temperature had already reached seventy-nine degrees. Gravel crunched under the rubber soles of my new shoes as I ambled along a dry path just outside the tall chain-link fence around the baseball field and onto the riverbank. No bushes were allowed to grow on the near side, the private-school side of the river. Only small weeds and grasses parched in the heat. Thick coyote brush, deer weed, and cottonwood trees topped the far side of the riverbank.

Concrete covered the bottom of the river, and the slopes were sprayed with stucco, courtesy of the Army Corps of Engineers. In the wintertime, rain-water from the mountains transformed the LA River into a raging, swift-water death trap. Someone managed to drown in it every year. After the rainy season ended, the river dried to just a trickle. This day in late August, only a thin thread of brown water inched downstream.

Something scuttled through the dense brush on the far side of the river. The fluffy brindled tail of a coyote appeared just before he disappeared into the landscape. I also made out bits of color hidden beneath the larger bushes, flashes of metal and plastic. I could barely identify a couple of sleeping bags and what looked like a cooking pot. Those bushes sheltered the homeless almost year round. I just couldn't detect anyone there at the moment. The homeless knew how to become invisible.

As I walked on, I saw a large heap of clothing come into view about ten yards ahead. At first, I thought some people had used this isolated spot to dump their trash. When I walked closer, I made out the body of a man lying tangled inside the dark jeans and maroon-and-gold baseball jersey. The dark red ground underneath his battered head crawled with ants and flies. His jaw hung open at an unnatural angle, and I didn't need to check his pulse to know he didn't have one.

The shaking started somewhere in my knees, and my stomach pushed up toward my throat. This was the second time in four months I'd discovered a dead body. My head started to float away—déjà vu all over again.

The first time I'd been with my quilting friends, Lucy Mondello and Birdie Watson, when we discovered the murdered body of another quilter. I was the one who eventually figured out the identity of the killer. The guy who worked the case was Arlo Beavers, a tall, hunky LAPD homicide detective, with a white mustache.

Beavers and I have been dating since then, which is kind of surprising since we started off on the wrong foot. He kept warning me to stop poking around the investigation. In the end, he was right. Because I refused to stop searching for answers on my own, I was thrown in jail and almost killed. After that, I promised myself and my friends I'd just quilt like a normal person and leave the policing to the pros.

And now, I had to tell him I just stumbled on what was obviously another murder. How would he react? Still staring at the dead man, I pulled my cell phone out of my pocket with badly shaking hands. Thank goodness Beavers was on speed dial.

"Arlo, it's me. I just found a dead body."

He laughed. There was a long silence. "You're kidding, right?"

I looked over at the body again. "I'm on the far side of the baseball field behind my house. He's lying on the banks of the wash. There's so much blood. I feel sick."

Then I moaned as I felt my stomach rising.

Beavers shouted through the phone, "Martha? Martha!"

I doubled over and threw up all over my new white Skechers.

I just realized I knew the dead man.

CHAPTER 2

I shuffled backward, dust forming a crust on my soiled shoes, until I hit the chain-link fence separating the well-manicured green outfield from the semi-wilderness of the watershed. I collapsed against the fence and slid down to the ground, waiting for the police to show up. So much for my walking career!

Moments later, sirens sounded. A young patrolman squatted next to me and his nose twitched when he glanced at my soiled shoes. "You all right, ma'am?"

"My pants are too tight."

He frowned with concern, looked over his shoulder, and waved a paramedic toward me. "She's in shock."

Beavers got there just as the guy removed the blood pressure cuff from my arm.

"Really, I'm fine!" I struggled to get up. The snap on my waistband popped open. Then two strong men lifted me by my arms to a standing position.

In contrast to my short plumpness, Beavers stood a lean six feet tall. His Native American eyes searched mine for reassurance I was all right. He wrapped his arm around my shoulders and gently led me toward my house. "I'm going to walk you home, Martha. What were you doing back here?"

I pushed my glasses back on my nose. "Just taking a little stroll." I wasn't going to admit I needed to lose weight, just in case he hadn't yet noticed the extra pounds. "I came across the body and called you. Then I kind of got sick when I realized I knew the guy."

Beavers stopped walking and stared at me. "Good God, Martha. Not again."

I just looked down and continued to walk. "His name is Dax Martin. He's the head baseball coach for the Joshua Beaumont School. This is their baseball field."

"How do *you* know a baseball coach?" Beavers knew my idea of extreme sports was a one-hour stroll through a quilt show.

"We've had run-ins with him before."

"Who's 'we'?"

"Me and my neighbors. Long story."

When we got to my front door, I had to fish the keys out of my pocket with my fingertips. There wasn't room for my whole hand. Once inside, I turned on the air-conditioning, put my dirty shoes in the laundry room, and poured two glasses of water. We sat in my newly renovated kitchen, with its apricot-colored marble countertops and largely unused stainless-steel appliances. He leaned forward. "So, what exactly do you know about this guy?"

I closed my eyes. A migraine began to pound on the right side of my head. "He's an arrogant jock who works for a fancy private school. Their new school year started last week. During baseball season, they invade our community with lights, noise, and traffic. When they're done, they leave tons of trash on our streets. We complained to him many times, but he just ignored us."

He squinted at me. "Did you ever try going over his head? Contacting whoever runs the school?"

"Yeah. Several times. But what you saw back there isn't just a high-school baseball field. It's a million-dollar stadium. Those parents are rich and power-ful. They expect the full Monty when they watch their boys play baseball. Do you think they care how their monstrosity impacts us?"

My Encino community was a well-defined and closely knit one. When our midcentury homes were built, the surrounding parks and river ensured an almost rural ambiance. Horseback riders from nearby farms used to amble where the private base-ball stadium now stood.

"The new stadium with the two-story building and the two-story scoreboard has destroyed our view of the neighboring parks and mountains. Their loudspeakers prevent us from enjoying our own backyards. Our properties have been devalued by at least thirty percent because of them."

"Dax Martin was responsible for all of this?"

"Well, he certainly liked to take credit. He served

as the public face of the Beaumont School during construction. Once I saw him give a television interview and I wanted to kill him myself."

"Can you think of anyone who could have done this?"

"You mean like everyone living in all of the four hundred houses here?" The muscles in my neck tightened. I got up from the sofa. "I'm going to have to take something for this headache."

"I've got to get back to the crime scene. We'll talk later." He stood and kissed me on the forehead.

I closed the front door behind him and headed for the medicine cabinet. I actually did know someone who might have a special reason to kill Dax Martin, but I didn't want to tell Beavers just yet. I didn't want to bring my friend more tsuris than he already had.

CHAPTER 3

After about twenty minutes, the meds kicked in and my headache receded. I picked up the phone and called my best friend, Lucy.

"Hey, Martha."

"I found someone murdered in the wash behind my house this morning."

Silence.

"Say something."

"Oh, for heaven's sake! This can't be happening again. What in the world were you doing in the *wash*?"

"Walking. I was beside it, not in it. Charlissa from Weight Watchers told me to walk every day."

"Since when are you going to Weight Watchers?"

"Since yesterday." Even though Lucy gave birth to five sons, she looked like a beanpole. I should be so lucky.

"Who died?"

"The baseball coach at the Joshua Beaumont School. Dax Martin. Looked to me like he was bludgeoned to death. I called Arlo, and he brought me home."

"Are you okay? Do you need me to come over?"

"Well, I do have a little dilemma. Since we've had such trouble with that school, Arlo asked me if I knew of anyone in the neighborhood who might have wanted the man dead."

"You've told me over the years about the conflicts with the Beaumont School. I'm guessing almost nobody in your neighborhood will be sad the coach is gone."

"Actually, I thought of someone who's bound to become a suspect, but I didn't want to tell Arlo."

"Who?"

I shifted the phone to my other ear. "Ed Pappas. You know him from my Hanukkah parties."

After my back surgery a few years ago, my young neighbor Ed Pappas watered my yard and took care of my trash barrels. I invited him to my Hanukkah party that year, where he met all my family and friends. From then on, he became like a son. He still took out my trash barrels every week and did odd repair jobs when I needed them done.

"Of course. He's always seemed like a nice young man. Doesn't he have motorcycles parked in his driveway sometimes? If he hangs around with a biker crowd, he might have a darker side."

"Not all bikers are outlaws. A lot of regular working guys belong to biker clubs. They're not gang members. They just ride for recreation. And, anyway, he can't have a dark side. Ed does yoga."

"Well, why would he be a suspect, then?"

"Ed's place is directly across from the Beaumont School loudspeakers. The noise they blast goes right into his house. He stormed over there one day and got into a fistfight with Dax Martin. Ed threatened to kill him if he didn't turn the volume down. The police were called and arrested Ed for assault. Since then, the noise has been even louder. Ed's life is hell on the days Beaumont uses the field."

"You're right. This doesn't look good for Ed. What are you going to do?"

"I'm going to talk to him before I say anything to Arlo, and I need to talk to him soon. It's just a matter of time before the police figure out the connection."

"Now listen, girlfriend. I think you should back away from this. You're going to upset Arlo. Just let him do his job."

"Look, poor Ed's in enough trouble for hitting Martin. I couldn't live with myself if I sat by and did nothing while he became a suspect in Martin's murder."

"How do you know he'll be home? Doesn't he work?"

"He's a computer guy. Works from home."

"Then wait for me and I'll go with you."

Fifteen minutes later, Lucy arrived; she was wearing rose-colored capris and a pink blouse. My friend always dressed with a theme. Without exception, including today, everything always matched perfectly. A pink-sapphire-and-diamond bracelet her husband recently gave her hung from her wrist.

We wasted no time and started down the street

toward Ed's house. Lucy walked like a sixty-year-old runway model going to war. Her very short, bright orange hair shone in the sunlight atop her five-foot-eleven-inch frame. I wasn't so graceful. I really worked my shorter legs to keep up with her, while my salt-and-pepper curls bounced around my face.

"Martha! Wait up!" shouted a female voice behind me.

I turned.

Sonia Spiegelman rushed across the street toward Lucy and me. The last thing I wanted was a conversation with Sonia, the neighborhood yenta. If she knew what we were up to, our entire Encino neighborhood would also know in thirty seconds.

Sonia panted slightly as she caught up to us. A dozen delicate Indian bangle bracelets tinkled on her arm, a remnant of her flower child days with Mick Jagger. "Did you hear what happened? They found a murdered body behind the baseball fields. I saw your cop boyfriend's car in front of your house earlier, so I figured he must have told you. What did he say?"

"Hello, Sonia. This is my friend Lucy."

"Oh, sorry." Sonia glanced at Lucy. She held out her hand and smiled. "Nice to meet you."

Then she turned to me again, with eyebrows raised. "So, do you know what happened? Who died?" Sonia probed without shame and was more than willing to share what she knew. And she usually knew a lot.

I glanced at Lucy, who briefly rolled her eyes.

"Um, the police aren't sure. Sorry, but I don't know more." I shrugged.

"So, are you guys going for a walk, or what?"

"Yes."

She seemed to be waiting for an invitation to join us, but I wasn't going to give her one. Sonia was harmless but annoying.

After a rather long minute of disappointed silence, Sonia shrugged. "Well, I guess I'll be going."

Lucy smiled. "Bye, Sonia. Nice to meet you."

We turned away and walked slowly down the street, waiting for Sonia to disappear inside her house. As soon as she walked out of sight, we doubled back to Ed's front door. I knocked, but nobody answered. We were about to turn away, when I heard someone moving inside.

The door opened a crack and Ed gave me a warm grin. Handsome, early thirties, light brown hair, and stubble on his jaw, he looked more like a movie star than an outlaw biker with a dark side. He wore his summer uniform of khaki shorts, flip-flops, and a blue striped tank top showing off a tattoo of the Greek flag on his left shoulder.

"Hey, Martha, 'sup?"

"Hi, Ed. My friend Lucy and I were taking a walk and I decided to see if you were home. There's something you really need to know."

"Is this about all the police activity out back by the river?"

"Yes. Can we come in?"

Ed opened the door wider and moved aside. We stepped into a dark, north-facing living room with sliding glass doors opening to the backyard. Beyond the back fence, several patrol cars were parked on the street.

In the ball field directly behind the squad cars stood a two-story structure the size of a small apartment building made of corrugated metal painted maroon and gold, completely blocking Ed's view of the San Gabriel Mountains beyond.

Ed stared bitterly at the eyesore. "That's what I have to look at every minute of every day."

When the Joshua Beaumont School began renovating the existing Little League field two years ago, no one in the neighborhood suspected that they were actually planning to build a million-dollar baseball stadium. Nor did we ever suspect they could get away with erecting an ugly two-story building obliterating the view of several homes on our street. By the time the neighbors found out, the project was a fait accompli. The houses nearest the field suffered the most, especially Ed's.

"I used to enjoy working in my yard." He turned his back to the maroon-and-gold atrocity looming only sixty feet away. "Now I can't stand to go out there." He waved toward his dry, weedy backyard, complete with an empty hot tub, fading in the sun. This young bachelor liked to have the occasional barbeque, but clearly no one had been in the backyard for months.

"I'm so sorry, Ed. Beaumont School has given you more than your share of grief."

"Yeah. After the relative quiet of summer, the new school year has started and those kids are back there, practicing every afternoon again. It's just a matter of time before they have their first game of 'fall ball.' Between the noise and the ugly view . . . well, I'd like to blow the bastards up! Oh, sorry."

"We've heard that word before." I smiled. "Everyone feels the same."

"So, what's the deal?" He offered Lucy and me seats on his leather sofa.

"Dax Martin is dead. I found his body this morning on the riverbank behind the field."

"You? Found? No kidding!" He looked genuinely surprised. "What happened?"

"Someone murdered him. There was a lot of blood. I don't really know any more."

"I can't say I'm sorry," he mumbled.

Lucy tilted her head slightly and looked toward Ed. "Martha's told me about the troubles with the school. Why didn't you go to the police? There are laws against noise pollution."

"You don't understand." Ed swept his hands through the air in frustration. "Beaumont School is bulletproof. The mayor, the police chief, the DA, and half the city council are either alumni or send their kids. Some of those very kids play baseball at that stadium."

"Why don't you all get together and hire a lawyer?" She looked at both of us.

Ed sighed. "Because they've got a bunch of high-priced lawyers—school parents who'll defend their cause for free. And some of the other parents? They're the ones who're supposed to enforce those laws. They make sure our complaints are buried.

Our resources are limited. We're no match for them."

"There must be something you can do."

The corner of Ed's mouth twitched slightly. "Actually, I've been doing some research online. I think I might have uncovered something wonky between the school and the City of Los Angeles. I discovered plans for the stadium were never submitted for approval to the city, and the city never sent out an inspector during construction. Same thing for the environmental impact report. So, far as I can tell, no records are on file for reports, permits, inspections—nothing."

Lucy looked puzzled. "How can you build a million-dollar stadium without city approval?"

Ed shrugged. "I've tried to find out from the Army Corps of Engineers. They manage all the land in the Sepulveda Flood Control Basin—all the open land west of the Sepulveda Dam, including the area behind us where the Beaumont Stadium sits. So far, they've refused to hand over any of their records. They'll only admit to leasing the land to Beaumont, but they won't release the terms of the agreement."

She frowned. "Wait a minute. What about the Freedom of Information Act? Can't you compel them under the law?"

"I've tried, but apparently the US Attorney's Office has better things to do than force the army to comply with my requests. I've been stonewalled at every turn."

I still wasn't sure how this tied in with Martin's

Lucy just shook her head. "Arlo Beavers isn't your enemy. Why can't you just relax and trust him to do his job?"

Lucy was right. After my cheating psychiatrist husband left me and my daughter, Quincy, a couple of decades ago, I could never let myself get too close to any man. Even one, like Beavers, who seemed to really like me. Still, you never knew when someone might just up and leave.

CHAPTER 4

As Lucy and I neared my yard, the coroner's van drove in the direction of the Joshua Beaumont field. By the time we got to my front door, Beavers drove past and followed the van around the corner.

Lucy looked at me. "That was fast. He couldn't have been at your neighbor's house for more than two minutes."

"Yeah. I guess he must have been called back to the crime scene."

I still felt a little queasy from the morning's shock, so Lucy made some tea and we went to my sewing room to audition some red fabric for a new quilt. The room was painted in a soft dove gray, the perfect neutral background for evaluating colors.

Quilters have a special relationship with cotton cloth. Most of us can't resist buying quite a few of the thousands of choices available in stores. Fabric comes in all sizes, from five-inch squares to many yards.

Over time, I've collected hundreds of pieces for

my stash. The amount I buy depends on what I think I'll use it for—small pieces for quilt blocks, larger ones for background and borders, and up to nine yards for the backing of a large bed-sized quilt.

I pulled out a number of red prints and smiled at Lucy. "One of my favorite things about designing a new quilt is going through my stash and fondling the fabric. My fingertips feel happy."

"I know what you mean." She smiled back. "Sorting through your fabric is like visiting old friends."

We lined up the other materials I previously selected for my new quilt and placed each red piece with them to see how they worked together. If the color was off or had too much contrast, we rejected it. High-contrast prints jumped out and dominated the design to the detriment of the overall pattern. Prints that were too much alike made the quilt look dull. Choosing just the right components, however, created sparkle.

Eventually we found three perfect candidates and I decided to use them all: crimson polka dots scattered on cream, scarlet roses on a light blue field, and a tiny black motif marching in orderly lines across a cherry-colored background. I loved traditional quilts made with as many different prints and hues as possible. The more fabrics—the more interesting the quilt.

By the time we were through, the events of the morning seemed far away.

"So, how are things between you and Arlo? Still good?"

"Yeah. Why wouldn't they be?"

"Well, he did seem a little *perturbed* back at Ed's house." Lucy was too polite to say the words "pissed off." She almost never used crude language. I thought her restraint came from years of trying to set a good example for her now-grown five sons.

There was a knock on my front door. An officer stood in a blue uniform. "Ms. Rose? I've come to give you a ride to the station. You need to give us a statement about the body you found this morning."

I shivered with disgust as I remembered my last ride in the back of a police car four months ago. I was arrested and detained overnight in the Van Nuys Jail under grossly unsanitary conditions. I didn't want to repeat any part of the experience.

"Can't I give my statement here? Why do I have to go to the station? I don't have much to tell you. I discovered the body and called the police. That's about all there is."

"The detectives will want to ask you questions, ma'am. Detective Beavers asked me to provide you with transportation to the station."

I looked at Lucy. *Is she just as puzzled as I am? Why doesn't he come here to interview me? Why not drive me himself? What's going on?*

Lucy shrugged and gave a slight shake of her head.

I turned back to the officer. "Okay, I'm coming, but I'll drive myself. I don't like riding in police cars."

Lucy took out her keys. "I'll drive. You're in no shape to be behind the wheel right now."

I took one last gulp of tea, locked the front door,

and slid onto the creamy leather seat of Lucy's vintage black Caddy, the kind with huge shark fins on the back.

I left Lucy waiting near the front desk while the officer escorted me into a blue interview room of the West Valley Police Station on Vanowen Street. I waited for fifteen minutes, expecting Beavers to show up. When the door finally opened, I stiffened. Kaplan walked in.

Detective Kaplan was Beavers's younger partner. The jerk arrested me four months ago, causing me a lot of unnecessary grief. In the aftermath, he never apologized for his behavior. I couldn't stand him.

I looked in the hallway, but no one else was there. "Where's Detective Beavers?"

With his combination of liquid brown eyes, olive skin, and curly black hair, Kaplan was probably irresistible to young women and girls. To me, however, he was just an arrogant little punk.

He looked at me with a slight smirk, which I immediately wanted to slap away. "The LAPD has a policy. Detectives cannot interview the women they're sleeping with."

I glared at him. "I guess that means where you're concerned, all the hookers in LA can breathe a sigh of relief!"

Kaplan's eyes blazed, and he opened his mouth to respond, but he must have thought better of it. After a beat, he said, "Just tell me about this morning."

"I went for a walk and saw the body. I called Detective Beavers. I didn't touch anything. When

I realized I knew the victim—Dax Martin—I threw up. Then I sat down and waited for the police to show up. EMTs briefly examined me and then Detective Beavers escorted me back to my house. The end."

Kaplan was far from done. He kept me there for another half hour, asking questions about how I knew Martin and digging for details about the relationship between the neighbors and Joshua Beaumont School.

"I went to Beaumont myself," he interjected at one point.

That explains everything!

I tried my best to protect Ed Pappas. I read his name upside down on a folder sitting in front of Kaplan on the table and assumed the contents must have been Ed's arrest record from his fistfight with Martin. But I knew Kaplan wouldn't be interested in my opinions.

"Have you seen any of the homeless people back there in the wash? Can you describe any of them?"

"Do you think one of the homeless people killed him?" I had, in fact, heard Dax Martin brag on television how he and his assistant coaches periodically visited the occasional person camping out behind his ball field. The coaches cleared out "those losers" so his young ballplayers wouldn't have to look at them. He actually winked at the interviewer. I wouldn't blame the homeless if they had killed Martin.

"I ask the questions here."

Give me a break.

"No. I've never actually seen any of them. They purposely stay out of sight. I don't think they want any trouble."

I spoke from firsthand experience. Four months ago, I met a homeless woman, Hilda. She sold me a discarded baby quilt, which turned out to be the key to finding a killer. Hilda worked hard every day to support herself by collecting recyclables and way overcharging me for information. She was a real entrepreneur and harmless.

"Well, they're about to get a whole truckload of trouble."

Oh, please. My daughter, Quincy, was around the same age as Kaplan. I hoped she never got involved with someone like him.

As Lucy drove me back home, she asked, "Arlo didn't interview you, did he?"

I shook my head, still seething at Kaplan's crude remark.

"I imagine interviewing you is no longer kosher," continued my Catholic friend. "After all, you two are dating."

"Guess so," I snapped.

Lucy pulled up to the front of my house and smiled. "See you in the morning at Birdie's." For the last fifteen years, Lucy, Birdie, and I got together to quilt every Tuesday morning—no matter what.

"Thanks for everything, Luce. See you tomorrow."

I closed the car door and stood in the ninety-degree heat as I watched Lucy drive away. Five motorcycles sat in Ed's driveway. He loved his Harley and, in the days before the baseball stadium, used to have his friends over for parties after riding all day.

As far as I could tell, the guys in Ed's biker club always behaved respectfully to the neighbors. Even so, some of the locals were freaked out by the men's matching leather vests that had *VE* painted on the back in big purple letters.

A biker I'd never seen before stood in front of Ed's place, the kind of guy you'd remember: a white male, well over six feet, and weighing about three hundred pounds of solid muscle. He looked like a golem, wearing a black leather vest and a red bandana do-rag. He watched me closely as Lucy drove away.

CHAPTER 5

I cracked open a can of diet cola and sat down at the kitchen table. My large cat, Bumper, jumped up on my lap. "Hey, handsome!" I smoothed his fluffy orange fur. He rewarded me with an affectionate purr and settled on top of my thighs, one of his favorite soft places to rest.

I couldn't get the picture out of my head of Dax Martin and his fellow coaches harassing the poor homeless people behind the ball field. Did one of them fight back and kill Martin? They'd probably never get the chance. Bullies, like Dax Martin, rarely did their dirty work alone. If you scratched the surface of most bullies, you'd find a coward. If Martin tangled with the homeless, he wouldn't have gone in without backup.

Without support, Martin would have stayed within the safety of the fenced-off ball field. So, what drew him to the river's edge in back of the field? How did his killer lure him there? He must have felt safe enough to go there alone. Did Martin trust his attacker? Did he know him?

What about the homeless? Was anyone hiding there who might have seen the attack? If I could find a witness, maybe I could help Ed Pappas. I wouldn't actually be searching for the killer. I knew how mad Beavers would be if he thought I was poking my nose in police business again.

No, I only would be looking for one piece of the puzzle. I only wanted to help clear Ed as a suspect.

I needed to find Hilda. My stomach growled as I got in my Corolla and drove south toward Ventura Boulevard (known as "the Boulevard" or simply "Ventura" to local residents). She hung out in front of a strip mall wedged between two tall office buildings on Ventura, with a great little falafel place I liked to go to. Whenever I saw her sitting in her spot near the sidewalk, I'd stop for a chat and slip her a twenty. I hoped to find her there today.

I pulled into a parking spot halfway down the block and walked toward the mall. Rafi's Falafel was easy to find. You just followed the scent of cumin and hot oil wafting seductively out toward the sidewalk. My watch read three in the afternoon and my last meal had been a virtuous breakfast of scrambled egg whites and coffee, which—come to think of it—hadn't stayed with me long. Technically, I'd eaten zero calories today. Pangs of hunger stabbed me accusingly.

Hilda sat in her usual spot and smiled as I approached. She wasn't old, wasn't young. Her years of living rough etched her with a kind of agelessness and a wary ability to blend into the background. In the heat of the day, her hair clung to her head in moist strings, and her skin looked desiccated. "Hey, Wonder Woman! Caught any bad guys lately?" She burst into laughter at the joke she always greeted me with.

"Hi, Hilda. I'm just on my way to Rafi's for a shawarma. Care to join me? My treat."

"Only if he lets me park by the door. I gotta keep an eye on my cart." Hilda kept her worldly goods in an old shopping cart, along with large black trash bags full of the cans and bottles she collected for recycling, her major source of income.

"Never hurts to ask."

Hilda got up and wheeled her cart near the restaurant and waited for me while I went inside. The interior was refreshingly cool and smelled of cooked meat and spices. Rafi looked up and smiled. He was short, with the dark curly hair and brown skin of a Sephardic Jew from Syria or Iraq.

"Hey!" I waved.

"Martha! Shalom." He pointed to Hilda with his chin *"Ma koreh?"* ("What's happening?")

"My friend Hilda—we want to have lunch in here, but she needs to keep an eye on her cart."

Rafi shook his head sadly. "I see her every day. *Haval.*" ("A shame.") "You know, in Israel, there is no homeless. We take care of poor and old. America's a rich country. I don't understand why anyone live like her."

"Well, can we park her cart near the door so she can see it?"

Rafi shrugged. "Why not?"

I waved to Hilda that the coast was clear. We took a seat at the window.

Rafi came over to our table with a pad and pencil in his hand and looked at Hilda. "Welcome."

"Hi." She smiled, showing remarkably clean teeth.

"What can I get you?"

While we waited for our orders, she drank two glasses of ice water.

"Hilda, do you know anything about the small homeless campsite on the riverbank behind the baseball field north of here?"

Her eyes suddenly narrowed. "Why?"

"I found a dead body back there this morning. He was a baseball coach, but he wasn't killed on the baseball field. He died on the river's edge, right across from someone's camp."

Her voice went flat. "So you're blaming the homeless?"

"Frankly, Hilda, I don't know who's to blame. The police will find out. It's just that one of my neighbors is a suspect, and I'd like to help clear him."

She eyed me suspiciously. "What do you want from me?"

"Looked to me like a couple of sleeping bags were still in the camp. I just want to know if the people living there might have seen what happened. That's all."

Rafi brought our shawarma sandwiches—fresh, spongy pita bread stuffed with a bed of chopped lettuce, tomatoes, onions, and cucumbers. Lying on top were fragrant strips sliced off a rotating stack of succulent lamb and turkey meat. Rafi drenched everything with tahini sauce, which dripped down the sides of the pita. I'd figure out the total Weight Watcher points later.

He also brought a bowl of *hamutzim*—pickled turnips and beets. Extra meat made Hilda's sandwich especially fat. Rafi had a big heart.

We both made short work of our sandwiches; and when Rafi saw we were done, he brought over two golden baklavas dripping with honey. "On the house." He winked at Hilda. "Special for first-time customer."

An idea suddenly popped. "Rafi, what do you do with your cans and bottles?"

"Nothing. I throw them in trash with everything else."

"Well, if you could save them, Hilda could take them off your hands. She already has an arrangement with Sol's Deli down the street."

Hilda raised her eyebrows; she was surprised I remembered something she'd told me four months earlier.

Rafi looked at her. "Sure!" He shrugged. "Why not? I keep separate bag in kitchen. You come every morning at seven to pick up. Otherwise, I throw away. Deal?" He stuck out his hand.

Hilda grinned. "Deal!" She pumped his hand once.

She slurped her tea. "I don't know who camps over there, but I know someone who does know. They call him 'Switch.' He's sort of an unofficial king of a bunch camping all along the river—from the wildlife reserve, off the 405 Freeway and Burbank Boulevard, all the way west."

Hilda referred to a whole area of green space surrounding the LA River, part of the Sepulveda Flood Control Basin operated by the Army Corps of Engineers. The three-mile strip west of the 405 Freeway featured a wildlife reserve, golf courses, and parks—including the one next to our community along the watershed.

These days, nobody ventured into the reserve because unsuspecting joggers and bird-watchers risked being accosted and raped. Police believed the group camping there was also responsible for a lot of local burglaries and drug deals. Citizens were advised to stay away from the area.

"I'd be too afraid to go there." I made a face.

"You'd be right about that. You can't go alone. He knows me. I'll go'n ask if he'll meet with you. If he says yes, then we can go back together, but you'll have to bring a lot of money. Couple hundred bucks. You're gonna have to pay a lot to get anything from him."

"Okay." I hated to think what Beavers would say if he knew what I was about to do.

"Meet me back here tomorrow afternoon. I'll have his answer by then."

I slipped Hilda a twenty and walked back to my car. As I headed home, I wondered what the heck I'd gotten myself into.

CHAPTER 6

I parked in front of my house at four-thirty. Only one police car and a crime scene unit van were parked next to the ball field. Just one Harley remained in Ed's driveway, along with the huge biker in the red bandana. He turned to look at me, frowned, and started moving in my direction. I didn't like the looks of him. I hurried inside, closed the door, and set the alarm. Half a minute later, the doorbell rang.

I never opened my door to strangers. I looked through the peephole in the door. A massive set of shoulders filled it. "Who's there?"

"Crusher."

Oh, my god!

"What do you want?"

"I've been waiting for you."

This guy can break down my door with one blow of his fist.

I stepped backward toward the hall table, where

I'd dumped my purse and cell phone. *How long will it take for the cops to respond?*

"Step back from the door and let me see your face." I clutched my cell phone, ready to call for help if he didn't comply.

"Ed told me to talk to you. You said you wanted to help him, right?"

I went back to the peephole and Crusher had stepped back a little so I could see him better. The bearded giant looked down and held up his hands in a gesture of surrender. Since Ed sent this man, maybe I should hear him out.

I hadn't even realized I'd been holding my breath. I turned off the alarm and opened the door a crack. Crusher glanced at the mezuzah on my door, identifying mine as a Jewish household.

This giant clearly enjoyed the menacing effect he imposed on people. He wore a short-sleeved black T-shirt under his black leather vest, thick denim jeans, and dusty brown work boots. Up close, he looked a lot older than Ed, somewhere in his late forties. Deep lines engraved his forehead under his red bandana do-rag, crow's feet creased the corners of his blue eyes, and his red beard was shot through with gray. His beefy arms were freckled and sunburned, except for a white scar running the length of his right upper arm, bisecting the remnants of an angular tattoo. Crusher had some serious years on him.

I wasn't ready to let him get comfortable, so we stood just at the door. I tentatively stuck out my hand. "I'm Martha Rose."

Crusher nodded once. His calloused hand, stained with black grease, completely enclosed mine like a whale swallowing a minnow. "Yeah. Ed told me."

I pulled my hand away. "Why did he send you?"

"The cops came to question him this morning. They said they were following an anonymous tip. Walked straight to his backyard and found a bloody baseball bat under the bushes. Before they hauled Ed away, he told me to talk to you. Said you'd know why he's being set up."

"Oh, my God. I do know why he's being set up. Just this morning he told me he uncovered some irregularities between the Beaumont School and several government agencies. They know he's digging for information. We can be pretty sure he's made some very powerful enemies. Ed needs a good lawyer. Does he have one?"

Crusher nodded. "One of the guys. He's with Ed now."

"What exactly does Ed want me to do?"

He paused for a second, seeming to size me up. "You're hooked up with a cop. You could get information for us."

I crackled at his suggestion. How dare he ask me to manipulate Beavers! "That's ridiculous. I don't take advantage of my friends." Golem or not, I glowered at the giant and put my fists on my hips.

To my surprise, he smiled a little. Then he threw back his head and laughed from a place deep inside.

"What?"

"You're small but fearless. I like that."

Small? Did he just say small *?* I must admit, standing next to Crusher, I didn't feel the least bit overweight. I stepped aside to let him in the house.

"Would you like some water?"

"No, but I'd sure like to sit down. I've been standing a long time."

My heart sank as he walked inside and headed toward my cream-colored sofa with my favorite blue-and-white quilt draped over the back. I waited tensely for it to collapse under his weight, but I relaxed when only air strangled out of the cushions.

I closed the door and sat in a comfortable overstuffed chair. My living room, painted the color of driftwood, featured neutral-colored upholstery and accents of blues and oranges in the rug and accessories. White linen drapes softly framed the windows. "It's true I want to help Ed, but I'm not willing to take advantage of my friend. Let's just get that off the table right now."

Crusher shifted his weight and the sofa frame groaned. "Okay. I get it, but I know the cops are going to take the easy way out and settle on Ed as the doer. Isn't there anyone else around here who might have had the stones to go after the bastard?"

"I can't think of anyone else. Although, I did notice a couple of sleeping bags and other items under the tall bushes on the other side of the river, right across from the crime scene. I'm thinking there might have been witnesses camping there."

"Or maybe a homeless guy killed the dude. The

cops are probably already tearing up their place right now trying to ID him."

I nodded. "Yeah, but I think I have a better chance of identifying them than the police do."

Crusher's eyebrows pushed together. "How?"

"I've got a friend." I told him about Hilda and my plans to find the guy who lived under the bushes. "She's arranging a meeting with a guy named Switch, a sort of king of the LA River homeless."

"Don't be an idiot! I know this guy. He's a whack job. Gets his name from carrying a six-inch blade. You can't go in there!"

"Watch me."

"Okay now, babe, that's just wrong. Even the cops don't go in there alone."

"I'm not going in there to arrest anyone. I'm going in to buy information. It's just a business deal."

"You can't deal with those lowlifes. They're thieves, pimps, and dealers. Without protection, you could get hurt real bad. Me and the others will have to go with you."

There it is again! Another man telling me what to do. Is bossiness programmed into their DNA?

"Seriously? You guys look a lot scarier than the police. I, on the other hand, am not a threat. I think I'll have better luck alone."

He shook his head. "You're being stubborn, not smart."

Crusher was right. I'd be taking a big chance going unprotected into a den of known criminals. "Fine. I'll ask Hilda what she thinks. She may be homeless, but she's sharp, and I trust her. If she says it's safe, I'm going in, and I'll try to get her to come with me." I paused for a beat. "How'd you get the name 'Crusher,' anyway?"

"I used to be in that line of work."

"What line would that be?"

"Crushing."

I hope he isn't referring to skulls or kneecaps.

He jerked his head slightly toward the street. "You ever ride a bike?"

"What?"

He smiled and ducked his chin a little. "You want to go for a ride sometime?"

"Are you insane? I'm fifty-five years old, for God's sake!"

"So?"

"What's your real name, anyway?"

"I told you. Crusher."

"No, I mean the one you were born with."

His eyes twinkled. "Yossi. Yossi Levy."

Impossible! My brain stopped for a second and I blinked rapidly. Did I hear him right? "You're *Jewish*? There's no such thing as a Jewish biker."

Crusher laughed. He was having way too much fun at my expense.

The knocking on my door pulled me out of my shock. Before I could get up, a key scraped in the lock and Beavers walked into the room. He stood unmoving when he caught sight of Crusher sitting on my sofa. I thought Crusher smiled slightly.

Never taking his eyes off the biker, Beavers said, "Martha?"

I got up and walked over to him. "Hi, Arlo."

He put his arm protectively around my shoulders, still staring at Crusher. "You okay?"

"Why wouldn't I be? This is a friend of my neighbor Ed's." I hesitated, trying to decide whether to introduce him as Crusher or Yossi.

Crusher stood, crossed his arms in front of his massive chest, and took a slow, deliberate breath. He towered over Beavers by a good six inches and far outweighed him.

Beavers's jaw muscle rippled and his frown deepened.

I looked at Crusher. "This is Detective Arlo Beavers."

Beavers still stared at Crusher, who stared back. Must be a guy thing, sort of like pissing on your enemy. "What are you doing here, Levy?"

Surprised, I turned to Beavers. "You know each other?"

Crusher lifted his shoulder to his ear and cracked his neck. "I've seen Detective Beavers at my shop from time to time."

"Your shop?"

Beavers let go of my shoulders and assumed an official posture. "Mr. Levy, here, owns a motorcycle repair shop on Reseda, not too far from the station. We've had occasion to visit him a few times. Mr. Levy's shop is well-known to my colleagues in the department."

He took a protective step in front of me. "So, what are you doing in this house?"

Crusher wasn't here to hurt me, and I wanted Beavers to know it. "Arlo, I—"

Beavers held up a hand to silence me, and I really, really didn't like that.

Crusher watched my reaction and then sneered at Beavers. "Trying to get her on the back of my bike."

The red crept slowly up Beavers's neck. He opened his jacket, exposing his brown leather shoulder holster. In a very quiet, very low voice, he said, "Time to go, Levy."

Crusher looked at me and I nodded rapidly behind Beavers's back. Crusher walked to the front door. "I'll be in touch, babe. Don't forget what we talked about."

He wasn't referring to the back of his bike.

CHAPTER 7

As soon as the door closed, Beavers whirled around and looked at me, fury heating his face. I'd only ever seen him mildly annoyed—say a four on a scale of one to ten. This anger scored an eleven.

"What just happened, Martha? How could you let a guy like him come into the house?"

I walked into the kitchen and put a kettle on the stove, put a couple of bags of Taylor's Scottish Breakfast Tea in a pot, and pulled out two cups. "Before we have this discussion, I'd like to get a few things straight."

Beavers followed me and growled, "Like what?"

Outside, the loud guttering of a Harley-Davidson motor accelerated down the street and off into the distance.

"Like the fact that even though you have a key to this house, you do *not* own this house. You do *not* get to determine who comes or goes in this house."

Beavers's eyes flashed. "Levy is—"

"I'm not through!" I shouted, getting close to

losing it completely. "Even though you and I are together, you do *not* own me. You do *not* get to order me around. You especially do *not* get to silence me in front of others and especially in *my own home!*"

By now, I stood trembling in the middle of the kitchen. "If you ever do that to me again, Arlo, we're through. Done!" Then the horror of the morning and stress of the day came crashing in on me and I started sobbing.

My fury had the effect of calming him. Beavers walked over and wrapped his arms around me. "After everything you went through this morning, I just wanted to be here with you. Then when I saw Levy inside the house . . . he's an ex-con. We've never been able to prove anything, but he operates on the fringes. Now you're telling me he's tight with our chief suspect? I guess I just went into protective mode. I'm so sorry, honey."

I relaxed into his arms until the emotional storm passed. In truth, I liked feeling protected and always felt safe with Beavers.

When the kettle whistled, I fixed two cups of tea. We settled on the sofa and I pulled my feet up and wrapped myself in my favorite blue-and-white quilt. I should be grateful someone wanted to look out for me for a change. Lucy was right; I needed to trust Beavers more.

He sat close to me and we sipped in silence. Then he put down his cup. "So, what was Levy doing here, anyway?"

I had no reason to hold *everything* back, so I told

him what I could, minus the part about my plan to go to the homeless encampment in the wildlife reserve. "Crusher just wanted to know if we could somehow prove Ed innocent of killing Dax Martin."

"What did he have in mind?"

"He wanted to know if any of the other neighbors might have done it."

"What did you tell him?"

"I told him no. But if you want, I'll tell you what I think."

"Go on."

My glasses had slipped down my nose and I pushed them back up. Then I leaned closer toward Beavers. "First of all, I'm pretty sure Martin was killed where he lay. The ground was soaked in way too much blood. Am I right?" I shuddered a little at the memory of the mangled jaw and all those ants.

"Yeah."

I put my cup down. "Okay. Second, we know Dax Martin was a bully. He and his coaches frequently went behind the field to harass the people living along the riverbank. They made a sport out of rousting the homeless. Bullies usually roam in packs, like wild dogs stalking a single sheep."

"So?"

"So I'm pretty sure Martin wouldn't have ventured outside the security of the perimeter fence unless he knew he'd be safe. That means he must have known and trusted his killer. Martin would never have gone out there with Ed Pappas. Martin was soft around the middle and out of shape, despite being a coach. He would've been no match for Ed."

"Maybe, but Pappas is in serious trouble. We found the murder weapon, a bloody baseball bat, in his yard."

"That's not proof of anything. The killer could have tossed the weapon over his back fence." I carried our empty cups to the kitchen and refilled them from the still-warm pot of tea. I loaded a plate with almond biscotti and brought everything back to the living room on a lacquered wooden tray painted with tole roses.

I dunked the end of a biscotti into my tea and told Beavers about the potential scandal Ed discovered involving Beaumont and various government agencies. "I think someone might be framing Ed in order to silence him."

"If you're right about a scandal, Dax Martin was probably right in the middle of it. But why choose him as the victim, especially if he was one of the conspirators?"

Beavers had a point. It was hard to believe some mysterious cabal wanted to stop Ed Pappas from uncovering a scandal so they committed murder and framed Ed for it. Why would they choose Dax Martin as their sacrificial victim?

Occam's razor: the cops would be searching for the simplest motive for the murder and Ed was the perfect suspect.

"Yeah, I know a conspiracy theory may not make much sense right now, or what the connection is with the murder of Dax Martin, but that doesn't make Ed's premise less plausible. Arlo, look at all the recent political scandals that have been exposed in Los Angeles. We live in the most corrupt municipality in the nation, second only to Chicago. Rampart wasn't so long ago."

I referred to the Rampart Street Division of the LAPD, which was responsible in the late 1990s for its own crime wave. More than seventy officers were implicated in a litany of crimes, including drugs, murders, robberies, planting evidence, and perjury. When the story broke wide open, the city was forced to accept a consent decree allowing the US Justice Department the authority to step in for five years and implement serious reforms. Rampart wasn't the city's finest hour.

Beavers bristled. "I know. I helped run down some of that evidence. You're not implying the LAPD is involved in some sort of new conspiracy, are you?"

Didn't Kaplan say he graduated from the Beaumont School?

"No, of course not. But I am sure Ed is right. Something bigger is going on."

Beavers put his arm around my shoulders again as he drank his tea.

I looked at him. "Is Ed under arrest?"

"Kaplan's interviewing him now."

"Kaplan, huh? Poor Ed. Arlo, you must have seen the homeless camp right across the river. Maybe they witnessed the killing. Maybe they could prove Ed wasn't the killer."

"We're way ahead of you. We're looking for them now. There's evidence a man and a woman were living in those bushes."

Wow! I need to remember that when I meet up with Switch.

I tried to imagine what living in a thicket would be like in the richest country in the world. Sure, the weather was warm now, but what would those poor people do in two or three months when the weather turned cold and rainy?

Beavers squeezed my shoulder. "Listen, I know Pappas is a friend of yours and I know he's helped you in the past, but the thing is, you need to stay out of this. Right now, my captain has given Kaplan lead on this case because of you."

"Why?" I knew the answer.

He leaned down and pulled me closer. "Because everyone knows we're a thing. You can't investigate your own thing."

He nuzzled my neck and I smiled, content to forget about Kaplan's snarky remark and everything else.

The next morning, I woke to the sound of Beavers knocking around dishes in the kitchen. The clock read eight. I'd overslept. Bumper jumped on the bed, purred, and tickled my face with his whiskers, tired of waiting for me.

"Okay, okay!" I rubbed the itch from my cheeks. "I'm up." I threw on my baby blue chenille robe and slippers, shuffled toward the kitchen, and found a pot of coffee already made.

Beavers stood at the counter, whipping up an omelet. His German shepherd, Arthur, jumped up and greeted me with a wagging tail. I skritched him behind his ears, just the way he liked it.

"When did he get here?"

Beavers looked at me over his shoulder and smiled. "After you fell asleep last evening, I went home, ate, and brought him back with me. We didn't want you and Bumper to be alone."

I came up behind him, wrapped my arms around his waist, and gave a squeeze. He turned around and I gave him a long, searching kiss; then I put my head on his chest, careful not to wrinkle his clean white shirt.

I still couldn't bring myself to say the L-word. Even though we'd been dating for four months, I feared that merely uttering the word would put me at a permanent disadvantage. Thanks to my divorce, I wasn't ready to go to that scary, vulnerable place.

Beavers had told me he understood. He'd been through a bad marriage too. He also seemed frustrated with my reluctance to wade deeper into our relationship. I sometimes worried he'd lose patience and give up on me.

"You okay?" he mumbled into the top of my head.

I smiled at him. "Better than okay."

He turned back to the stove and poured a mixture of egg, veggies, and cheese into a hot skillet with olive oil. "You've switched to egg whites?"

I was too embarrassed to tell him about joining Weight Watchers. Beavers, who was in his midfifties, had a lean, hard body. He ran every day with

Arthur. When I chose ice cream, he chose fruit; beef, chicken; butter, olive oil. Bless him, because he never once criticized my extra pounds. In our intimate moments, he called me "beautiful" and "luscious."

Bumper walked over to Arthur and rubbed his head against the dog's foreleg. Arthur lowered his head and the two of them briefly touched noses. The dog, a retired LAPD canine officer, now lived happily with Beavers. Four months ago, when a killer was after me, Arthur was my bodyguard.

I washed my hands and poured some half-and-half into a cup before I filled it with steaming-hot dark Italian roast. Since the shawarma sandwich and the biscotti were the only things I ate yesterday, I was still on track with Weight Watchers.

We sat at the table and devoured the steaming omelet and whole wheat toast. I switched on the small television in my kitchen and turned to the morning news, hoping to catch a weather report. The temperatures had hovered in the triple digits for the last week, and I hoped for some serious relief.

I turned up the volume when the announcer said, ". . . body found yesterday at the Joshua Beaumont School baseball field in Encino. The victim was thirty-year-old Dax Martin, Beaumont's head baseball coach." The scene switched to a talking head standing in front of the Beaumont School. "Kip, what is the feeling at the school today?"

A square-jawed, frowning African-American reporter in a suit and tie spoke into a microphone.

"Well, Adam, the students here at Joshua Beaumont are stunned and saddened by their coach's death."

The camera panned over to some students in maroon jackets, with the gold Beaumont crest on the breast pockets, wearing backpacks and talking on cell phones. Some girls were hugging and wiping tears from their eyes.

The camera panned back to Kip. "As you can see, Adam, some of the students have already set up a memorial here at the entrance of the school."

The scene switched to an iron gate stuffed with posters, notes, stuffed animals, baseballs, and novena candles. "This is a sad day for the school, Adam. Back to you."

A photo of Dax Martin's smiling face appeared on the screen. Adam's voice said, "Martin was a former San Jose State baseball all-star headed for the pros when knee and shoulder injuries cut his career short. His bad luck was good luck for Beaumont. The talented young coach took his players to three championships in the Mission League. Dax Martin was a loving husband and father of three small children, with another one expected in two months."

The scene shifted back to the announcer. "The school said they knew of no reason why Martin would have been at the field late on Sunday night, the estimated time of the murder. Police are following a few leads and say they have already located a person of interest."

I looked at Beavers. "By 'person of interest,' do you mean Ed?"

"Look, Martha, I can't control what the media says. Everyone who ever knew Martin is a person of interest in the investigation. What are your plans for today?"

"Today is Tuesday, so we're going to Birdie's house to quilt, like we always do."

The paper napkin made a swishing sound over his mustache when he wiped his mouth. He got up and carried his plate to the sink. "I'm leaving Arthur here to watch over things, if you don't mind."

"Sure. Fine. But there's nothing to worry about."

He looked at me sideways. "Tell that to someone who doesn't know you."

CHAPTER 8

I arrived at Birdie Watson's house at ten on the dot. Birdie was Lucy's across-the-street neighbor in another area of Encino; The three of us had been quilting together for the last fifteen years, ever since I retired early from my administrative job at UCLA.

During those years, we'd helped each other through family crises and health problems, as well as birthdays, graduations, and joyful events. We were sisters despite our age differences. At fifty-five, I'm the youngest. Lucy's in her sixties and Birdie's in her seventies.

The fragrance of summer roses, lavender, and gardenias hung on the warm morning air and circled around me as I walked through Birdie's English garden to her front door. When I entered the cool house, the aroma of freshly baked applesauce cake teased me—my favorite. Already the calculator in my head worked out how big a piece I could have and still stay within my daily calorie allotment. The results weren't promising.

Birdie gave me a warm hug. "I made your favorite cake today." (As if she needed to tell me!) She wore her signature denim overalls, with a white T-shirt and Birkenstock sandals. Her pure white braid hung down her back in a long rope, while little wisps fluttered around her face like downy feathers.

We each claimed our favorite spot in Birdie's living room. Mine was an overstuffed green chenille easy chair that had arms wide enough to hold my sewing supplies. I settled in, adjusted my glasses, and spread open the Dresden Plate quilt I'd just started stitching. The Dresden Plate pattern is a circle divided into scalloped wedges, each wedge a different fabric. I centered one of the plates featuring pink and yellow prints into a fourteen-inch wooden hoop to hold the fabric taut. This would ensure two things: the bottom layer of the quilt wouldn't pucker, and my stitches would be small and even.

I typically worked on more than one project at a time. In addition to selecting materials with Lucy yesterday for the new scrappy Jacob's Ladder quilt in my sewing room, six other quilt tops waited to be layered with batting and backing and basted together in preparation for quilting. I had already basted the Dresden Plate and recently had begun the long process of sewing the three layers together by hand, one stitch at a time.

Birdie set a cup of fresh coffee with cream beside

me. "I'll bet we're the last holdouts in the guild. So few women quilt by hand anymore." Birdie was right. The majority of quilters in the West San Fernando Valley Quilt Guild used a sewing machine to do the work.

"They don't know what they're missing." Lucy slowly shook her head and her deep blue earrings swung back and forth. I always looked forward to finding out what theme Lucy would choose for the day. Today she featured blue: navy slacks and sandals, bright cerulean silk blouse, a necklace of lapis and crystal beads, and a pair of large lapis disks dangling from hooks in her ears. I thought blue was her best color; it made her orange hair look more authentic.

I agreed with my friends. Hand quilting was a long proposition. You must be willing to put in dozens, even hundreds, of hours before finishing— a good thing in my book. The process of stitching by hand provided time to think, to meditate, and just to slow down. The journey was worth it. In the end, you held a blanket textured with the comfort of thousands of thoughtful stitches, a piece of art.

Birdie returned with a generous thick slice of cake for each of us. I tried to keep from looking at mine. *Out of sight, out of mind.* Unfortunately, I couldn't turn off my sense of smell.

She twirled the end of her long braid. "Now, Martha dear, Lucy just told me about your finding the body of that baseball coach practically in your own backyard. I heard on the news he was a family man, the father of three young children."

"Yes. The body looked pretty gruesome. He was savagely beaten. Even though Dax Martin was universally resented and disliked in our neighborhood, he didn't deserve to die in such a horrible way. I feel sorry for his family."

Birdie sat and picked up her sewing. "Lucy said the police suspect your young neighbor."

"That's right, but I think he's being framed. I can prove it if I can find the homeless people who were camped across from the crime scene. They may have witnessed the murder. Lucy drove me to the police station to give a statement. You'll never believe what happened after she dropped me off." I hesitated to tell my friends about Hilda offering to take me to meet a dangerous character like Switch, but I wanted their support.

"Oh, Martha!" Lucy put down her needle and looked up. "You've got to be kidding. You've done some harebrained things before, but this is out-and-out lunacy. Please tell me you're not serious."

"Actually, I won't have to go in alone." Then I told them about my plan to take Hilda with me and Crusher's offer to back me up with Ed's other biker friends.

Lucy's voice rose a notch. "This is just getting worse and worse. You're going to ride with a team of bikers? *Really?*"

Birdie shook her head, eyes wide. "Lucy's right. You have no business going to such a dangerous place. No. Absolutely not, Martha dear."

I sat back and sighed. "Of course I've thought the same thing, but what else can I do? I'm going to see Hilda this afternoon to get an answer. If she says it's safe, then she and I will go in. If she says I should take Crusher, then he'll go in with us. I'll be safe with him and his guys."

Birdie looked horrified. "And what do you think Arlo will say to all of this?"

I narrowed my eyes. "He doesn't have to find out, unless you tell him."

"We might just be forced to," Lucy warned.

My friends were taking sides against me. I reached for the cake.

At two that afternoon, I packed my quilt, hoop, and sewing kit in the tote bag. In bygone times in France, a sewing kit was called an etui, pronounced ehTWEE. I loved the feeling of that word in my mouth.

"I've got to leave a little early," I said, standing up.

Lucy stood and put her hands on her hips. "You're going to meet Hilda, aren't you?"

I didn't answer.

She looked at Birdie. "You know, for someone who's so intelligent, sometimes this gal can be dumb as a sack of hammers."

I still didn't answer.

Lucy threw up her hands. "Okay, okay. We're going with you. We're not letting you out of our sight. Right, Birdie?"

Birdie got up and grabbed her keys.

Without another word, the three of us got in my car and drove to the Boulevard.

I found a parking spot close to Rafi's restaurant. Temperatures were slightly cooler today, in the upper eighties. Hilda sat in her usual place, looking up and down the street. When she spotted me, she gave a little wave. Then she frowned when Lucy and Birdie emerged from the car.

"Hey, Wonder Woman." Hilda looked at my friends and back at me, still frowning.

"Hi, Hilda. These are my friends Batwoman and Supergirl. They wouldn't let me come alone. They think I'm about to do something stupid."

She looked from one to the other. "They know everything?"

"Yes. You can talk freely." I stepped close so I wouldn't embarrass Hilda in front of the others and slipped her a twenty.

"Okay. I talked to Switch. He said for two hundred bucks he'd give you a name. You want more—you pay more."

"Will I be safe going to see him down in the wildlife reserve?"

"No. I talked him into meeting you in the little parking area just west of the Burbank Boulevard off-ramp. It's right out in the open under a streetlight, so you should be safe there." She eyed Birdie and Lucy warily, then turned back to me. "You'll have to show up by yourself."

"What time?"

"Ten tonight."

"You can't go there, Martha dear." Birdie shook her head. "Not in the dark. Not alone."

Hilda pointed her chin. "He sees Batwoman and Supergirl, and he won't show."

That didn't sound good. If Lucy and Birdie

couldn't come, what chance did I have to be protected by Crusher and his guys? "Hilda, will you come with me? He knows you, after all."

"I would, but I got a shelter bed tonight. Doors close at eight. If I'm not inside, I lose the bed and have to sleep rough."

I swallowed. "Well, how will I know him?"

"Don't worry. He'll know you. I need your answer now."

"Okay. Tell him I'll be there."

"Got it. Whatever you do, stay in the open. Don't let him draw you into the bushes."

Lucy waited until we were back in my car. "What! Are you crazy?"

"Don't worry, Lucy. I'll have Crusher watch my back."

"Dear God. Do you even know how to get in touch with him?"

Beavers knew exactly how to get in touch with Crusher, but I couldn't let him know my plans. Ed couldn't help me because, as far as I knew, the police were detaining him still. What had Beavers said? Crusher owned a motorcycle repair shop in Reseda, not far from the police station. I'd search for the address on Google.

I tried to look brave. "It's all good, Lucy. As soon as I get home, I'm calling Crusher. I've got everything under control."

She rolled her eyes and snorted. "That'll be the day."

CHAPTER 9

I dropped my friends off and headed home. When I got to my street, I hoped to find Ed back at his house. The street was empty; but since he usually garaged his vehicles, I couldn't tell for sure. I parked my car and headed toward his place. Nobody answered my knock. Ed must still be in custody. Was he only being detained for questioning or had he actually been charged with murder?

I needed to find Crusher fast. As soon as I walked in my door, I went straight for the computer. I searched and found two motorcycle parts and repair shops on Reseda Boulevard: one in Reseda itself, the other farther north in Granada Hills. I chose the closest shop and dialed the phone number.

"Bikes," a female voice answered the phone.

"I'd like to speak to Yossi Levy."

"Sorry. No one here by that name."

"Are you sure?"

"Well, I don't actually work here—my boyfriend does, but he's busy with a customer right now."

"Uh, is Crusher there?"

"Yeah. He's the owner. You wanna speak to him instead?"

I waited a tick. "Yes, please."

I heard her yell, "Hey, Crusher! There's a woman on the phone looking for a dude named Levy."

A deep, familiar voice said, "Yeah?"

"Hi, Yossi. It's Martha Rose."

The edge went out of his voice. "Babe, what do you need?"

"Protection. Tonight at ten. Can we talk?"

"Beavers know?"

"No, and I don't want him to. He'll freak."

"Meet me in the Home Depot parking lot on Balboa and Roscoe in a half hour."

"Why there?"

"It's crowded at this time of day, so nobody will notice us."

I couldn't imagine Crusher becoming invisible, no matter how busy the crowd. "I'll be there."

I opened a cup of plain Greek yogurt and poured in a teaspoon of agave syrup—a quick, healthy pick-me-up for late afternoon and one Charlissa would approve of. She didn't need to know about the applesauce cake.

Once I parked in the Home Depot lot, I didn't have to wait long. Crusher opened the passenger door and slid the seat all the way back before squeezing his huge body into the Corolla. His head scraped the roof and he winced. "One reason I like a big Harley is because of little cars like this."

"What do you do during the rain?"

"I've got a truck." He shifted his shoulders around to face me. "So talk."

"My friend Hilda set up a meeting for me tonight at ten with that Switch guy we talked about. He insists I come alone."

"Yeah, I found out more today about this guy. He and a few thugs went in and took over the area where a bunch of homeless people were camping. He deals from there—even pimps out some of those women. Switch is a real lowlife. You wouldn't be safe alone."

"That's what Hilda said, so she arranged for us to meet at the parking space just west of the Burbank Boulevard off-ramp of the 405. It's well lit and right on the road. Do you know where I'm talking about?"

"Yeah, and I don't like it. There's dense shrubbery at the edge of the parking space. Switch could drag you in there—and at night, nobody would see it happen."

"That's where you come in, Yossi. Except I can't figure out how you and your guys can protect me without being seen. The meeting place is out in the open, and his people will be watching from inside the reserve."

He was silent for a moment. "I think I know a way. Before you get there, me and my guys will ride south on the 405. When we get close to Burbank Boulevard, we'll cut our lights and engines and coast quietly onto the off-ramp. We can hide behind some of the bushes and trees up there. We'll only be a few feet away from the parking area."

"Won't Switch be able to see you?"

"Not a chance. We'll be able to see him come up from the reserve, but he won't be able to see us because we'll be hidden fifteen feet above him on the off-ramp."

"What about me? Will you be able to see me?"

"If you stand under the streetlight, we'll see you. Your job will be to stay in sight at all times. If we lose sight of you, we're coming in. If he makes one suspicious move, we're coming in. So you better get your information fast and get out of there fast. Once you're safely in your car, we'll book it on out and escort you home."

"Okay. Sounds like a plan. I have to tell you, I'm pretty scared."

"You'd better be scared. This dude is nobody to mess with." He pulled out a cell phone from inside his black leather vest. "We'd better exchange cell phone numbers."

Two minutes later, he opened the passenger door to leave.

"I'll see you tonight, Yossi."

"Don't leave your house until I call your cell phone. Don't wear any jewelry and don't take a purse. Don't worry. We'll be in place by the time you get there. I won't forget what you're doing for Ed. None of us will. And, Martha?" He cupped my chin in his hand. "Beavers is a lucky man."

I stopped at the bank on my way home. If Switch

demanded two hundred dollars for a name, how much would he demand for a location? I pulled four hundred dollars from my savings account. Ed would pay me back.

I returned home to the phone ringing.

"Hey, honey. How was your day?"

Every time Beavers called me "honey," my skin rippled with excitement. "Oh, you know. Lucy and Birdie and I spent our usual quilty day together. Birdie made my favorite applesauce cake. How was your day?"

"Same-o."

"Can you tell me what's happening with Ed?"

"He's still here."

"Has he been charged with murder?"

"You know I can't talk about an ongoing case. Listen, I'm afraid I'll be working late, so I won't be coming over tonight. I left a bag of Arthur's food next to your washing machine."

"Oh, don't worry, Arlo. I'm planning on an early night, anyway." I blew kisses and hung up the phone.

I felt dreadful. I'd never told Beavers a lie. If I didn't want him to know about something, I just failed to mention it. This was the first time I'd told a deliberate falsehood. Instead of staying home, I planned to meet a dangerous criminal to get important information that might exonerate Ed— information the police couldn't get on their own.

I consoled myself with the thought that after this meeting I'd have solid information to give to Beavers. I was taking a chance he might be angry as heck I lied to him. I might be jeopardizing the best relationship of my life in order to help my friend Ed. I prayed the outcome would be worth the risk.

According to Ed's research, something very wrong went down between the Army Corps of Engineers and the Joshua Beaumont School. Was Ed being framed for murder in order to stop him from digging for information? If so, who was really responsible for Dax Martin's murder?

I had to go through with Crusher's plan. Ed's freedom might depend on it. So much hinged on what the homeless people might have seen. The stuff about Beavers and me? I'd just have to figure that out later.

CHAPTER 10

Crusher's phone call came at nine-fifty, his voice a whisper. "We're in place. Looks good. It should only take you five minutes to drive here."

"Are you sure you'll be able to see me once I get there?"

"I've got a straight shot. Just remember to stay under the light."

I paced nervously for the next five minutes and then headed for the door. Arthur stood and trotted over to me. This dog was preternaturally smart. He sensed something wonky and planted himself between me and the door.

"Come on, Arthur, move."

The dog twisted his ears back, creased his forehead, looked at me, and gave me one anxious whine. I moved to the left, and so did he. I moved to the right. Ditto.

This ninety-pound retired police dog didn't want me to leave the house. We had history. Four months ago, when a killer came after me, I'd locked Arthur in the backyard. He couldn't protect me then, and I could see he still hadn't gotten over it.

I grabbed his leash. "Okay, buddy. You win. Nobody said anything about not bringing a dog."

This stretch of Burbank Boulevard, from Encino east to the 405 Freeway, was dark and deserted at ten. Deep shadows engulfed the golf course to the north and the heavily wooded Encino Creek bed on the south. After Woodley Avenue, the golf course gave way to a nature reserve, with native plants and trees on both sides of the street. This was Switch's territory, where his people lived in small tents hidden among the trees and in the underbrush.

I pulled into a parking space next to the off-ramp, right under the single streetlight. Switch was nowhere in sight. A pair of headlights came down the off-ramp, briefly illuminating the bushes up there, before turning east on Burbank Boulevard toward Van Nuys. Crusher was right. I couldn't see him from down below.

I grabbed Arthur's leash and walked around the car to stand in the light. Anyone driving by would think I was just giving my dog a potty break.

Arthur stiffened and growled softly. We weren't alone. My heart began to race, and I was glad for this big German shepherd by my side.

The bushes in front of me briefly rustled and out stepped a thin, wiry white man of medium height. His shoulder-length dark hair formed a greasy curtain over his eyes. He wore a dark, unbuttoned, long-sleeved shirt over a light T-shirt and black jeans. The pointed metal caps on the toes of his cowboy boots shone under the light. A swift kick from those bad boys could do some real damage.

Arthur refused to sit, pinned back his ears, and bared his teeth. I kept his leash short and bent to pet his head. "Easy, boy."

Switch kept to the shadows, speaking in a gravelly voice. "Where's the money?" He held out his hand, but I refused to walk toward the bushes.

I reached in my pocket and took out a pair of one-hundred-dollar bills. "If you want these, you'll have to come and get them." The bills fluttered from the shaking of my hands.

In one swift move, he darted forward, grabbed the bills, and retreated back to the shadows. "Make it quick."

"I want to talk to the people who camped across the river from the baseball field where a man was murdered Sunday night. Hilda said you could tell me who they were."

"What for?"

"I want to know if they witnessed the murder. To help out a friend of mine."

"Two beaners." He spat on the ground. "Javier and his woman, Graciela, rent that space."

This guy collects rent from the homeless sleeping on public land?

"Do you know where I can find them?"

He said nothing. I reached in my pocket and took out another bill.

He still didn't move.

I took out my last bill and stuck out my hand. "This is all I have."

He held out his hand again, not moving from the shadows.

I stayed under the light.

He slowly walked toward me. "They're down with my people. I can take you to them."

Suddenly he grabbed my wrist and yanked me toward the bushes.

Several loud engines roared to life.

I let go of Arthur's leash. He snarled and jumped, wrapping his mouth around Switch's arm.

Switch let go of me and I stepped back. Then a sharp whine and Arthur fell to the ground, bleeding from a deep cut to his shoulder.

Oh, my God. This is going all wrong.

I bent to touch Arthur, but a strong pair of arms grabbed me from behind and pulled me to the other side of my car, out of harm's way.

At the same time, the bikers arrived, four dark figures rose from the bushes below, Switch's thugs. Soon fists and chains hit flesh.

All I could think about was getting Arthur out of the scuffle of so many pairs of boots and dragging him to safety. I crept back around my car toward the fighting. Arthur raised his head, propped himself up on his side, and tried to drag himself, using his one good foreleg and pushing with his back legs.

I ran forward, grabbed him around his chest, and pulled with all my might, dragging the heavy German shepherd back toward my car. He whined in pain, leaving a dark trail of blood behind.

Crusher yelled at me, "Get out of here!"

I opened the door to the backseat of my car. "Not without my dog!"

I tried to lift Arthur up into the car, but he was way too cumbersome for me.

Suddenly a biker appeared beside me. He scooped up the dog in his arms, laid him gently into the backseat, and slammed the door shut. "Go!"

I ran to the driver's side, jumped in, and turned the ignition key even before I'd shut the door. Arthur's cries of pain were muffled by the sound of my tires squealing on the road.

Oh, please don't let him die! Please don't let him die.

CHAPTER 11

I broke the speed limit all the way to the twenty-four-hour animal hospital in Encino, pulled into the parking lot, and leaned on my horn, hoping to arouse someone inside. A tech dressed in blue scrubs came to the door.

I jumped out and opened the passenger door. "My dog! He's been stabbed! Please help me!"

The tech yelled something over his shoulder; then another tech appeared, running with a rolling stainless-steel table. Arthur whined softly as they pulled him gently out of the car. Blood dripped on the carpet and puddled on the seat. He lifted his head and gave me a sad look.

The open car door triggered a persistent dinging to let me know the keys were still in the ignition. I ran inside after the techs, ignoring the sound.

Arthur had tried to keep me from leaving the house tonight; I took him with me instead. I was so ashamed. I put him in danger, knowing he'd protect me, even at the risk of his own life.

Frantic for reassurance, I grabbed the tech's sleeve as his helper wheeled Arthur through doors marked STAFF ONLY. "Is he going to be all right?"

"Don't know yet. He's got a deep laceration on his shoulder and he's lost a lot of blood. Looks like he'll need surgery. We'll know more after the doc looks at him. Meanwhile, register at the desk and then have a seat and wait."

I ran back to the car, pulled the keys from the ignition, and grabbed my purse from under the seat. I reached inside for my cell phone, dreading the call I had to make. I could hardly see through my tears.

He answered on the second ring. "Beavers."

"Oh, Arlo, I've done something so foolish. Now Arthur is hurt. I'm so sorry," I blubbered.

"Slow down. Are you all right? What's this about Arthur?"

"I went out tonight and took Arthur with me. Someone attacked me and then stabbed the dog when he jumped in to protect me. I'm at the animal hospital in Encino."

His voice got very quiet. "Were you injured?"

"No. But Arthur—"

"How bad?"

"He got stabbed in the shoulder. He's in with the doctor now. He may need surgery."

"Where were you when this happened?"

"On Burbank Boulevard."

"Near the 405? We've just responded to a call. Were you in that mess?"

"Yes."

"That's it. I've had enough." Then the phone went dead.

Ten minutes later, Beavers pushed open the waiting-room doors and reached my chair in three angry strides, eyes on fire. A look of dread briefly crossed his face when he saw Arthur's blood smeared on my clothes and hands. "Where's my dog?"

The STAFF ONLY door opened and a gorgeous young veterinarian in a white lab coat walked efficiently over to us, peeling off a pair of bloody latex gloves. Her long blond hair hung in a perky ponytail and her blue eyes flicked from me to Beavers. "Are you the owners of the German shepherd?"

Beavers turned his back to me and faced the doctor. "I am. How is he?"

The pretty doctor looked at him and smiled, ignoring my presence completely. "I'm Dr. Kerry Andreason." She held out her hand. I noticed she wasn't wearing any rings.

He shook her hand. "Arlo Beavers."

She led him a few steps away, effectively shutting me out of the conversation. I sat by helplessly and listened.

"Well, Mr. Beavers, he's sustained a pretty serious cut to his shoulder. He may have some nerve damage. We'll have to wash out the wound and stitch the muscles back together. He'll need to stay here on an antibiotic drip for a few days."

"Just do what you have to do, Doctor."

She glanced over at my bloody shirt and then back at Beavers. "How did this happen?"

"He's a retired police dog. Someone stabbed him while he tried to protect this woman." Beavers jerked his thumb in my direction, refusing to look at me.

This woman?

"It's a good thing your dog was there, I guess." She smiled into his eyes and slightly caressed his upper arm. "Don't worry, Mr. Beavers, I'll take good care of him."

She's flirting with him!

"Thanks, Doc."

She smiled once more. "Call me 'Kerry.'"

He nodded.

When she disappeared through the door again, Beavers turned to look at me. His eyes were cold.

"Arlo, let me explain."

"Not this time. Whatever this is you're doing, you're doing it alone from now on. Go home. I've nothing more to say to you."

He took a few more steps over to the reception desk. With a deep sinking in my heart, I knew he might as well have taken a thousand steps. Arlo Beavers just walked out of my life.

I spent the night crying. What was wrong with me? Why did I take such a stupid risk? Poor Arthur almost died protecting me. What for? I'd just lost the best man I'd ever known. Oh, God, I probably couldn't fix what I'd broken. On top of everything, that pretty doctor's flirty smile flashed through my mind. More tears.

Sleep finally came at around four. At nine, the phone woke me up.

"You okay?" Crusher asked.

"No. Arthur's in the hospital and Arlo has left me." I started crying all over again, wallowing in misery. I didn't even think to ask if he and the other bikers were okay. After all, they went into combat for me. Saved me.

"I'm just a rotten person," I sobbed.

"I'm coming over with some strong coffee, babe."

To heck with Weight Watchers. "Bring some donuts," I sniffed.

I put on my bathrobe. My bloody clothes lay on the bathroom floor, right where I dropped them last night before taking a shower. I scooped them up, went to the kitchen, and put them in the trash, along with the bloody rag I'd used to clean my car. Then I fed Bumper and cleaned his litter box. Arthur's dishes sat empty on the floor. I washed them in the sink, arrows piercing my heart.

A huge white Dodge Ram, with just about the biggest tires I'd ever seen, pulled up in front of my house. I stood at the living-room window. Crusher limped up my walkway, carrying a large paper bag from Western Donuts and a cardboard tray with two giant cups of coffee.

I opened the door and he walked straight to the sofa, sitting down gingerly. This giant of a man, with gray creeping into his red beard, was way north of forty; yet he fought like a young gladiator last night and came away with one swollen eye and hands covered with cuts and bruises.

I sat down on the other end of the sofa. "I never got a chance to thank you for saving Arthur and me last night."

"I've gotta be honest, babe. You were smart to bring the dog along. If he hadn't jumped in, we might've been too late."

I opened the bag of donuts. *How does he know I love apple fritters?* I reached in and took out a glazed hunk of deep fried dough and cinnamon apples the size of a salad plate. "What happened after I left last night?"

"The minute we saw Switch grab you, we came down like his worst nightmare. None of us really got jammed, but we busted up those other guys pretty bad. They probably put Switch in the hospital." Crusher grinned. "I recall he somehow got stuck with his own knife. By the time the cops got there, we were dust. Did you get anything useful outta him?"

"Two names, Javier and Graciela, but names alone don't do us much good. We don't even know how to find them. You got hurt, and Arlo's dog almost got killed." I couldn't stop the tears. "Arlo was so angry—he broke up with me."

Crusher watched me silently as I wept. "He's a fool if he did." Then he slid over next to me, put one arm around my shoulders, and pulled me into his chest with his other. I felt like I sank into the middle of a giant inner tube that smelled like a mixture of gasoline and Tide.

As nice as Crusher tried to be, this didn't feel right. I pulled back and gave my head a firm shake. I didn't want him to get any ideas.

Somewhere a cell phone rang. Crusher reached in his pocket. "Yeah. When? Okay. Meet you there."

He stood up. "Ed's on his way home. The cops couldn't hold him any longer without charging him. They don't have enough evidence and his lawyer knows it. I'm going over there now."

I blew my nose in a Kleenex. "Thanks for everything, Yossi."

"Don't worry, babe. I'll be in touch."

CHAPTER 12

I splashed cold water on my face and looked in the bathroom mirror, horrified at my splotchy red skin and puffy eyes. Even my graying curls were drooping sadly. I looked every bit my fifty-five years—and felt even worse. The trauma and stress of the last few days caused my fibromyalgia to flare. My body ached all over and all I wanted to do was crawl in bed, pull a quilt over my head, and escape the reality of the damage I'd caused.

I swallowed a Soma, my go-to medication for muscle pain, and headed for the bedroom. There was a firm knocking on my front door. I looked out the peephole. *Beavers!*

I opened the door and stared hopefully at his face. I wanted him back. Wanted him to forgive me.

He had a firm jaw as he walked past me, with grim determination, into the kitchen.

"How's Arthur?" was all I could think to say.

"I've come for his things. He'll need them when he gets out of the hospital."

"So he's going to be all right? The surgery went well?"

Beavers scooped up Arthur's bowls and bag of dog food. "If you really cared about him, you wouldn't have put him in such danger."

"But I do care! I'm devastated he got hurt."

"You should have thought of that before you took my dog with your biker friends. I might be able to put up with your stubbornness. Even your selfishness. But you deliberately lied to me!"

"But—"

"Cut the crap. If I can't trust you, I can't be with you—especially because of what I do for a living. If you want to ride with the outlaws, be my guest, but you can't have it both ways."

"Arlo, I'm not riding with the outlaws. I'm—"

"Whose truck is in front of your house?"

By the accusing tone in his voice, I knew he already knew. He'd probably run the plates through the system as soon as he spotted the truck.

Beavers looked at the two coffee cups and remnants of donuts on my coffee table. "Levy was here this morning." He wasn't asking a question.

I couldn't speak.

He looked at my bathrobe. "Last night?"

I opened my mouth to protest, but Beavers tossed my house key on the hall table, turned on his heel, and slammed the door behind him.

I stood for a minute in the stunning silence that followed. Then I picked up my phone and called Lucy.

My voice shook. "Can I come over?"

"What's wrong?"

"I'll tell you when I get there." I put on my clothes and hurried over to my best friend's house.

Lucy opened the door, took one look at my face, and pulled me inside. "What happened?"

"I'm an idiot."

We sat at her kitchen table and she kept saying, "Oh, my God!" as I told her the story of the meeting with Switch, the fight, the injured dog, the flirty blond vet, and the breakup with Beavers.

When I told her about Crusher's morning visit and Beavers finding me in my bathrobe, she just shook her head. "You're right. You're an idiot. This about tops every reckless thing you've ever done. If I could, I'd break up with you too."

"Thanks a lot."

"Look. I've known you longer than Arlo has. I know you'd never deliberately hurt anyone. In fact, under normal circumstances, you're a very compassionate person."

"Thanks." I inhaled deeply and began to relax. My best friend always knew how to comfort me.

"Not so fast, girlfriend. I also know Arlo's right. You're stubborn as a one-eyed mule. You never just dabble. You always jump headfirst into things. When you're on a mission, you lose sight of everyone and everything else around you. Your judgment goes to *H-E*-double-sticks!" She wiggled her fingers in air quotes.

"Don't hold back, Lucy."

"And don't get me started about the chip on your shoulder. Okay, your ex-husband was a class-A jerk. Now get over it. If you want any hope of getting

Arlo back, you'll have to adjust your attitude. There! I've said it."

"Don't I deserve some trust as well? I mean, Arlo admitted I was right all along about the murder four months ago. Why can't he believe my judgment in this case? I know Ed, and that guy would never commit murder. And the accusation about me and Crusher? So offensive!"

"He'll calm down. Just give him some space right now."

I sighed. "You're right. I do go overboard sometimes. I can be selfish and single-minded, but I don't mean to be. Oh, I don't know what to think anymore. My brain is a mess and I feel like crap."

"Go home and look at your new quilt. Maybe working on it will help you make sense out of all those pieces floating around in your head."

I drove back home, determined to follow Lucy's advice. The thermometer on my dashboard put the outside temperature in the nineties. I rushed from the air-conditioning of my car to the cool interior of my house. I cleaned up the coffee cups and donut crumbs, put in a load of laundry, and made my bed.

As I worked, I kept wondering about Dax Martin, the loving husband, father, and beloved coach, versus Dax Martin, the pompous jerk and bully.

A savage beating indicated his killing was personal, an act of rage. Who was Dax Martin really, and whom did he piss off so fatally?

Completing the household chores freed me to lose myself in the creative process of designing and piecing a new quilt top. A colorful pile of cotton textiles waited on my sewing table to be transformed into Jacob's Ladder blocks, but I couldn't start just yet. If unwashed cotton material is sewn into a quilt, it can shrink when washed, causing the seams to split. I'd made a rule to wash and preshrink every new piece of fabric I bought before bringing it into my sewing room.

However, washed cotton becomes wrinkly and has to be ironed before cutting. I turned on my steam iron and sat at the ironing board for two hours, slowly pressing the creases out of all the dozens of different pieces of cloth. Even though I hated to iron clothes, I loved to prepare my beautiful textiles. I took time to admire each unique pattern. Once a piece was smooth, I lined up the selvedge edges, made sure it was square, and carefully pressed the folds in preparation for precision cutting.

Ironing for the last two hours had also smoothed some of the wrinkles from my brain. I could once again think in logical sequence without being mugged by tears. I turned off the iron, stood, and stretched. Then I walked to the laundry room and transferred the clean load out of the washer. My new athletic shoes thumped dully against the stainless-steel drum, turning inside the dryer.

I thought again about the witnesses. Where had Javier and Graciela gone? How could I find them? Had I missed anything at the crime scene? Forgotten any detail? Despite the heat, I decided to take a quick walk back to the river to jog my memory. I planned not to go any farther than the yellow police tape. If I did, it would be just my luck for Detective Kaplan to show up.

Since my new athletic shoes were in the dryer, I wore my gardening shoes, a pair of bubble-gum-pink Crocs that made me look like Barbie's plump mother.

CHAPTER 13

A Joshua Beaumont groundskeeper rode a large green power mower in straight lines over the outfield. A very tall young woman stood on the street at the chain-link fence and gazed in his direction. She wore a pair of white slacks and a gauzy white shirt over a black halter top. Her long, Malibu-blond hair drooped in the hot sun, and large sunglasses covered her face. A yellow Mercedes SL convertible sat at the curb behind her.

As I got closer, I could see she was crying. She held a wad of tissues in her right hand and lifted her sunglasses with her left so she could wipe her eyes. The sun glinted off the large diamonds in her wedding ring. Expensive hair, expensive car, big diamonds—clearly, she was a Joshua Beaumont person.

I stopped about three feet away from her. "Hi."

She glanced at me, blew her nose, and looked away.

"Are you okay?"

She took a shaky breath and sniffed. "I'm fine," she said in a voice hoarse from crying.

"I'm guessing you knew Dax Martin."

She turned sharply toward me. "Who are you?"

"My name is Martha Rose. I live in that house over there." I pointed to the one near the end of the street. "I went for a walk a couple of days ago and found his body."

She must have been as tall as Lucy in her bare feet, because she stood well over six feet in her platform sandals. She dabbed her eyes and blew her nose again. "I just can't believe what happened."

I put my hand reassuringly on her arm. "Are you his wife?"

She took a step backward. "Oh no, I'm an old friend. We went to high school together. Beaumont. We used to joke we both ended back where we started."

"How do you mean?"

"Dax worked for my husband, Jefferson. He's the headmaster of Beaumont. I'm Diane Davis." She offered her hand, apparently forgetting she'd just used it to blow her nose.

"Well, I can see how Mr. Martin's death would be such a personal loss. I'm so sorry."

"You saw him. Did he . . . Did he die right away?"

Oh, my God. How should I know? He may have been conscious through the whole savage beating, in which case he would have suffered greatly.

"I'm not an expert, but I think it was an ambush. The attack was probably over very quickly."

Her hands shook as she covered her face.

The severe August sun was creeping toward its zenith. "I need to get out of this heat. Can I offer you a cold drink back at my house? It's much cooler inside."

She hesitated for a moment and then relaxed. A sniff, more nose blowing, and "Yeah, I could really use something cold. Just let me close up the car."

She walked rather skillfully on her five-inch platforms. I wore a more moderate version of platform sandals in the 1970s. They boosted me all the way up to five feet five, but I turned my ankle once and nearly broke my neck in the fall. Now my shoes were all about comfort, and I painted quite a contrast walking alongside this dazzling California girl in my bubble-gum-pink rubber shoes.

The inside of my house felt mercifully cool. I gestured for Diane to sit on the sofa. "I have diet cola or water. Which would you prefer?"

She took off her sunglasses and her puffy red eyes disturbed an otherwise perfect face. "Water and lots of ice, if you have it."

We sat for a minute, just enjoying our drinks. Between sips Diane pressed the frosty glass against her forehead and around her eyes.

I cleared my throat softly to get her attention. "So tell me about the Beaumont School. Has anything changed since you went there? I'm guessing that wasn't so long ago."

Diane Davis smiled for the first time. "I graduated twelve years ago and the school hasn't changed a bit. Same families, same teachers, same headmaster, just more iPads and cell phones."

Did she say same headmaster?

"So your husband was headmaster when you were a student?"

She waved her hand. "I know, I know. It's not like what you're thinking. I mean, I never dated him when I was a kid. He was, like, an uncle or something. He and his wife were friends with my parents."

"How did you, um, get together?"

Diane spoke in what sounded like questions: "My mom modeled when she was young? She got me a couple of gigs in high school just to see if I liked it. After I graduated, Daddy bought me an apartment in Manhattan? And I got to travel to Europe to walk a lot of runways. It was, like, one long party. Once you hit twenty-five? You're pretty much over-the-hill in that business."

I couldn't imagine anyone looking like her being too old for the beauty business.

She tucked her hair behind her left ear. "Anyways, five years ago, I came home for Christmas and Jefferson showed up alone at my parents' annual bash. His wife died the year before. I wore Marchesa? A hot little white strapless, with lots of sparkles. My parents had just given me diamond drops as a coming-home present? So I put my hair up to show them off. I've got a nice, long neck."

Her voice gave out and she took a sip of water. "Anyways, Jefferson couldn't take his eyes off me. We started talking and, well, we just clicked. He's way older than me? But that's cool. He takes good care of me."

"Did you and Dax Martin stay in touch over the years?"

"No. We really came from different social circles. He got to Beaumont on a baseball scholarship. He was hot, though. We dated in our senior year. After he graduated, he went to San Jose State in Northern California, and I went to New York. You know how that goes. Out of sight? It was sad for a minute."

I could teach her a lot about sad endings today.

Just then, her cell phone made a chiming noise. She reached in her purse, saw who the caller was, then looked at me apologetically. "Hi, honey. No, I'm with a friend. No, you don't know her. Her name's Martha? No, we just met. We're at her house? Okay, I'll be there soon."

Diane put down her water and stood up. "He likes to check to see if I'm okay." She rolled her eyes. "Several times a day."

Seems like I'm not the only one with trust issues.

She hoisted her yellow Birkin bag on her shoulder. "I have to give him props for loving me so much. I mean, most husbands are too busy to even care what you do, right?"

That's one way of looking at it.

"You're lucky to have him."

She looked around the room. "Thank you so much for the cold drink, Martha. Your house is really cute."

"My pleasure. I hope you're feeling better."

Diane Davis put her perfect sunglasses back on

her perfect face and glided out the door of my really cute house toward her perfect yellow Mercedes.

Too perfect.

Diane Davis was hiding something. Her puffy eyes revealed she'd been crying for quite a while. I knew exactly what that looked like. Why all the tears?

Just how close had Diane really been to Dax Martin? She admitted they had a romantic history. Didn't she say they joked about ending up where they started? Maybe she didn't just mean back at the Beaumont School. Maybe she meant back in each other's arms. It certainly wouldn't be the first time that happened with the young wife of an older man.

What kind of husband checked up on his wife several times a day? You didn't have to be a psychiatrist to figure out he must be a control freak. Did the lovely young woman who had sat before me feel trapped in her marriage to this older man? Was he the source of her grief? What if he found out about his wife's affair with one of his employees? Would Jefferson Davis go so far as to kill Martin?

Given the conflict between Ed and the school, Davis could have known where Ed's backyard was— right across from the maroon-and-gold monstrosity. If he killed Martin, he could have tossed the murder weapon over the fence into Ed's yard. Then he could have called in the anonymous tip to the police.

Now I had a suspect, so finding a witness was more important than ever. If the homeless couple

Javier and Graciela saw the murder, they might be able to identify Jefferson Davis as the killer.

The clock read nearly five. I hadn't eaten anything since the apple fritter at breakfast. Remembering breakfast made me once again think of Beavers. I needed food. Now.

Thawing a chicken breast from the freezer and broiling it would take way too long to prepare. Ditto with a salad. Too labor intensive. I emptied a can of chicken noodle soup into a bowl and nuked it in the microwave for one minute and thirty seconds. Meanwhile, I counted out five saltine crackers and cut in wedges one medium peach for dessert. Total prep time from can to steaming bowl to table was three minutes—my kind of cooking.

I had just finished the last juicy segment of peach when the phone rang. "Hi, Martha, this is Ed."

"Hey, Ed. You okay?" I could sympathize with his ordeal. My recent experience of overnight detention in jail was scary and exhausting.

"Yeah, so far. Listen, what you did for me last night was awesome. I can't thank you enough. Crusher says you were really brave. I think he likes you."

Crusher was in the background. "Aw, come on, man."

Ed chuckled. "Anyway, I'm having a meeting here tomorrow morning at ten with my lawyer and some other people to talk about my situation. Do you think you could come? You risked your life for me. You found the body. You're good at putting things together. And my man Crusher—he's crushin' on you."

From the background, ". . . it, man!"

Ed was only teasing, but I didn't need another romantic complication in my life—even if it was just one-sided. I didn't like Crusher in *that* way; but when Beavers walked out of my life, he apparently thought I did.

On the other hand, I remembered Diane Davis and the phone call from her husband. I had just stumbled upon someone besides Ed Pappas who might have had a motive to get rid of Dax Martin. "Sure. I'll be there."

CHAPTER 14

I arrived at Ed's house at ten o'clock on Thursday morning. Three Harleys sat in his driveway and a blue Prius sat at the curb. I knocked on the door. Ed gathered me in a warm hug. "Thanks for coming, Martha. And thanks for everything you've done."

He led me into the living room, where Crusher sat along with two other men and a woman. "You already know Crusher."

We nodded at each other.

Next to Crusher sat a man I recognized as the biker who had scooped the bleeding Arthur off the ground and put him in the backseat of my car. He was slender, with strong shoulders and arms, had blond hair, and looked to be barely out of his teens. Ed introduced him as Carl.

"Thanks for helping me with my dog the other night."

Carl smiled. "He's one great dog. How's he doing?"

I remembered how furious Beavers had become

when he learned Arthur was seriously wounded because of my stupidity. I also remembered the pretty blond vet who flirted so openly with him. "He's recovering." Would I?

Ed pointed to a man sitting alone in a chair. "This is our friend Simon Aiken. He's also my attorney. Fortunately, he was here when the cops arrested me. He stuck with me during the interrogation and eventually got me out without being charged."

Simon Aiken acknowledged me with intense dark eyes. He had a raptor's nose, high cheekbones, and dark hair. Instead of biker leather, Aiken wore a gray Italian suit, with a tie of sky blue silk loosened around his neck.

Ed finally introduced me to a young woman, with very long brown hair, wearing gray linen slacks and a blue cotton blouse. The Prius probably belonged to her. "This is Dana Fremont, Simon's assistant. Simon has to be in court this afternoon, so we only have these two for a short time. Dana's going to be taking notes."

Dana smiled and wiggled her fingertips before looking back down at her iPad.

Ed provided a cardboard container of Starbucks coffee and pastries from Eva's European Bakery in a pink box. Next to the pink box sat a white box from Western Donuts with six apple fritters. I glanced up. Crusher watched to see which box I'd choose. I took a fritter. Crusher smiled.

Dear God.

I took a seat in a brown chair so large that my feet dangled awkwardly above the floor.

"Okay. Let's review the facts." Simon Aiken took control of the meeting. "Martha, can you tell us about finding the body and the homeless camp? Then maybe you can walk us through the details of your search for those possible witnesses. Start at the beginning."

All eyes turned toward me and I put down my coffee and fritter. "I discovered Dax Martin's body Monday morning behind the Beaumont School ball field on the riverbank. He died where he lay. Looked like he was beaten to death." I explained my theory about how, since Martin was a bully, he wouldn't have gone outside the perimeter fence alone—unless he knew his attacker and felt safe.

Ed nodded in agreement. "The guy was a tool."

I took another sip of coffee. "You know how the sides of the river back there are covered with stucco? Well, on the far side, the riverbank is overgrown with bushes and small trees. Before I discovered the body, I noticed a couple of bedrolls, a metal pot, and other camping items hidden in the underbrush. I wonder if whoever slept over there witnessed the attack on Sunday night. I learned there were two of them, a man and a woman."

Simon typed something on his laptop. "Tell us how you found that out."

I reviewed my conversation with Hilda and her setting up the ten o'clock meeting with Switch. "You probably are all aware of what happened afterward."

Simon circled his index finger in the air in a

gesture for me to continue. "I want to hear it from your perspective. Don't leave out any details."

"I contacted Yossi and—"

Dana looked up, confused. "Who's Yossi?"

Crusher shifted in his seat and grunted. "Me."

Dana looked at him, raised her eyebrows, snorted, and then bent once more to her typing.

"I contacted Yossi and asked him to back me up. He came up with the plan to hide on the off-ramp while I talked to Switch. I brought my friend's German shepherd with me for protection. Switch told me the possible witnesses were Hispanic, Javier and Graciela. He said he collected rent from them. He also led me to believe he knew where they were. That thief charged me four hundred dollars for the information. Then he grabbed my arm and tried to drag me into the bushes. You know the rest."

Ed looked shocked. "You paid him four hundred dollars of your own money? Wait right there." He briefly left the room and returned with four $100 bills. He kissed my cheek. "You're really awesome."

Aiken looked at Crusher and Carl. "Tell me again for the record what happened."

Crusher leaned forward and put his elbows on his knees. "As soon as that guy touched Martha, me and the boys went in. Maybe five, ten seconds is all it took us. The dog attacked and Switch cut him. In the scuffle, the little slime ball was disarmed and he got cut too." Crusher looked around the room, but he avoided my eyes. "Maybe a few times. Meanwhile, some of his guys came out of the bushes, but we fought them off. Carl's job was to take care of Martha. As soon as she got out safely, we left too."

Aiken turned to Carl. "Tell me what you did."

"Like Crusher said, we got there in only a few seconds. I grabbed Martha's shoulders from behind and dragged her around the other side of her car and told her to go. She wouldn't leave her dog. So I helped her get him inside the car and she laid rubber getting out of there. When those punks saw Switch bleeding on the ground, they ran. That's when we jumped on our bikes and booked."

Aiken turned back to me. "Do you have any more ideas about how to find this homeless couple?"

I'd just taken a large bite of apple fritter; the flakes of sugary glaze clung to the corners of my mouth. I held up my hand, stalling a moment to take a sip of coffee and clean my face with a napkin. "I watched a groundskeeper mow the edges of the field yesterday. I think we should talk to him. Since his job takes him all around the property, he might have observed something. He's one of those anonymous guys who labor quietly in the background. They may be unnoticed, but they still see a lot of stuff that goes on."

Aiken made another note on his laptop. "Dana, see if you can get his name and schedule."

Ed pointed out his living-room window to the field beyond. "No need. I think he works Monday, Wednesday, and Friday mornings. I usually hear his mower then."

I raised my hand a little. "Tomorrow's Friday. I can go talk to him. I find people are more likely to open up to a senior-looking citizen than to a biker-looking guy."

Aiken smiled for the first time that morning. "I can see why Crusher likes you. You're one fearless little lady."

Crusher turned redder than normal and refused to meet my eyes.

I actually felt sorry for him.

"I'm pretty sure I uncovered a real suspect yesterday."

Everyone stopped smiling and looked at me. Even Crusher.

"Out by the field, I came across a young woman standing at the fence, crying."

I told them about Diane Davis—her previous romantic history with Dax Martin and her possessive, controlling husband, Jefferson. "This may be far-fetched, but if Mrs. Davis had an affair with Martin, maybe her husband killed him in a fit of rage."

Aiken nodded slowly. "That possibility could raise serious doubt in the DA's mind and keep Ed from being arrested and charged with murder. It could also raise doubts in a jury's mind if this ever goes to trial."

Ed slapped his hands together once and pointed at me, arm straight in front of him. "I told you she was good at figuring things out."

Aiken turned to his assistant. "Dana, see what you can find on Jefferson Davis and Diane Davis. Ed, you told me you uncovered something funny involving the school, the city, and the Army Corps of Engineers."

Ed talked about the lack of permits, inspections, or an environmental report on file with the city. "So I tried to get information from the Army Corps of Engineers about the land they lease to the Beaumont School, but they refused to make any documents available."

Aiken scowled. "They can be compelled to disclose under the Freedom of Information Act. I'll put some pressure on them and see what I can find out. If this baseball stadium was built illegally, we want any future jury to see Ed as a concerned citizen trying to save his neighborhood from the bad guys—not as a villain out to kill a baseball coach."

He looked at his watch and stood. "Good work, everyone. Keep digging. Let's meet back here tomorrow evening, say at seven?"

I also stood. Donut crumbs fell from my lap to the floor. "Not tomorrow evening. I'm having dinner with my uncle Isaac. I'm available Saturday."

"Saturday good with everyone?" The rest agreed. "Okay, let's meet here at ten on Saturday morning." I walked outside and watched Aiken put on his helmet, stow his laptop in a carrier behind the saddle, and ride his Harley toward the Van Nuys Courthouse.

Simon Aiken inspired confidence with his take-charge attitude. I was sure we'd get to the bottom of what went down among the Beaumont School, the city, and the Army Corps of Engineers. If Dax Martin's murder had anything to do with it, we might even discover his killer.

CHAPTER 15

Before I reached my front door, Sonia Spiegelman rushed over from her house across the street. She wore tan cotton trousers and a loose paisley blouse from India. Thin bangles clattered on her wrist. Her smile was genuine, but her eyes had a certain hungry, wolverine quality. Sonia was sniffing around for news. "Hey, Martha. I see you have a new guy coming to your house. You know, the big biker. I thought you were dating a cop."

I swallowed the lump in my throat. "Really? I have all types of friends. Like you, for instance."

"So I see Ed Pappas is home now. Has your cop friend told you anything new about the murder?"

Of course Sonia would ask. No matter what happened in the neighborhood, she needed to know about it. Despite this annoying compulsion, Sonia deserved props for organizing The Eyes of Encino— a neighborhood watch that patrolled our community in times of, well, peril. Since Dax Martin's murder, the Eyes had been walking and driving up and down our streets at night, carrying their walkie-talkies and wearing matching yellow T-shirts, with a big eyeball logo on the back. Sonia's idea.

The patrol leader was Ron Wilson, a Korean War vet, who lived with his wife on the next street over. Ron's military crew cut had long ago turned white and sparse, but he and some of his fellow geezers took community safety very seriously. Even old Tony DiArco joined the patrol on his Chair-A-Go-Go scooter, oxygen tank strapped to a holder in back. They shortened his shift to one hour because the scooter's batteries were unreliable.

Sonia could be pesky when she nosed around in someone else's business. As far as I could tell, though, she never meant anyone harm.

"Ed's okay. He's been through a lot, poor guy."

"Like what?"

"Well, I'll leave it up to Ed to decide how much he wants to tell other people about his business."

A shadow of hurt crossed Sonia's face.

"I can tell you his spirits are good and he has a strong support network."

Sonia reached up and adjusted the tortoiseshell clip holding her long brown hair in place at the back of her neck. I had recently been in Sonia's house and saw her with her hair hanging loose. She looked a dozen years younger then, and the wrinkles became softer around her eyes and mouth. That was also the day I saw a photo of her with Mick Jagger in her younger, groovier days.

"So, do the cops think a homeless person is the killer?"

How much does she know about the homeless couple, and where does she get all her information, anyway?

"I wouldn't know what the police think. I did see evidence someone lived in the bushes across the river from the crime scene. I don't think it's possible they killed Dax Martin."

Sonia leaned forward in eager anticipation. "Why do you say that?"

I explained my theory that Martin would never have gone outside the field with someone he didn't know and trust. "I just think it's more likely they witnessed the crime and fled the scene out of fear."

"Those poor people. I can't stand the thought they actually live without decent shelter. Sure, the weather's dry now in the summer, but what do they do when the weather's cold and rainy? I wish we could give them blankets or something. . . ."

Bingo! I looked at Sonia and smiled. "We can."

"Can what?"

"Give them blankets." I explained how our guild gave away quilts to hospitals, shelters, and the homeless. Maybe we could organize some kind of distribution. With Switch gone, I wanted to get into the wildlife reserve in the worst way so I could try to find out where Javier and Graciela had disappeared.

Sonia looked doubtful. "Nobody's going to go anywhere near the place, Martha. It's way too dangerous."

"Things may have changed recently." I wasn't going to tell Sonia about Crusher putting Switch out of business. "I'll check with some friends of mine to make sure, but I think that with some help, we could go in there and do some real good."

Sonia smiled and stood a little straighter. "Well, I'm a pretty good organizer. I'll be glad to help you."

"Sure! I'll call you later."

I phoned Lucy the minute I got inside. I sat on the board of the quilt guild and my friends sat on the philanthropy committee. "Hi, Lucy. Are you still doing charity at the guild?"

"Yeah. Birdie and I still go once a month to help tie quilts. Why?"

I told her about my idea to organize an outreach in the Sepulveda Basin and to look for Javier and Graciela at the same time.

"Were you not listening yesterday? Did you not vow to change your ways? I thought you were through with your obsession to solve the murder and save your friend Ed."

"Yes, I listened. I'm no longer obsessed." I wasn't going to correct Lucy and remind her I made no such vow. "Anyway, I think I stumbled upon a real suspect."

"Get out!"

I told Lucy about Diane and her husband, Jefferson Davis, the headmaster of Beaumont School and Martin's boss. "So you see, if Davis thought his wife had an affair with Dax Martin, that cradle-robbing control freak could have killed him in a jealous rage."

"But that's pure speculation on your part."

"Doesn't matter. As I understand it, we don't need to prove he actually killed Martin. Finding proof is up to the police and the DA. We only want them to look at someone other than Ed Pappas. In the worst-case scenario, if Ed is arrested and goes to trial, we want to have enough evidence to convince a jury someone else *could* have done it. We need to create reasonable doubt."

"Well, good luck with that."

I ignored the sarcasm. "You remember my neighbor Sonia?"

"The one we met the other day? The former disco queen-slash-flower child?"

"She's not so bad. She came up with the idea to distribute blankets to the homeless. Does the guild have any quilts to give away?"

"At the moment, we only have about five completed, but we've been gearing up for Veterans Day in November. We've at least ten more quilt tops ready to tie."

Not all quilts were stitched together. To save time, many quilts were tied together every few inches. Strong yarn or heavy thread was stitched a couple of times in place through the three layers of the quilt and cut, leaving two-inch to three-inch ends. Then the ends were tied together to make a permanent suture. Using this method, one person could finish a bed-sized quilt in just a few hours.

"I'm going to ask Hilda to help. Today's Thursday. The longer we take to arrange this outreach, the less chance we have of finding Javier and Graciela. So let's aim for Sunday as the day to give away the quilts. What do you think?"

"We'll have to call an emergency meeting of the

committee to tie those other tops. We could end up with fifteen finished quilts by Sunday."

"That'd be great, Lucy. Could you please get started right away? I'm off to find Hilda."

My homeless friend was fanning herself in the shade near her usual space on Ventura. She wore a short-sleeved T-shirt, which had a picture of a hairy dog and the words I LOVE MY LABRADOODLE. The pockets of her chambray pleated maxiskirt were bulging and the hem was frayed. Hilda parked her shopping cart in front of Rafi's place, where she could see it. We sat at a table near the window and each ordered a falafel combo plate, with assorted cold salads.

She stood. "I gotta go wash my hands." This wasn't the first time I noticed that even though she didn't have access to regular facilities, Hilda worked to keep herself reasonably clean. When she returned from the restroom, she'd also washed the sweat off her face and combed her tangled hair.

She tore off a piece of pita bread and swiped it through the baba ghanouj, a puree of roasted eggplant, olive oil, lemon, and garlic. "I heard what went down the other night. You and your friends really did a number on Switch. I also hear he's cuffed to a hospital bed."

She went on to describe how, after the brawl, the homeless people banded together and forced the other thugs to leave. "It's a lot safer there now."

"I'm glad, and I'll tell you why. The weather won't be hot like this forever. In just a couple of months, it'll be cold out and the rains will come. I'd like to help those people prepare for the winter, so here's my idea. We go into the reserve on Sunday with blankets to distribute. While we're there, we can look for Javier and Graciela."

"You should go soon. I heard someone say a couple was looking for a ride to Mountain View. I don't know if it's them."

The town of Mountain View sat four hundred miles north in Silicon Valley. If Javier and Graciela left Los Angeles, we'd never find them. We needed to visit the reserve before they fled.

Hilda tilted her head. "You know, these people down there could use other things besides blankets."

"Such as?"

She ticked items on her fingers. "Socks for the cold weather. Toiletries for hygiene, like body soap, deodorant, toothbrushes and toothpaste, shampoo, disposable razors, rolls of toilet paper, and small packets of laundry detergent."

I thought about Sonia and her organizing skills. I'd ask her to contact the neighbors and solicit donations of those other items. "I think we can put something together by Sunday, but I need you to go there and let people know we're coming."

"No problem. You gotta respect their privacy. Hand out your packages and then leave. You and I can look for your witnesses."

"Do you know how many people are living there right now?"

Hilda shrugged and looked at the ceiling, calculating. "At least fifty. Maybe more."

Help for fifty people would be a challenge to organize in the next two days, but I was pretty sure it could be done with a little help from my friends. If I found Javier and Graciela, and if they witnessed Dax Martin's murder, and if I could convince them to tell the police what they knew, I could clear Ed from suspicion by Sunday night.

CHAPTER 16

I laid my keys on the hall table, right next to the key Beavers angrily discarded the day before. I walked slowly to the kitchen and put a kettle of water on to boil. Some late-afternoon tea would help me think about what to do next.

I made my first call to Sonia. "We can go forward with our plans to distribute blankets to the homeless on Sunday."

"Will we be safe?"

"Yeah. I'm going to ask my friend Yossi to be our escort, though."

"Your big biker guy?"

My guy? That's the second time she's mentioned him today.

"Yes. You probably also saw he has a big white truck to transport the stuff."

Sonia's voice sparked with excitement. "Terrific! How many blankets do we need?"

"There are at least fifty people down there. We

should also put together packets of personal hygiene products." I recited the list Hilda suggested.

Sonia said she'd hit up the neighbors for donations. "Can your quilting friends get fifty quilts?"

"No. Maybe fifteen."

"Well, then, how about I also ask the neighbors for donations of regular blankets? New or used, as long as they're clean."

Sonia agreed to have the items dropped off at her house and we'd put everything in packages on Saturday night.

The kettle whistled and I made myself a cup of *genmaicha,* Japanese green tea. I took a moment to enjoy the distinctive roasted-rice flavor, which always reminded me of sitting at a sushi bar.

Next I called Crusher's cell phone.

"Yeah?"

"Hi, Yossi. It's Martha. Are you up to doing another good deed?"

"Anything for you, babe. What do you need?"

"I need a big truck and a bunch of strong guys to keep the peace."

"I've got more than that for you." He chuckled. "When and where?"

I ignored the innuendo and told Crusher about the plan to distribute blankets and packages to the homeless on Sunday. "I'm hoping the groundskeeper can tell me something tomorrow about Javier and Graciela. If he can't, we still might find them or someone who knows about them in the reserve. What do you think?"

"I'm in. You're still gonna talk to the groundskeeper tomorrow morning, right?"

"Oh, sure. No stone unturned."

"Do you want me to come along as backup?"

Is he kidding? A three-hundred-pound hulk with a do-rag?

"No thanks, Yossi. Better I go alone. I look less threatening, if you know what I mean."

He laughed. "I pity the guy who underestimates you." He paused. "Is that what happened with Beavers?"

I remembered the confusion, anger, and disappointment I felt when Beavers accused me of spending the night with Crusher. "I don't want to talk about it."

"Sorry, babe. You wanna get some dinner tonight? We could go to the Cantina on Mulholland Drive. They have killer enchiladas." I'd never been to the Cantina, a notoriously rowdy hangout for bikers, cowboys, and movie stuntmen. "I can pick you up in a half hour and you can ride on the back of my bike."

There it was. Crusher told Beavers he wanted to get me on the back of his bike—also known as the "bitch seat." Beavers had gone livid. Was Crusher really interested in me, or was he just playing me because he wanted to stick it to Beavers? When did I get so cynical?

"No thanks, Yossi. It's been a long day. I'm just going to chill at home and go to bed early."

"Okay, but one day you'll get over him, and I want to be first in line when that happens."

First of all, I didn't know if I'd ever get over Beavers. Second of all, there wouldn't be a line. There had never been a line. Third of all, even though he was growing on me, I still didn't like Crusher in *that* way.

"You're sweet, Yossi. I'll talk to you soon."

I made myself another cup of tea and the phone rang.

"Hi, *faigele*. Are we still on for Shabbat dinner tomorrow?" My elderly uncle Isaac always called me by that Yiddish endearment, "little bird."

"Of course."

"I called to say you don't have to pick me up. Morty's gonna visit a friend in Northridge. He says he'll drop me off at your house on the way."

"Why don't you invite Morty for dinner? I'm cooking a brisket."

"I did, but he's got other plans. He's got a new girlfriend."

"How old is he, anyway?"

"Morty? He's almost eighty-eight, but he's as strong as an ox. Still drives his car. And still, you know, likes the ladies."

"What happened to the last one?"

"Heart attack. Second girlfriend in two years. The senior center is full of nice Jewish ladies our age, but they can't keep up with him. So he decided to go younger. This new one, Marilyn, she's only seventy. A little on the zaftig side, which is the way he likes 'em."

I laughed. "I hope she lasts."

I said my good-byes to my uncle and began cutting

veggies for salad. I knew all about *zaftigkeit*. Being plump was a Jewish woman's curse, a lifelong battle in my case. How many salads had I made over the years, only to ruin my good intentions by topping off the meal with a sugary pastry or grabbing fast food on the run?

Tomorrow was going to be a long day, and I needed to plan ahead, so I opened my Weight Watchers book for inspiration. I only wished I could open a book with a recipe for finding Dax Martin's killer.

CHAPTER 17

Friday morning's weather report promised more ninety-degree heat. At nine in the morning, the temps were already reaching into the high seventies. I put on lightweight khaki cargo pants, a V-neck T-shirt, and my clean white athletic shoes; then I walked behind my house over to the Beaumont School baseball field. A lone figure rode on a green mower along the first base line near the street; the smell of freshly cut grass filled the air.

"Hello!" I shouted through the chain-link fence. My voice was lost over the loud rumble of the mower. I walked onto the field and stood near the catcher's mound. He finally saw me when he turned the mower toward home plate. He drove up to me and turned off the engine.

The driver, a dark-haired Hispanic man, jumped off the machine, took off his work gloves, and walked toward me. On the left side of his maroon golf shirt was the Beaumont School crest and the name "Miguel" embroidered below in school bus yellow thread.

"Can I help you, Mrs.?" He spoke with the accent of someone who wasn't born in the United States but had lived here a long time.

I attempted to dazzle him with my most disarming smile. "I hope so. My name is Martha, and I live in the house over there."

"I am Miguel. What can I do for you, Mrs. Martha?" He spoke softly and with the charming deference Latino men showed to older women.

"I'm looking for someone, and I hope you can help me."

"My pleasure."

"Did you notice a couple camping out behind the field over on the other side of the river?" I pointed in the direction of left field. "Their names are Javier and Graciela."

"When I come here to work on Monday, the police were already back there with the body of Coach Martin. I told them I don't know nothing."

"I'm not the police, Miguel. I'm concerned about my neighbor Ed Pappas. His house is right there."

"Oh yes. I know who he is. He comes here many times during a game. He yell and argue with Coach Martin. Once, they fight and the police come."

"Well, because of that fight, the police think my friend might have murdered the coach. They found the murder weapon in his backyard, but I think the real killer threw it over the fence. If the two people I'm looking for, Javier and Graciela, witnessed the murder from their camp, they could prove my friend is innocent."

"If they saw something, they probably ran for

their lives. Where I come from, if you are picked up by the police, you are never seen again. They probably think the police here are the same. Homeless Latinos are afraid of *La Migra*. They don't want to be sent back to their country. Death there, death here, it's all the same. I don't think you ever find those people."

"Listen, Miguel. I was the one who found Coach Martin's body. I had gone for a morning walk, and I can tell you he was savagely beaten in the head. The killer must have been very angry. Did the coach have any enemies you knew of? Maybe someone at the school?"

Miguel shook his head slowly. "No, Mrs. Martha. No one."

"Well, did you ever hear him arguing with anyone?"

Miguel said nothing. He just looked at the ground and put his hands in his back pockets. "I don't think so."

He seemed to be holding back. "Please, Miguel. I'm not interested in getting anyone else in trouble. I just want to get my friend Ed out of trouble."

Miguel took his hands out of his pockets and crossed his arms. "Well, like I said, your friend, he come here more than once. Some of your other neighbors, they also complain about noise. A lady with long hair come once, with an old man on a scooter."

Must have been Sonia and Tony DiArco.

"What did Coach Martin say?"

"Nothing. He was too busy arguing with one of

the mothers. She scream at Coach to put her son on the field. The lady hit him with her purse when he tell her to sit down and be quiet." Miguel stopped to chuckle at the memory.

"So the coach had trouble with the parents?"

"All the time. At one game, a fat man, he shove Coach Martin in the shoulder, and the coach push him away like a *pulga*, a flea. He fall down and the other parents laugh.

"Another father, he wears a black baseball cap with a *marisco,* a pink shrimp, and talks with a stutter. Coach make fun of the way he talk and say if he don't shut up, he'll never let his kid play."

Miguel stopped and slowly shook his head. "Then there's 'Señor Rolls-Royce.' He has *una perilla*." Miguel stroked an invisible goatee on his chin. "That one don't yell. He just talk quiet. He tell Coach Martin to take his son off the bench or he wish he never born. The coach don't say nothing to that one."

"Gosh, it sounds like the parents can get pretty ugly."

"Yes, but the school is like a family. They argue with each other, but they fight together against anyone from the outside. The fat man and the shrimp hat, they help Coach Martin when your friend hit him."

"Did you ever hear the coach argue with anyone else? Maybe someone from the school?"

"The coach, he was a macho guy. He argue with a lot of people. When they built this field a couple of years ago, he argue with the contractor, the workmen, and the woman from the army."

He must be talking about the Army Corps of Engineers.

"Lately the coach have a new kind of trouble." He hesitated and looked down.

"Please, Miguel, anything might help."

"Coach, he comes here a few times a week to check equipment and check the field. He has an office inside." Miguel pointed to the maroon-and-gold monstrosity directly behind Ed's house.

"For the last six month, a lady come to see the coach at least once a week. They go in his office and he close the door. She stay for about an hour and then leave. Last week, another lady come. I think she is his wife, because this time he doesn't close the door. I hear them fight. She yell, 'Your whore will be sorry. I told her husband.' I keep my head down and work. They think I don't see nothing or hear nothing."

"Can you describe the women to me?"

"His wife is small like you, and is *muy embarazada.* She is going to have a baby. The other lady, she is very tall, yellow hair."

"Does she drive a yellow Mercedes?"

Miguel looked shocked.

I was right! Diane Davis and Dax Martin were having an affair.

"Did anyone else know about the coach and his girlfriend?"

He looked down and didn't answer.

"I know who she is, Miguel. Did her husband know—like the coach's wife said he did?"

He shuffled his feet in the dirt. "Please, Mrs. Martha."

I couldn't blame Miguel for not wanting to come right out and accuse his employer's wife of having an affair with the coach.

Dax Martin's murder was personal. Although I could sympathize, I could hardly see a small, pregnant woman beating her husband to death with a baseball bat, no matter how much he deserved it.

I doubted a rich and successful Beaumont parent, no matter how obnoxious, would kill Martin over his refusal to give their kid more playing time.

Diane's husband, Jefferson Davis, the control freak, was still the most likely suspect in Dax Martin's murder. If Javier and Graciela could confirm this, Ed would be out of the woods.

Of course this also meant Diane Davis could be in terrible danger. Who was to say Mr. Davis wouldn't turn his rage on her next? I worried for her safety.

"Did you tell any of this to the police?"

"No, Mrs. Martha. I mind my own business. They do not ask and I do not say." He looked worried. "Mrs. Martha? You know I could lose my job if they find out I talk to you. I have a family."

I smiled and put my hand on his arm. "I promise I won't tell the school you talked to me—not even if they send me to Guantanamo and pour water up my nose."

He relaxed a little and gave me a slight smile. *"Gracias."*

CHAPTER 18

I continued to walk around the adjacent park to burn calories and put some mileage on my new exercise shoes. I stepped off the path to take a closer look at the deep violet flowers of a Mexican sage plant growing in a sunny patch. I smelled it before I saw the pasty dog crap now staining the sides of my clean white Skechers.

Back home again, I scraped most of the doody off my shoes and put them in the laundry room to wash for the second time in a week. I was disappointed to find out I'd been gone only twenty-five minutes, including my conversation with Miguel.

His story about Coach Martin's affair was too good to keep to myself, so I put on my pink Crocs and walked over to Ed's house, five doors away. Ed opened his door, looked at my Barbie-pink rubber shoes and smiled. "Where's Ken?"

I walked inside. "I have some serious news, but we've got to be careful who we tell. If anyone at the

Beaumont School finds out he gave us this information, Miguel could lose his job."

"Who's Miguel, and what did he say?"

"The groundskeeper. He confirmed Dax Martin had an affair with the headmaster's wife, Diane Davis, for the past several months. Then a week before he was killed, Martin had a huge argument with his pregnant wife. From what Miguel overheard, the enraged Mrs. Martin knew about the affair and told Jefferson Davis."

"Do you think Martin's wife killed him?"

"That's the thing. She's small and very pregnant. Probably not able to beat a big man like Martin to death with a baseball bat."

Ed looked impressed. "So you were right. Dax Martin could have been killed by the jealous husband of Diane Davis, the high-and-mighty headmaster of Beaumont School. Great news!"

"Well, great news for you. Not so much for Martin. He's still dead."

"Yeah. There's that. Wouldn't it be sweet to see the school taken down a peg by a scandal?"

Ed's phone rang. He had a brief conversation and hung up. "That was Simon. He's contacted a friend in the US Attorney's Office. He should have some new information in time for our meeting tomorrow."

I got up to leave. "Great. Hang in there, Ed. Things are beginning to look a whole lot better for you."

I made a quick trip to the market to get all the ingredients for dinner, including a loaf of braided challah and some kosher wine. Uncle Isaac would never sing the Shabbat blessings with just any wine.

I peeled fresh Idaho potatoes on top of a newspaper for easy cleanup. Then I shredded them in my food processor with fresh onion and prepared a kugel to go in the oven later in the afternoon. Even though I had remodeled my kitchen a little more than a year ago, I mostly used my microwave to prepare meals. Still, I hadn't lost the knack for cooking traditional Jewish dishes.

At about eleven, Lucy and Birdie showed up with quilts over their arms just as I put the brisket in my new stainless-steel oven.

"Coffee?" I asked.

Lucy shook her head and I followed as she and Birdie walked toward my sewing room. "Can't stay. We've just set up a workshop in the parish hall at Saint Winifred's. We've got about ten quilters and three sewing machines. Seven will be tying and three will sew on bindings. We brought you the five quilts that were already finished."

I examined the quilts lying on my cutting table. The blocks were simple Windmills, a square of eight triangles with their points meeting in the center. The alternating dark and light fabrics created a whirligig pattern. The backings were pieced with spare yardage and everything was tied together with perle cotton embroidery thread. Binding had been sewn on by machine, and the resulting blankets were utilitarian but cheerful.

Birdie tugged on her braid. "Martha dear, do you have any extra batting? We may not have enough."

I pulled out a bolt of low-loft pure cotton batting—as tall as I was—from the closet. Batting was usually sold in cuts just big enough for one quilt. Since I made so many quilts, I bought in bulk. "There should be enough for about six more quilts here."

Birdie felt the batting between her expert fingers and made a face. "We can't use all cotton, dear. Pure cotton batting needs to be stitched in place so it doesn't separate. We need a polyester or poly-cotton blend that won't pull apart between the ties."

Of course I knew what Birdie meant. I'd seen some antique quilts tied every four inches. Over years of use, big lumps of cotton had bunched in between the ties. "Sorry. I can't help you, but I'll give you a donation to buy some more today."

Lucy smiled and held out her hand. "Seems only fair since this whole thing was your idea in the first place."

"By the way, I found out I was right about Diane Davis having an affair with Dax Martin."

Birdie perked up. "What's all this? Are you talking about that dead coach you found? Lucy told me about the young woman you suspected he had an affair with."

"How'd you find out?" Lucy demanded.

"I'm sworn to secrecy. But, believe me, I'm one hundred percent certain."

"You amaze me, Martha Rose."

I laughed. "I amaze myself sometimes."

After lunch I took a break from cooking and drove to the Boulevard to find Hilda. I wanted to know if she'd notified the people we were coming on Sunday. She was sitting with Rafi inside his restaurant. They were sipping something cold, and Rafi had just made her laugh. They both saw me at the same time and waved me over to the table.

Hilda's slightly greasy hair clung to her scalp, and dust and perspiration from the August heat coated her skin. A spot of grease stained the front of her Labradoodle T-shirt and the hem of her blue chambray skirt had picked up more dirt.

After a bit of small talk, I asked Hilda, "Have you told everyone about Sunday?"

"Yup, and they're pretty excited. They want to meet the woman responsible for gettin' rid of Switch."

I rolled my eyes. Then I got inspired. *Tonight is Shabbat and I'm fixing a big dinner. Hilda is homeless. She could use a good, hot meal.*

"Listen, Hilda, I have a large roast in the oven I have to get back to. I'd really love for you to come home with me and have dinner tonight."

Hilda looked at me for the longest time, fighting with some inner demon, trying to decide. Her eyes became glossy with tears. "What about my cart?" she asked in a small voice.

"We can load your stuff in the back of my car and bring it with us."

Rafi gently patted her hand. "You park your empty cart in back behind the Dumpster. Nobody take it from there. Cart will be waiting for you."

"Yeah, okay." She wiped her eyes. "Yeah."

We drove to Ralphs grocery store, with the recycling center in the parking lot. Hilda exchanged two bulging black trash bags full of cans and bottles for a few dollars. She folded the empty bags and put them in the pocket of her skirt. The bills went down the front of her T-shirt.

When we arrived at my house, she said, "I know this house. I've seen it from the park. You have a nice yard."

Because of my fibromyalgia, I didn't do much of my own gardening anymore. My talented landscaper, Abraham, gave me the most beautiful yard on the street. Graceful pepper trees shaded the perimeter, and fragrant, drought-resistant plants, such as rosemary, sage, and lavender, grew in little communities. Even the white Iceberg roses did well in the xeriscape.

"Listen, Hilda, as long as you're here, you might as well take advantage of my washer and dryer. Do you have any clothes you'd like to wash?"

She seemed embarrassed. "Yeah. It's hard to stay clean. I visit the Laundromat as often as I can, but those machines are expensive. I do a little washing by hand in the restroom of a Mobil station over on the corner of Balboa and Burbank. They're real nice to me there 'cause I don't leave a mess afterward. They even pay me sometimes to clean the restrooms."

"What do you do with your wet clothes?"

"I go down by the wash, where nobody can see me, and hang them on a bush to dry."

Hilda pulled a sack of clothing out of the trunk of the car. She left something bulky behind.

"What about those?" I pointed to her bedroll and towel.

"I thought you might not want those in your machines. They're awfully dirty."

I smiled. "Don't worry. I've got heavy-duty appliances."

Hilda's guarded footsteps followed me to my front door.

CHAPTER 19

The air-conditioning welcomed us as we came in out of the heat. The aroma of roasting meat, herbs, carrots, and onions filled the house. Hilda sniffed. "Smells so good."

I showed her to the laundry room, where she sorted her clothes. I went to check on the brisket and put the potato kugel in the oven. Soon there was a rapid clicking of the knob turning on the washing machine. Hilda started up the first load of clothes and walked shyly into the kitchen. "I really appreciate this. Thanks."

I smiled. "You know, I'm thinking now you're here, would you like to freshen up? Maybe take a nice cool shower?"

Hilda's eyes opened wide. "I would, but I don't have any clean clothes to put on yet."

"I think I might have something to fit you. Then you could also wash the clothes you have on."

I walked her to my daughter Quincy's old bedroom, where she slept on her visits home from the

East Coast. A Grandmother's Flower Garden quilt covered a double-sized antique walnut sleigh bed. Hundreds of two-inch hexagons pieced in a mosaic of concentric circles of color mimicked the shapes of flowers. I worked over a whole year to sew the pieces together by hand and then quilt each individual hexagon.

I placed a fluffy white towel and washcloth in the all-white en suite bathroom and unwrapped a fresh bar of rose-scented soap.

Hilda pulled the bar of soap to her face, closed her eyes, and took a deep breath. "Smells like my grandma's yard when I was a kid."

"Where was that?"

"Portland, Oregon. She took care of me after school while my parents worked. She'd have a batch of fresh, warm sugar cookies waiting for me every day after school." Hilda smiled wistfully.

"My grandmother, my bubbie, took care of me too. I lived with her and my mother and my uncle Isaac. Only Uncle Isaac is left. You'll meet him at dinner tonight. How about your folks?"

Hilda's shoulders sagged. "Oh, my grandma died a long time ago. My parents are . . . We don't really speak." She looked down and turned slightly away, struggling to maintain control.

I cleared my throat and opened one section of the bedroom closet. "Come and take a look. These are some of my daughter's clothes I've been meaning to take to the Goodwill. You're about the same size. Please feel free to take anything from this section to wear."

"Anything?"

"Yes, and I don't mean just one thing. Whatever you can use, you can take. Pants, blouses, skirts, anything."

Hilda gave me a funny look. "Why're you doing this? Why're you so sure you can trust me?"

That was a good question. I was a pretty good judge of people and simply felt in my bones Hilda would never harm anyone. "You've helped me a lot. I just want to return the favor." I jerked my head toward the bathroom and smiled. "Take as much time in there as you want."

Lucy and Birdie showed up around five with six more quilts. They didn't recognize Hilda. Her face and skin were no longer covered in grime. She wore a pair of gray corduroy trousers and a white peasant blouse from Guatemala, with bright embroidery around the neckline and on the puffy little sleeves. Her shoulder-length brown hair was clean and blow-dried. She lived a rough life, but her features still showed a lot of gentleness. She appeared to be somewhere in her early forties.

Lucy's mouth fell open when she figured out who Hilda was. "Well, don't you look absolutely wonderful!"

Amen to that.

No sooner did we put the newest quilts on my cutting table than the doorbell rang again. I left the three others in the sewing room and went to investigate.

Three hundred pounds of biker in a black T-shirt and red bandana walked in.

"Hey, babe. I just talked to Ed. He told me all about your conversation this morning with the—"

I held up my hand. "Don't say it. I promised him anonymity."

He grinned. "Okay. I heard you-know-who confirmed Martin had an affair with his boss's wife. I just wanted to say you were right about talking to you-know-who alone." He lifted his head and sniffed. "Smells good in here. Like home."

"I'm fixing Shabbat dinner for my uncle Isaac."

"Shabbat dinner? It's been a while."

It's Shabbat, Martha. You won't be alone with him. Uncle Isaac and Hilda will be here.

"Would you like to join us?"

Crusher put his huge hand over his heart. "I'd be honored."

Great. There goes half the kugel.

The three women came out from the sewing room.

Lucy took one look at the bearded giant. "I'll bet you're Crusher."

He looked at me. "You've been talking about me. That's a good sign."

Darn it, Lucy!

I introduced him as Yossi Levy, and the doorbell rang again. Sonia stood there, smiling.

She walked in wearing a gauzy white Indian blouse and her colorful bangles tinkled on her wrist. After a brief hello, she stood next to Crusher and smiled at him. As soon as Sonia saw Crusher from her window, her curiosity must have compelled her to rush right over. There was something un-Sonia-like in the way she smiled at him. *Hmmm.*

"Sonia Spiegelman, this is Yossi Levy, a friend of Ed's. You may have seen him around lately."

Sonia stuck out her hand and smiled demurely. She still held his hand and looked at him. "I sure have. You're kinda hard to miss, big fella."

No way. You didn't just say that!

I introduced her to Birdie and Hilda. She already knew Lucy.

Sonia inhaled deeply and looked at me expectantly. "Something sure smells good in here."

It's Shabbat, Martha. Sonia's alone in this world. It would be a mitzvah.

"Would you care to join us for Shabbat dinner, Sonia?"

"I haven't had Shabbat dinner in a long time. I'd love to. Oh, and I've already collected a lot of items for Sunday. Shall I bring them over?"

"Sure. We can put them in my sewing room."

I should have seen what was coming next.

"Yossi, would you please help me carry all those things? I need someone really strong." She tapped his large bicep with her finger.

"Yeah, sure." Poor Yossi looked clueless.

As soon as they left, Hilda burst out laughing. Then Lucy joined in. Soon the four of us were howling.

Lucy wiped tears from her eyes. "That was just plain pathetic. I'm going to need to change my pad."

I opened a bottle of wine. "Come on, girls. This

may turn out to be a long night. Lucy, Birdie, will you stay for dinner too? There's plenty to go around. I actually made extra food, thinking I might send some home with my uncle and freeze the rest."

"No, hon. I'll have a small glass of wine, though. We worked like slaves today and there's more to do tomorrow."

Birdie reached for a glass. "Ditto."

Hilda checked on her laundry and then took a glass of wine. "I usually don't drink, because I've got to stay alert, but tonight I'll make an exception."

She took tiny sips of wine. At the rate she was going, the glass would last all evening. After about ten minutes, she said, "Where are those two, anyway?"

Lucy raised her glass to her lips. "Sonia must have an awfully big load."

More laughter.

The doorbell rang again and Sonia walked in carrying several blankets, followed by Crusher, carrying two cardboard cartons full of toiletries and packages of white athletic socks from a big-box store. He looked at me with wide, clued-up eyes. After depositing the donations in my sewing room, they each took a glass of wine. I cut some pita bread and put out a bowl of hummus.

From inside my house, we couldn't miss the loudspeakers at the Beaumont School baseball field. Even the death of their head coach didn't deter them from playing ball and disturbing the peace of our neighborhood.

CHAPTER 20

Lucy and Birdie left at five-thirty and Uncle Isaac came at six. My elderly uncle, Isaac Harris, was starched and clean-shaven. Covering the top and sides of his curly white hair sat a *kippah* made in the Bukharian style—a brimless round hat, with elaborate embroidery, covering his skull. He'd gotten shorter with age; and when he hugged me, we were almost eye to eye.

He looked around, surprised to meet so many other people.

I introduced him to the odd assortment of people.

"So, where's Arlo?" my uncle asked.

Crusher looked down. My uncle liked Arlo Beavers. He had high hopes I'd found a permanent relationship with a good man. It didn't bother him that Arlo wasn't Jewish. Uncle Isaac liked the fact Beavers was Native American and grew up on the

Rez. "They're spiritual people. We have a lot in common," he'd said.

My heart sank. "Arlo couldn't make it."

He studied my face. "The life of a lawman is hard work, I guess." He always knew when I was hiding something. For sure I'd be hearing from him later and he'd make me tell him every humiliating detail, starting with the fact that I'd discovered a dead body and was now looking for witnesses to the murder. I'd rather stick a fork in my eye.

He sat. "It's a good thing Morty dropped me off and didn't have to park his car. There's no space. The streets around here are full of expensive cars. I even saw a boy speeding by in a black BMW convertible. He couldn't have been more than sixteen."

"Yeah. The Beaumont School is having a baseball game this evening."

"So that's what all the noise is about. What a *shande*. It used to be so peaceful around here." He shifted in his seat and faced Crusher. "So. It's Yossi, is it? Yossi Levy?"

Crusher sat up a little straighter and played with his wineglass. He was three times larger than my uncle, but he was clearly a little nervous. "Yes, Mr. Harris."

Uncle Isaac adjusted his glasses, squinted, and looked at the red do-rag. "What is that covering your head? Some kind of new *kippah*?"

"It's a bandana, sir."

"Like the cowboys wear?"

"Yes, sir."

"*Oy va voy!* What will they think of next?"

My good plain white Rosenthal china sat on the white tablecloth and my bubbie's twin silver candle-holders sat in the middle, in the place of honor. A silver kiddush cup, which was filled with wine, sat ready at the head of the table for Uncle Isaac, and a cloth embroidered with colorful fruits and flowers covered the challah.

I draped a sequined blue scarf over my head, lit the candles, circled my hands over the flame and covered my eyes as I recited the Hebrew blessing. I always felt a deep connection at this moment knowing Jewish women all over the world were doing exactly the same thing.

When I looked up, Sonia had maneuvered a seat at the table next to Crusher. My uncle lifted the silver cup of wine and recited the kiddush, a Hebrew blessing for the Sabbath. Crusher joined in. Hilda sat in respectful silence, listening to the four of us sing blessings over the wine and challah.

As we passed the food around the table, Hilda looked at Uncle Isaac. "I've never been in a Jewish home before. Is this some special kind of holiday?"

"Special, but not unique. This we should do every week when the Sabbath begins."

"It's beautiful. Why do you wear your hat at the table?"

"Covering my head keeps me humble, sweetheart. It reminds me God is the boss. Even at the table."

The talk turned to our plans for the distribution of goods to the homeless on Sunday. I'd warned everyone ahead of time not to mention Javier and Graciela. I wasn't ready to tell my uncle I discovered a murdered corpse, and I especially didn't want him to know about my close call with Switch.

Uncle Isaac said, "What you're doing for those homeless people is a mitzvah."

"What's that mean?" Hilda asked.

"A good deed, sweetheart. One of the foundations of our religion is to care for the less fortunate. Nowadays people give money. In Bible times, most people were farmers. The Torah taught them how to help others. 'When you reap the harvest of your land, do not reap to the very edges of your field or gather the gleanings of your harvest. Leave them for the poor and the alien.'"

"It's from *Sefer Vayikra*, the Book of Leviticus," added Crusher.

I put down my fork and stared at him.

He blushed and put his hand on top of his bandana. "Hidden depths, babe. This ain't just a do-rag."

Crusher uses a bandana as a religious head covering? He knows Torah? Who is this man, outlaw or scholar?

Uncle Isaac asked Hilda, "So, what do you do, sweetheart?"

I was mortified, worried that his innocent question might embarrass Hilda.

She smiled sweetly. "I collect trash for recycling and do casual janitorial services when I can get work."

Uncle Isaac looked confused. "'Collect trash'? Like with a truck?"

"No, Mr. Harris. I collect cans and bottles from trash cans and Dumpsters and walk them to a recycling center in Ralphs parking lot."

He still didn't get it. "Like the homeless people do?"

"That's me."

Now he was completely distressed. "*Vey iz mir!* You're homeless? How could a nice lady like you be homeless?"

I jumped in. "Maybe Hilda doesn't want to talk about it, Uncle Isaac."

Although we're all dying to know.

He reached over and patted her hand. "I'm sorry, sweetheart. I don't mean to be nosy."

"I'm homeless because I can't find steady work. People don't like to hire ex-cons."

Crusher swallowed his food. "I know what you mean. I spent some time in prison too. After I got out, I couldn't get a job. Luckily, some friends loaned me enough money to open my own shop. Everything's cool now."

Uncle Isaac turned to Hilda. "So if someone loaned money, could you do the same thing?"

"Not really. I used to be a licensed vocational nurse. I lost my license when they convicted me of grand theft."

Sonia could keep quiet no longer. She asked the question we all wanted to hear. "What happened?"

Hilda took a dainty bite of her kugel and looked at me. "This sure is good." Then she put her hands in her lap, sat back in her chair, and looked around the table.

"I worked in a nursing home with wealthy patients. We all rotated in and out of the Alzheimer's ward on a regular basis. They said permanent assignments to the ward were too stressful on the staff. Well, it turns out a man in senior management arranged the schedule that way so none of the staff would notice when expensive jewelry went missing."

Uncle Isaac asked, "The man stole things from the patients, who trusted him?"

"Once, when he thought nobody was looking, I saw him pocket something, but I didn't know what really went down until it was too late."

Sonia leaned toward Hilda. "So then what happened?"

"The family of that patient discovered a three-carat diamond ring missing from her room. I put two and two together and went to the manager's office. I told him to return the ring or I'd tell the police what I saw. The next thing I knew, the police were searching staff lockers. They found the ring in my locker. I tried to tell them the manager planted it there, but no one believed me. I spent the next five years in prison." Hilda looked around the table defiantly. "I was innocent!"

Uncle Isaac balled his fists. "A great evil was done to you, sweetheart. *Feh!*"

Then he spat out a curse in Yiddish. *May God bestow on the man everything his heart desires, and may he become a quadriplegic and not even be able to use his tongue!*

Sonia asked, "Aren't there organizations helping women who get out of prison?"

Hilda shook her head slowly. "Only for a short time. Then you're on your own. You can't help people find jobs when there're no jobs to begin with. Anyway, I'm used to street life now. The people call me 'doc.' They get hurt or sick, and then they find me. They know I'll help 'em as much as I can. I even helped birth a baby down in the wash a couple of years ago. Someone called the parameds, but they took twenty minutes to find us. By the time they showed up, it was all over."

Uncle Isaac's eyes brimmed with tears. *"A gesind auf deine keppele."*

"What does that mean?"

"He's heaping blessings on your head," said Crusher.

Uncle Isaac looked at each person sitting around the table: Hilda, Sonia, Crusher, and me. "You're all in this blanket mitzvah together?"

The four of us nodded.

"Well, I'm so relieved. I don't feel so guilty now."

What did my uncle mean? "Guilty about what?"

He grabbed my hand and squeezed. "Well, *faigele.* I know my Martha pretty well. You were acting pretty shifty tonight, so I thought maybe you were up to something crazy again. You know, like the murder you were involved in four months ago. Thank goodness I was wrong."

Crusher cleared his throat and looked at his plate. Sonia took a sip of water, and Hilda found something interesting to stare at across the room.

Uncle Isaac narrowed his eyes. "I was wrong, wasn't I?"

"Don't be silly, Uncle. You've got nothing to worry about."

CHAPTER 21

Morty came by after his date to pick up Uncle Isaac. With her bedroll still in the dryer, Hilda spent the night in the guest room.

She helped wash the breakfast dishes while I made her a sandwich-to-go from the leftover brisket and challah. The sack carrying her clean clothes was now fatter with several pieces of Quincy's old wardrobe. Her clean bedroll was a little brighter with a pretty red-and-yellow tied Windmill quilt; she asked to keep the rose soap.

"Thanks for everything, Wonder Woman. I enjoyed sleeping in a real bed again. That quilt reminds me of one my grandma made that I loved so much. Maybe one day you'll show me how to make one just like it."

"I'd love to. Seriously." I thought about asking Lucy and Birdie to include Hilda in our weekly group. If there was anything a quilter loved, it was teaching someone new how to quilt.

"Your uncle's such a sweet old man." Hilda briefly

touched my arm. "You're cut from the same cloth." She laughed. "Get it? It's a quilter joke."

I chuckled. "I get it. And you're right. He's special."

I handed her a piece of paper with my phone number. "Keep this. Call me anytime, for any reason. If you decide you want to get off the streets, I'll do everything I can to help." Then I drove her back to Rafi's place to retrieve her cart.

I arrived at Ed Pappas's house in just enough time for the ten o'clock meeting with his attorney, Simon Aiken, and Ed's other biker friends. Ed's wood-and-chrome dining-room table sat to the right, loaded with refreshments. I poured myself some Starbucks coffee from the disposable carton, but I passed on the apple fritters from Western Donuts.

People were lounging in Ed's living room to the left, sprawled on his brown leather sofa and matching easy chairs. I sat in one of the empty chrome chairs from the dining room. We had all agreed to meet this morning for a progress report, and I couldn't wait to tell everyone what I found out from the groundskeeper.

Simon Aiken wore jeans, like everyone else, on this Saturday morning. A new diamond stud sparkled on his earlobe.

Dana Fremont sat next to him on the sofa. Her long brown hair hung in two thick braids and her size-four skinny-legged jeans hugged ankles as slender as my wrists. A big new diamond sparkled on her finger.

Aiken reached over and briefly caressed her forearm.

Ah! Dana doesn't just work for Aiken; they're a couple. Have they recently exchanged diamond engagement rings?

Crusher wore a brown bandana on his head this morning. His six-foot-six, three-hundred-pound frame completely filled one of the large leather easy chairs. He stood to offer me the chair. He might've been a golem, but he was a golem with manners and "hidden depths," as he hinted last night. I declined his offer and stayed seated in the smaller chair, where my feet could touch the floor.

Carl, the young biker who helped save Beavers's wounded dog, waved; a smile creased his handsome face.

Ed Pappas, whose legal defense was the topic of this meeting, sat in the other easy chair, studying his laptop. Ed wore his uniform: a blue-and-white striped tank top showing off his tattoo of the Greek flag, cargo shorts, and a three-day growth of light brown beard.

Aiken cleared his throat. "Okay, everyone's here, so let's get started. I'll go first. I talked to the DA, and she's convinced she can make a case against Ed based on his threat against Dax Martin and the bloody baseball bat found in Ed's backyard. Although he hasn't been arrested and formally charged with the murder yet, we need to be prepared for when she comes after him. She hinted it was only a matter of time."

Ed's face paled; the skin around his eyes tightened and his mouth formed a hard line. My pulse quickened at the bad news.

Aiken looked at me. "Martha, I hear you talked to the groundskeeper yesterday. Could he tell you anything about the witnesses Javier and Graciela?"

"He wants to remain anonymous. He'll lose his job if the school ever finds out he talked to me. Anyway, he knows nothing about the homeless couple, but he did give me a juicy bit of info. He confirmed Dax Martin carried on an affair with the headmaster's wife, Diane Davis, in the stadium office there." I pointed through Ed's sliding glass doors and beyond to the maroon-and-gold building looming like a permanent insult sixty feet away. Dana typed quickly on her iPad.

"He also said he heard Martin and his wife arguing a week before he was killed. Martin's angry wife informed him she told Jefferson Davis about the affair with Diane."

Aiken nodded. "That would give Davis a motive to kill Martin. That's more ammunition to help us establish reasonable doubt in court. Good work, Martha."

"Thanks. There's also been a new development since our last meeting." I told them about the plan to go down in the wildlife reserve on Sunday and distribute quilts and supplies to the homeless. "While we're down there, we'll look for Javier and Graciela."

Dana looked at me and smiled. "Nice idea. Will you be safe?"

Crusher sat forward in his seat. "Now that Switch

is gone, I hear things have changed for the better down there. I'm going to help Martha take the stuff in my truck. We need the Valley Eagles to ride in and keep the peace." Valley Eagles was what these motorcycle buddies called their club—hence the big purple *VE* on the back of their jackets and vests.

"I'm loading the truck tomorrow morning at ten, at Martha's house. We'll caravan from there down Burbank Boulevard at around eleven."

"I'm in," said Carl and Ed at the same time.

Aiken cracked his knuckles. "Yeah, Dana and I'll be there." He turned to Ed. "Anything new?"

"I went to the website for the Army Corps of Engineers. The chain of command is pretty short. Specialist Lawanda Price is the coordinator for the Sepulveda Basin. She's the one who actually comes to the area and physically supervises the properties for compliance and maintenance—including the parks, wildlife reserve, and ball fields."

Crusher took a gulp of coffee. "She's the one who approved the building of the stadium?"

Ed scratched his neck. "No. I think that's way above her rank and pay grade. She's basically a low-level field grunt. A couple links up the chain is a civilian, Barbara Hardisty. She's the real estate assets manager and the one who has broad authority over all the federal real estate in California. This Hardisty woman is likely the one who approved the stadium."

Aiken narrowed his eyes. "Interesting."

Ed shifted in his seat. "There's more. I went fishing around the Beaumont School website to see what I could find out about Martin, the stadium, the athletic program, anything really. I found a roster and photos posted of the students participating in each sport. Guess which sophomore is on the baseball team?"

Everyone looked at Ed.

"A boy named Jason Hardisty."

Crusher stopped just before he bit into his second fritter. "Any connection to the lady who approved the building of the school's baseball stadium?"

Ed shrugged. "I don't know. Beaumont records are confidential. In order to get a list of students and their parents, I'd have to hack into their computer system or break into their offices."

Aiken stretched his arm out like a traffic cop. "Stop. I'm sure you're speaking hypothetically, right? You can't say things like that with other people in the room, even if you're kidding. Attorney-client privilege extends only to the two of us when we're alone. If you're arrested and we have to convince a jury you're innocent, we don't want anyone here forced to testify you said anything incriminating."

Ed looked chagrined. "Okay. Got it."

Aiken waved his hand. "Anyway, that information is easy enough to get. Every family is listed in the school directory. All we have to do is find a parent with a directory. I know someone at Beaumont who might give me a copy, but they're out of town until Monday."

He turned to Dana. "Tell everyone what you discovered about the headmaster and his wife."

She made a few swipes on her iPad. "I did some

cyber sleuthing on each of them. Diane Davis appears to have her own assets. She comes from money. Jefferson Davis reports about half a mil a year from his job and another two hundred thou from a personal holding company called 'SFV Associates.' Probably stands for San Fernando Valley."

Ed looked at me and back at Dana. "Do we know what his company does?"

"Yeah. SFV Associates incorporated more than two years ago, right before the Beaumont Stadium project began. They just happened to make the winning bid to build the stadium and then subcontracted with Valley Allstar Construction to do the work."

I spoke up. "Makes sense. As headmaster, Jefferson Davis was in a position to know what the other contractors bid on the stadium. He might even have suggested to them a number to bid on, knowing it would be high. Then his company came in at the last minute with a lower bid, undercut their prices, and got the job. Davis pocketed a percentage and, with the rest of the money, hired a contractor, Valley Allstar, to actually build the stadium."

Carl still looked lost. "How does this tie in with Martin's murder?"

I refilled my coffee cup. "Maybe the murder wasn't about an affair. Martin was closely tied to the stadium project. Maybe he knew from the start, or maybe he found out from Diane Davis, how her husband got the contract. Dax Martin didn't come from money. He had three kids to support and another on the way. Maybe he saw a way to get more money and tried to blackmail Davis. It's obvious to me that Davis is a control freak. He'd never stand for anyone having power over him. It's possible Jefferson Davis killed Martin to shut him up."

Aiken nodded. "Davis has two reasons for wanting Martin dead—jealousy and money. Of course, at this juncture, this is all speculation, but it's substantial enough to cause reasonable doubt if the case ever goes to a jury."

Maybe Beavers might be less angry with me if I could give him this useful information we were uncovering. Maybe he'd see I was right all along about Ed's innocence. Maybe he'd even forgive me.

"Shouldn't we give what we have to the police? They might decide to pursue these other leads right now and leave Ed alone," I suggested.

Aiken shook his head. "Not yet. The police are building their case against Ed, and the DA isn't in a mood to listen. We've got to present them with more than conjecture. We need additional hard evidence. The information against Davis is our ace in the hole, and we're not going to play that card until it'll do the most good."

I was disappointed over losing the opportunity to contact Beavers, but I knew Aiken spoke the truth. Ed's freedom might depend on a surprise defense.

I asked, "Simon, what happened with your contact in the US Attorney's Office? Were they able to get the Beaumont documents from the Army Corps of Engineers?"

"So far, the district commander has failed to return his calls. It's the weekend now, so nothing more is going to get done until Monday. We'll just have to exercise some patience and wait." He cleared his throat. "Let's review where we stand."

I said I'd search for Javier and Graciela in the wildlife reserve the next day, and Aiken said he'd pursue the Army Corps of Engineers/Beaumont/Hardisty connections with his contacts on Monday.

Aiken stretched and stood. "Good work, everyone. And good luck tomorrow. Let's touch base again here at Ed's on Monday evening. Hopefully, we'll have more answers by then."

Crusher also stood, towering above me by a good fourteen inches. Hebrew letters and a familiar red logo spread across the expansive chest of his XXX-Large T-shirt. "I'll walk you home."

Walking next to Crusher, I felt as light as a feather and completely forgot about Dana's size-four jeans.

"Thanks again for dinner last night."

I jumped at the chance to find out more about this enigmatic giant. "How do you know so much Torah? Do you really keep your head covered for religious reasons? And how did you land in prison?"

A curtain twitched in Sonia's window across the street. Before Crusher could open his mouth to answer, Sonia stood in front of us. Her gaze never left his face. She wore green eye shadow and batted lashes coated in black mascara. She reminded me of an eager lizard.

"Martha, Yossi, how nice to see you again so soon after such a lovely dinner."

Crusher put his arm around my shoulders and

hung on for dear life. "Huh? Yeah. Martha here's a real *balabusta*." He used the Yiddish expression for "domestic goddess/kitchen maven" and squeezed me like toothpaste for emphasis.

She tilted her head. "I'm also a pretty good cook. . . ."

I *SO* did not want to be in the vicinity of this conversation, and I didn't want Crusher hiding behind me—as if he could hide behind anybody. I wriggled out of his grasp.

"Uh, Sonia, are we expecting any more donations today?"

"Lots, and I've got a few pickups I promised to make." She looked hopefully at Crusher. "I may need a little help."

Crusher smiled apologetically and touched his forehead as if he'd just remembered something. "You know, I'd like to help, but I've got to get back to my shop. I'll call Martha this evening after I close to see how things are going."

He rapidly walked back to his Harley and strapped on his helmet. The very large black-and-chrome bike rumbled past us like a Brahma bull, and Crusher briefly flashed the palm of his hand in salute.

Sonia sighed. "There goes one gorgeous hunk of man. I was surprised last night to learn he's so religious. Do you know what was written in Hebrew on the front of his T-shirt?"

Yes, I did, although it had taken me a while to figure it out.

"Budweiser."

CHAPTER 22

Sonia returned home, and I was just about to walk in my front door, when an army jeep drove down the street and turned toward the baseball field. A late-model black Jaguar wasn't far behind. The jeep must have been from the Army Corps of Engineers. Ed said Specialist Lawanda Price managed the Sepulveda Basin. That could be her.

I moved quietly around my house to the back, hiding under the drooping branches of the pepper trees, hoping to blend in with the foliage. The jeep parked next to the field and a woman with a red ponytail, wearing army fatigues, got out. The Jag pulled up next to the jeep and a brunette in a green linen pantsuit got out. Was that a Beaumont parent driving the expensive car?

The two of them walked toward the shade of the trees in the nearby parkland. "Ponytail" started talking and "Pantsuit" crossed her arms over her chest.

I moved as quickly as I could in my pink rubber Crocs, darting from behind one bush to another, skulking like the Pink Panther. Luckily, the women were hotly engaged and didn't notice my approach. They made no effort to keep their voices down.

"I know all about Beaumont," said Ponytail. "I could ruin you, Barbara."

Oh, my God. The woman in the green pantsuit must be Barbara Hardisty, Lawanda Price's boss and the one who approved the building of the baseball stadium!

"You'd better keep your mouth shut," said Hardisty.

"It'll cost you."

"I'm warning you. You're in way over your head." She gestured toward Ed's house. "People who get in their way—"

The pollen from a nearby acacia made me sneeze. They stopped talking and looked in my direction. I quickly stepped back onto the path and pretended to be walking toward the park. As I approached, they both glanced at my distinctive pink shoes.

Note to self: get dark-colored Crocs to wear in public.

I smiled and waved my hand in greeting. "Hi, ladies. Looks like we're in for another scorcher today." I got close enough to read the name tag sewn onto the pocket of Ponytail's uniform: *Spc Price.* I was so right about who they were.

Price nodded politely. "Yes, ma'am. Looks like it."

Hardisty said, "Well, I think we're done here. Tell maintenance to trim those bushes. They're growing too close to the path."

"Yes, ma'am."

They turned and walked ahead of me back to their cars.

Price snarled, "Don't underestimate me, Barbara."

"I'll talk to them."

Price jumped into the jeep and drove away.

Barbara Hardisty pulled out her cell phone and climbed into her black Jaguar XJ. What was a civilian employee of the Army Corps of Engineers doing with an expensive luxury car? The jaguar would have cost her more than a year's salary.

Hardisty was getting money from somewhere and, apparently, Price wanted a piece of the action. Hardisty had pointed to Ed's house and warned something about "Anyone who gets in *their* way." So, who were "they," and who is it that she just called?

The sun was straight up overhead and the spindly buckwheat—a plant acclimated to drought conditions—gasped, nonetheless, for water in the merciless sun. Still mulling over what I'd just overheard, I headed back home toward the air-conditioning.

I poured myself a glass of ice water and called Simon Aiken. The phone went to voice mail. "Simon, this is Martha. Please call me as soon as you can. I just stumbled on some important information that'll help Ed's case."

Then I called Lucy's cell phone. I knew she'd be at St. Winifred's with Birdie, tying quilts for tomorrow. "How's it going today?"

"Coming right along. Word got out and fifteen women showed up today. Many of them brought packages of socks and other toiletries. We even got four more quilt tops to tie."

"Do you need more help?"

"Yeah. Could you bring Birdie and me some lunch? We both got so busy putting things together this morning, we forgot about food."

"Sure. I'll bring sandwiches and iced tea. Anyone else need to eat?"

Lucy turned away from the phone and yelled, "Anyone here want a sandwich?" Then she said, "Two more hands raised. Bring enough for four. No, make that five, just in case." I drove to the sub shop and got six foot-longs cut in half and three six-packs of bottled iced tea. As an afterthought, I threw in a dozen individual bags of chips. God forbid there shouldn't be enough food.

St. Winifred's was located on Ventura, not too far from my house in Encino. The architecture was conceived in the 1950s, with its roof thrusting out at sharp angles and lots of clerestory windows with orange-colored glass. Broad, no-nonsense steps led straight up to a wide set of glass front doors. A steel cross with pointed ends stood on the pinnacle of the roof.

The church let our guild use the parish hall for meetings and special activities, such as the project today. I drove to the parking lot in back, near the entrance. Even with arms full of plastic sacks, I managed to push the lock button on my remote as I walked toward the building. The car gave a little chirp behind me. Luckily, someone inside saw me coming and opened the door.

Several folding banquet tables were set up around the room. At five of the tables, quilts were smoothed out and clipped to the edges to keep them from shifting. Teams of two or three women were stitching ties into the quilts. The needles they used were long and heavy-duty, with large eyes to accommodate the heavier perle cotton thread. Perle cotton was a versatile thread used for many kinds of needlework, including decorative stitching, like embroidery, or a special kind of large-stitch quilting, *sashiko*. The heavier-weight single-ply yarn was a perfect choice for tying quilts.

Once the quilts were tied, the raw edges needed to be covered. Three sewing machines sat on three other tables. Women were attaching long strips of previously folded binding to the quilts to finish them off. A special attachment on the machine allowed the sewers to fold the binding over the edge and stitch through both sides at once. It was a slow, stop-and-go process because the binding strips constantly needed to be adjusted around the edges of the quilt.

The room pulsed with animation as the women gossiped and laughed. A frustrated "Darn it!" came from one table as a quilter struggled with a stubborn sewing machine.

Someone hurried over to see what the problem was. "I think you've just got lint gumming up the works. Let's take the throat plate off, clean it with a brush, and put in a drop of oil. Then your machine should run more smoothly." Quilters not only engineered the design of their quilt tops, they were also required to be mechanics for their sewing machines.

At one end of the parish hall stood a raised stage, with navy blue velvet curtains. Birdie and Lucy spread out the food and drinks, using the edge of the proscenium as an improvised buffet. "Food's here!" shouted Lucy.

Several women broke away and made a beeline toward us. I was glad I brought the extra sandwiches and drinks.

After a quick bite, I washed the grease off my hands and joined my friends at a table with another Windmill quilt done in greens and unbleached muslin. Birdie had used low-loft polyester batting, so the ties could be five inches apart. We used green perle cotton thread and relied on the pattern of the block as a guide for the placement of the ties.

"I uncovered something really important this morning." I told them about sneaking up on Lawanda Price and listening to their conversation. "Someone is covering up something illegal between the Beaumont School and the Army Corps of Engineers. I think payoffs are involved. The thing is, if we can figure out what they're hiding, we might divert suspicion from Ed."

Birdie cut the ends of a tie. "How's that, dear?"

"According to his attorney, Ed is close to being arrested and charged with murder. If we want to point the police and the DA in another direction, we need to make the case that someone else has a strong reason to kill Dax Martin."

"Well, what would the reason be?"

"Bribes. Barbara Hardisty may have been paid off for something, probably for approving the stadium in the first place, and Lawanda Price wants part of the action. What if Dax Martin was also receiving hush money to keep his mouth shut about illegal deals? What if he got too greedy and was killed?"

Lucy threaded another needle. "Who exactly would be making those payoffs?"

I told them about SFV Associates being awarded the contract to build the baseball stadium. "Jefferson Davis could be making payoffs to hide the fact he committed fraud to obtain and profit from the contract to develop the stadium. Or maybe someone else connected to the school wasn't about to let anything stand in the way of developing the fanciest, most expensive high-school baseball field in the nation. When it comes to prestige, some parents will do anything to make their kids look good."

Birdie finished tying a stitch. "Can you prove any of this?"

"Not yet. We need to convince the DA to look at other suspects besides Ed. We're trying to keep him from being arrested. If Ed is charged with murder, then we've got to establish reasonable doubt. Remember the glove and the O.J. trial?"

By the end of the day, nine more quilts were finished. I cleaned up the remnants of the food as women folded up the banquet tables and metal chairs and placed them in the storage closet next to the stage. Someone found a push broom and swept all the cuttings and pins from the floor.

A man walked into the room, wearing eyeglasses

and a short-sleeved black cotton shirt with a clerical collar. He came over to where the three of us were gathering our things and smiled. "Nice job of cleaning up, Lucy. Thank you."

St. Winifred's was Lucy's home church, and she was quite friendly with the priest. "We're grateful to be able to use the hall, Father Joe."

"What are you going to do with all these quilts?"

"We're taking them tomorrow morning to the homeless people who live in the wildlife reserve, next to the 405 Freeway."

"Come to early mass. We'll say a special prayer for you and for the homeless."

Lucy smiled. "Thank you, Father. Ray and I'll be there."

Lucy's husband, Ray Mondello, was a man of deep faith. The two of them raised five sons in St. Winifred's. Ray always gave credit to the church for keeping the boys on the straight and narrow. I gave major credit to the couple for creating a strong circle of love and discipline, which guided their boys into manhood.

Father Joe helped us carry the nine finished quilts and donated toiletries to my car. I pressed the remote and the priest opened the door to the backseat. He turned to me with concern when he saw the dried blood smeared on the leather seat and on the carpet. "Should I ask?"

My eyes filled with tears as I remembered Arthur whining in pain. "I transported an injured dog to the vet a few days ago. I just haven't gotten around to having the blood cleaned properly."

Birdie came over and put an arm around my shoulder. "Why don't we put everything in the trunk, dear."

I thanked my friends profusely for all their help. "Tomorrow morning at my house, around ten?"

Lucy hugged me. "We'll be there."

Back at home, I made four trips to bring all nine quilts and the other donations into my sewing room for sorting later in the evening. As soon as I put the last armload down, my phone rang.

"So, *faigele,* tell me what's going on," said Uncle Isaac.

"I just got home with the last of the quilts to give away tomorrow. Sonia should be coming over soon to help me put everything together."

"I'm talking about you and Arlo. What's going on?"

"What makes you think anything's going on?"

"*Vey iz mir!* I always know when you're hiding something. Out with it. You'll feel better."

My uncle Isaac might have been in his eighties, but he was the sharpest pencil in the box. I couldn't hide anything from him, so I took a deep breath and plunged in, editing as I went along. I talked about discovering Dax Martin's body and looking for evidence to exonerate my neighbor Ed Pappas. I left out the part about Switch attacking me and injuring Beavers's dog.

"Arlo doesn't like you being such a *kuchleffel*?" My uncle used the Yiddish expression meaning "cooking spoon." It applies to a spoon stirring a pot—a meddler.

"Yeah, Uncle Isaac. Something like that."

"Why don't you stop, already?"

"Because an innocent man may go to jail."

"You don't trust Arlo to do his job right?"

How does he do it? How can my uncle zero in on the heart of my deepest issues in so few words?

"It's complicated."

"It doesn't have to be, *faigele*. Love and trust. They should be simple."

CHAPTER 23

At six, Sonia arrived with several blankets in her arms. "I've got lots more where these came from, and I could use some help. Has Yossi called yet? Is he going to come over?"

Poor Sonia was besotted with Crusher. What if the two of them actually did get together? Wouldn't my Crusher problem be solved? I just hoped she didn't come on so strong that she drove him away. Judging from his reactions this morning, he already seemed uneasy with her keen attention.

"I haven't heard from him yet. I just got home. Why don't I help you carry everything over?"

"There's too much. I'll call The Eyes."

Sonia, referring to the neighborhood watch patrol, pulled out her cell phone. Ten minutes later, Ron Wilson, with his large belly and white crew cut, knocked on my door, followed by Tony DiArco, riding his scooter with the oxygen tank.

The four of us managed to carry thirty blankets and several large cartons of toiletries to my house.

Tony made several trips with supplies in the basket of his scooter, using driveways as ramps to cross the street from Sonia's house to mine. His last load consisted of a giant pack of forty-eight rolls of toilet paper that was so large he had to lean over the side of his scooter to see where he was going. When the last package was transferred, I offered the guys each a glass of wine.

"Can't," Ron answered, shaking his head. "The wife's expecting me home for dinner. Thanks, anyway."

"My doc would kill me," Tony wheezed.

After they left, I poured Sonia and myself each a glass of Santa Margherita Chianti and ordered a delivery pizza. A long evening lay ahead of us: sorting and packing personal hygiene products into extra-extra-large zippered plastic bags.

We set up the toiletries in an assembly line on the kitchen counters and filled over fifty sacks. Then we added rolls of toilet paper and a pack of white athletic socks to each one. Finally we piled them in my living room, covering the furniture and the floor with packages for the homeless.

Sitting at the kitchen table, Sonia and I finished off the pizza at around eight-thirty. I hoped the activity over the last few hours had burned off enough calories for one last slice. She removed the clip from the back of her neck and let her hair flow in a brown cascade over her shoulders. (So what if she touched up the gray? I would, too, if I possessed hair like that.) The loose hair relaxed her features, and I once again saw what I briefly glimpsed a few months ago—a soft and attractive woman. I just wished she'd lose the green eye shadow.

"Thank you so much for all your help and hard work, Sonia. I really have to give you credit. You did a fabulous job of collecting all these donations in just two days."

She washed down the last bite of pizza with a sip of wine. "It's because of the Internet and social networking. I just went to our Yahoo group and posted an urgent message to all the neighbors. I also posted on Facebook and tweeted. People were incredibly generous."

Yes. And they can also be incredibly greedy. Greedy enough to blackmail and commit murder.

Sonia looked at the clock, disappointment tugging at her face. "I thought Yossi said he'd call tonight. I hope he remembers about tomorrow morning."

"You really seem to like him."

As long as Sonia had lived across the street from me, I'd never seen her with a man.

She smiled shyly. "Is it so obvious?"

Well, she couldn't be more obvious if she spray-painted red hearts on his white truck.

"I think he's got a clue."

"Do you think he likes me back? What should I do?"

What were we—in seventh grade?

"I think you should take it slow. Don't push too hard. When he realizes how great you are, he'll come around." I really hoped I sounded sincere. In truth, I had no idea what Crusher liked in a woman or why he'd fixated on me.

She headed home.

At around nine-thirty, the phone rang.

"Is she still there?" Crusher asked.

Oh, for the love of God.

"No."

"Good. She scares me."

"Why? Sonia's an attractive, single Jewish woman who cares about others and has a big heart."

"Yeah, but she's so intense."

"*Intense* is a good thing. I think you're man enough to handle *intense*."

Silence.

I'd struck a chord, so I went in for the kill. "Intense women make intense lovers."

More silence.

He grunted. "Hnnh. See you tomorrow at ten. I'll bring donuts if you make the coffee."

"Done."

By ten on Sunday morning, I was up and dressed in jeans, a T-shirt, and my freshly laundered white athletic shoes—again. A large pot of coffee steamed on the counter. Cars and motorcycles began filling my street: Lucy and Birdie, Sonia, Crusher, Carl, and six other bikers. Fifty-plus large bags of toiletries took up all the space in my living room, so everyone crowded into my kitchen for coffee and donuts. Carl seemed quite taken with Birdie. He said she reminded him of his grandma.

Sonia clipped her hair at the nape of her neck again and the green eye shadow was back. Crusher flicked his eyes in her direction a couple of times. He definitely seemed curious. If only she'd let her hair hang loose, he'd see what I saw.

Ed walked in at about ten-twenty, face taut. He kept rubbing his hands together. "Hey, Martha. Can I talk to you for a sec?"

I led him down the hall toward my sewing room for privacy. "You don't look so good, Ed. What's going on?"

"I just heard from Simon. I'm not going with you this morning, and Simon and Dana won't be here either. His contact in the US Attorney's Office tipped him off. They're pushing the DA to arrest me and close this case."

"How can that be? The Feds don't have jurisdiction in Martin's murder."

"No, but they represent the Army Corps of Engineers. The corps may have something to hide and they're afraid of exposure if the investigation continues. Since the police don't have any other suspects, the Feds want me arrested and the case closed."

I reached out and took Ed's hand. "What are you going to do?"

"Simon told me to wait at home. He and Dana are trying to get hold of the DA today, even though it's Sunday. He's going to try to delay any arrest warrant to give us time to find those witnesses. We've got to find them, Martha."

"I'll do my best, Ed. You know I will." I prayed

we'd find a lead to Javier and Graciela today in the wildlife reserve. I gave Ed a hug before we returned to where the others were, and he fist-bumped his buddies on the way out the door.

Then I got everyone's attention. "Thank you all for your hard work in making this thing happen. We'll load the truck and caravan over to the reserve."

I shuddered a little as I thought of what happened there with Switch just four nights earlier. I morbidly wondered if there'd be bloodstains on the asphalt.

"My friend Hilda will meet us there and take us down to where the people are camping. They're expecting us. I'd like you guys to keep order down there, but make it friendly. We'll hand out one package of toiletries and one blanket or quilt to each person for as long as the supplies last. When we're through, we'll leave. Hilda has asked us to respect their privacy."

"What about your witnesses?" Lucy piped up.

Darn! I forgot to tell Lucy and Birdie not to let on they knew anything.

Sonia zeroed in like a smart bomb on a hideout. "What witnesses? Are you talking about the murder of that coach? Was there a homeless witness? Do you think they're down in the wildlife reserve?"

I cleared my throat and tried to finesse. "The police believe, and so do we, there may have been a homeless witness to Dax Martin's murder. While we're down there, we'll ask around."

I was deliberately vague. I didn't want to give her any information that needed to be kept secret.

I should have known Sonia would never accept such a fuzzy answer.

"If the police know about a witness, what makes you think they haven't already gone in there and found them? Why are you doing this? Do you know something they don't?" she grilled.

Our country could use someone like Sonia in Homeland Security.

Crusher stepped forward. "We just want to help prove that Ed is innocent. If we can find someone who witnessed the murder, that person could identify the real killer and get Ed off the hook."

Sonia smiled and bounced a little on the balls of her feet. "Well, this is exciting."

Crusher raised his eyebrows.

Lucy looked at her watch. "We'd better get started, if we're going to be there by eleven."

Outside, Crusher laid a tarp on the truck bed. The blankets and quilts were carefully stacked down the left-hand side. The zippered plastic bags filled with toiletries were carefully stacked on the right side. Then he covered everything with another tarp and tied it down, finishing by ten minutes to eleven.

Crusher walked over to me. "Wanna ride with me?"

"I think I'd better take Lucy and Birdie in my car. Maybe Sonia could ride over with you."

He gave me a cynical look.

"This whole giveaway started with her idea. She worked really hard to get the donations. It'd be nice if she could ride in the lead car. That's all I'm saying."

Crusher grunted, caught Sonia's eye, and waved toward the cab of the truck. "Time to roll." She didn't need to be asked twice.

The truck led the motorcade east on Burbank Boulevard, followed by my Corolla with Lucy and Birdie inside, and a string of seven bikers with a purple *VE* on each of their backs.

If we slowed traffic with our convoy, gawkers in other cars slowed the flow even further. While a group of Harleys riding together in formation wasn't an unusual sight in Southern California, it was highly unusual to see bikers escorting a car full of women of a certain age.

CHAPTER 24

Crusher's truck took an unexpected turn to the right, about one hundred yards before the freeway and far away from the spot where Switch grabbed me. I followed him, wondering what he was doing. Then I saw Hilda standing at the side of Burbank Boulevard, pointing us toward an access road not visible from the street. The truck slowly bounced ahead of us over the poorly maintained path, down toward an overgrown wild area at the bottom.

The access way was too rough for my car, so I parked on the shoulder of Burbank Boulevard and walked over to Hilda. She still wore Quincy's gray corduroy pants with the same embroidered blouse from Guatemala. She gestured toward the bikers.

"I didn't know you were gonna show up with so many reinforcements."

"Do you think they'll scare the people down there?"

"After having to put up with Switch for so long?

I don't think so. Everyone knows these are the guys who got rid of him."

"About how many people are there today?"

"I'd say at least a hundred. Word got out."

"Oh my God. We only brought enough toiletries and blankets for fifty."

"Face it, Wonder Woman. Whatever you can do for them is more than anyone else is doing. Be careful on the path and watch where you step down there. I'm right behind you."

Lucy and I tried to help Birdie negotiate the path downward, but she was having a tough time with her arthritic knees. Carl caught up with us and put one strong arm around Birdie's tiny waist, lifted her slight body in his arms, and carried her to the bottom at a moderate jog. Birdie hung on for dear life and shrieked with laughter as her white braid swung from side to side.

I looked at Lucy. "Are you thinking what I'm thinking?"

"Yeah. I haven't heard Birdie laugh like that in a long time."

Neither Lucy nor I could figure out what Birdie ever saw in the prissy old Russell Watson, or why she had long ago settled for their joyless fifty-year marriage. She was as generous as he was penurious, as outgoing as he was fusty.

Birdie channeled her creativity into sewing exquisite appliqué quilts. Because she and Russell were childless, she directed her natural affections toward everyone else around her. No matter where she was, Birdie became the beloved sister, friend, aunt, earth mother, or, in Carl's case, grandmother. Birdie's sweetness was a gift Russell Watson didn't deserve.

The closer we got to the bottom of the path, the more I saw that the wildlife reserve covered dozens of acres. In the near distance, a man-made lake offered habitat for local and migrating birds. Right now, a few Canadian geese foraged for food in the grasses and reeds on the edges of the pond. A white egret had flown the short distance from the coast over the Santa Monica Mountains to pluck an unwary frog or lizard for lunch. A family of mallard ducks occasionally quacked as they lazily pedaled across the water.

The older cottonwoods and willows chirped with the songs of dozens of avian species from tiny hummingbirds and blue grosbeaks to the raucous cawing of big black crows. The wildlife reserve was one of the few places left in Los Angeles that provided nesting ground, food, and shelter for over two hundred species of birds and dozens of other small animals.

The shade of the trees offered prime real estate for the homeless during the hot summer days. In sparser areas, pieces of canvas and sheets of blue plastic hung from the branches of scrub oak and taller bushes to provide shady crawl spaces. Several one-person pup tents in faded colors peppered the area like igloos. Plastic tarps covered with sleeping bags and bedrolls were scattered on the flat ground or were shoved under low-growing bushes as bivouacs.

A miasma of untreated sewage and stagnant creek water hung in the warm air. I pushed an empty sardine can off the path with my toe. Out of the corner of my eye, I noticed a scrap of something white, caught on a twig nearby, fluttering. It was a piece of used toilet paper.

Lucy pulled a clean tissue from her pocket and covered her nose. "Mother of God. What do they do for toilets down here?"

Hilda pointed to a ridge of dirt near a clump of coyote brush. "There's an open latrine over there, but some of the crazier folks just squat wherever they feel like it."

Lucy still pressed the tissue against her nose. "How do they stand this?"

Hilda shrugged. "Where else are they going to go?"

Lucy wasn't satisfied. "Well, what about social services? Shelters? Government aid?"

"Government aid? The homeless don't vote. Who's gonna give them aid?"

By the time we arrived at the truck, Crusher and the other bikers had removed the tarp and were encouraging people to form a line, advancing the women to the front. Most of the homeless were compliant. Two rough-looking men yelled profanities and tried to muscle their way forward. One look from Crusher and the boys calmed them right down.

The diversity of the homeless population surprised me. I assumed the homeless were pretty much the same as Hilda. White, jobless, English-speaking adults either mentally ill or down on their luck. I was learning differently.

Sonia stood at the back of the truck, poised to hand out blankets and supplies. "There are too many people, Martha. How do you want to do this?"

I hated to send away people empty-handed. "Why don't we give them a choice? Either a bag of toiletries or a blanket. That way we can help twice as many people. Lucy and Birdie can help you distribute the items. Hilda and I are going to walk around."

As I expected, everything ran smoothly after a couple of minutes under Sonia's direction. Bikers stood in the truck and unloaded items, handing the quilts to Birdie and bags of toiletries to Lucy. Sonia directed people to one of the two women, depending on the item they wanted.

Hilda and I headed toward a cluster of tents and bedrolls. "This is where you're gonna find your witnesses. The Hispanics stick together in their own section."

Undocumented immigrants made up the largest proportion of homeless in the Sepulveda Basin. They were usually single men with no English-language skills, no jobs, and no family to help them. We found several men who seemed afraid to join the line at the truck.

I hoped a smile and my high-school Spanish would be enough. *"Buenos días."*

They just looked at me.

"Javier and Graciela? You know them, you guys? *Los conocen ustedes?"*

No response.

One of the men stood. He wore a frayed white T-shirt and jeans covered in plaster dust. *"Porque?"*

Now I was in trouble. How to explain in Spanish what I needed? In slightly off-kilter Spanish, I tried my best, but when I said the word *"policía,"* the man's face turned blank and he stepped back. The other men on the ground tensed up, ready to run.

I held up my hands. *"No, no, hijos. Yo no soy de la policía. Solo quiero ayuda mi amigo."* ("No, no, sons. I do not exist of the police. Only I wish help my friend.")

With my broken Spanish, I explained Javier and Graciela lived near the river behind my house and might have seen the murder. I merely wanted to talk to them to discover if they saw anything.

The man stepped back, broke eye contact, and studied his calloused hands.

Hilda whispered in my ear, "Did you bring any money?"

I'd come prepared. I reached in my pocket and pulled out a twenty. *"Información?"*

The man looked at the others and wiped his nose on his arm. *"Sí, señora."* He stared at the money in my hand. The couple's last name was Acevedo, and he confirmed they were looking for a ride to Mountain View, four hundred miles north of Los Angeles. They were taking temporary refuge with a church in Van Nuys.

I turned to Hilda. "Do you know which church they're talking about?"

"I think so. A group from a little place called The

Heart of Zion comes down here pretty regular to help these people."

I smiled at the man and handed him the twenty. *"Muchas gracias."*

I needed to get over to the church today to find our witnesses before they left Los Angeles.

We walked back toward the truck and passed a wiry old man watching us from behind a tall bush. His wild hair and beard were full of bits and pieces of what looked like crusts of food and dried leaves, and he stank of urine.

Hilda put her hand on my elbow and hurried me forward. "That man is probably an old vet. Most of 'em are loners. Either the fighting or the drugs made 'em crazy. Best to keep a distance."

She told me most homeless veterans ran out of government resources. They usually suffered from brain injury, PTSD, or drug addiction. Like other individuals who were mentally ill, they tended to be unpredictable loners who avoided contact with the world except when they went out to panhandle or scrounge for food. Because of their survival training, the vets were the ones most likely to adapt to the harsh outdoor conditions.

There were two families with children, folks who were victims of the economy and first lost their jobs and then their homes. Hilda told me I wouldn't find many single homeless women in the wildlife reserve who weren't prostitutes. Unless they were protected by a pimp, a partner, or a family, they could be raped and assaulted.

"Hilda, you're a single woman down here. How do you manage?"

"These people come to me when they're sick. They need me because I'm the only 'doctor' most of them will have. If anyone dared to hurt me, the rest of them would probably kill him. I'm prob'ly safer down here than anyone else."

She pointed to a small tent under the trees. "Switch got hold of some runaway kids—boys and girls. In exchange for food and a raggedy bedroll, he pimped 'em out in parking lots and behind seedy bars in Van Nuys. The tent is where he used to keep 'em."

I stopped and looked at her in shock. "Where are those kids now?"

She shrugged. "In the wind, I guess. As soon as your guys took out Switch, they saw their chance and ran."

We were now close enough to see all the packages and blankets had been distributed. Many of the homeless stood around the truck, smiling and chatting with Lucy, Birdie, Sonia, and the bikers. One woman rubbed soothing hand lotion into the skin of her cheeks and cracked lips. Another gently fingered the ties on a quilt made up of multicolored square patches.

The sound was faint at first; but as it got closer to the basin, the chopping helicopter became unmistakable. The big black-and-white bird stopped above us and hovered. A police helicopter. Not low enough to kick up dust, but near enough to send people scattering.

As I looked up, someone in fatigues stood next to an army jeep parked above us on the Sepulveda Dam service road. I suspected it was Army Specialist Lawanda Price.

I moved sideways. The ground gave way slightly under my foot and something wet seeped through the bottom of my shoes. I'd just stepped in a pile of garbage reeking of rotting fish.

Hilda wrinkled her nose and looked at me. "I told you to watch where you stepped down here."

I dragged my feet several times over a clump of dry grass in a futile effort to clean my shoe.

Sonia pulled out her cell phone. "Where are you? Well, hurry up. You have to get over here now. There's going to be a confrontation with the police."

Sirens pierced the silence.

Oh, God, please don't let it be Kaplan. Worse. Don't let it be Beavers. My shoes stink to high heaven.

CHAPTER 25

At the first sound of sirens, all the homeless people hurried to scoop up their meager belongings and scattered over the wildlife reserve, heading for the trees and sprawling parkland beyond. Lucy and Birdie lost the color in their faces and stood close together, holding hands. Hilda had vanished.

Sonia clasped her hands together and bounced nervously up and down on the balls of her feet. "Oh, my God. Are we going to be arrested?"

Crusher took a step toward her. "Listen, everyone. We did nothing wrong. Don't argue, be polite, and, if they do arrest us, just be cool."

A dozen policemen in riot gear appeared on the path above us, shields raised and batons in hand. They looked like giant beetles with the visors of their shiny helmets pulled down over their faces and their bodies encased in protective padding. A couple of stripes adorned the sleeve of the leader, who I guessed was a sergeant. None of us dared move as they advanced in a wide phalanx toward where we stood.

Sonia smiled. "Oh, my God. Let's do a sit-in like the old days!"

Lucy looked at the ground. "I'm not going to sit on that!"

Crusher frowned at Sonia. "Were you even old enough to've sat in?"

"Well, I was a school kid during Vietnam, but I wanted to. Now we have the chance. We could protest the conditions down here."

Lucy frowned at her. "That's pointless. Who would know?"

Just then another helicopter appeared above. The second copter had EYEWITNESS NEWS and a big 7 painted on the side.

Sonia pointed to the sky and grinned. "A lot of people would know. I called a friend."

Of course she did. She was the yenta.

The army jeep previously parked on the service road had vanished. I was certain Price was the one who called the police. She didn't want us to be in the reserve, and I was pretty sure I knew why.

Price probably hadn't counted on the news cameras also showing up. When they did, she must have left the area to avoid being implicated in this fiasco. After all, calling in the police to enforce law and order was one thing. Calling in the riot squad to harass a small group of volunteers distributing free supplies to the homeless was quite another.

Whatever intimidation Lawanda Price hoped to accomplish unobserved, Sonia thwarted by that call to the news media.

A voice shouted out a command: "Stand where you are and put your hands on your head."

"Do as you're told," Crusher urged quietly.

Everyone complied, but Birdie. Her arthritic shoulders made bending a problem.

When the police got close enough, the sergeant told Birdie, "You too, lady."

Birdie's newly adopted grandson Carl—all six feet of him dressed in black—stepped between Birdie and the cops.

Birdie twisted the end of her white braid and peered at the cop from behind Carl. "I'm sorry, dear. I'd like to comply with the police. I'm a big fan of *Law and Order,* but I can't. My arthritis, you know."

The cop pointed to a spot of ground away from the rest of us. "Okay, Granny. Step over here."

Carl looked ready to pounce on someone. Birdie lightly patted his side and stepped out from behind him. She walked over to the cop, craned her neck to look in his face, and pointed an arthritic finger at him.

"Shame on you, young man. There's absolutely no reason for you to be rude and disrespectful to me or anyone else. Absolutely no one addresses me as 'Granny.' My friends call me 'Birdie,' but you may call me 'Mrs. Watson'!"

Carl snorted. Lucy's mouth hung open. I looked around. All the bikers were grinning. Even some of the cops smiled. Sonia thrust a power fist in the air.

Really?

The cop in charge looked up at the news chopper

and over his shoulder at his troops. One of them urged, "Go on, Sarge. I'll stay with her."

The trooper slowly led Birdie over to the side and nodded once. "Ma'am."

She hung on to his arm for balance. "Thank you, dear."

At the sergeant's command, several officers stepped forward and searched the men for weapons. When none were found, he glanced again at the news choppers. "Okay. You can lower your arms."

Crusher crossed his arms across his barrel chest. "Why are we being detained, Officer?"

"Trespassing."

"This is public parkland. We have a right to be here."

"Your truck doesn't," the sergeant growled.

Crusher maintained his cool. "That hardly warrants a riot squad and a search. A ticket, maybe."

"Suspicious activity gives me a right to stop and frisk."

"Nothing suspicious going on. We were just distributing blankets and gear to the homeless. We needed to transport the items in, so we brought a truck. We stayed on the path so as not to disturb the wildlife habitat."

The sergeant squared his shoulders. "There's wildlife here, all right. Drugs, prostitution, and thieves. This-here's their habitat. We got a report of gang activity."

"Do we look like a gang?"

The sergeant glanced from the bikers to Birdie and me and back to Crusher. "Yes and no."

"Well, just ask the people who live here what we were doing."

"Yeah? What people?"

I looked around. Every soul had disappeared. Who could blame them?

A reporter spoke into a microphone with a television camera aimed at us from the Sepulveda Dam service road, where the army jeep used to be. I raised my hand to speak.

The sergeant looked over at me. "Yeah?"

"Who called in the complaint?" I already knew the answer, but I wanted to hear the officer admit the army had called.

"We don't give out that information."

"It was someone from the Army Corps of Engineers, wasn't it?"

"Like I said before, lady, I can't tell you."

"It's *Mrs. Rose*. Martha Rose."

"Whatever."

"I thought I heard a familiar name."

I looked up. Detective Arlo Beavers frowned at me as he walked down the trail into the reserve.

As soon as I saw Beavers, my heart started racing and my mouth went dry. God, how I had missed him. God, how I wished my shoes didn't smell.

I suspected the department sent over a detective to handle this incident because of the news media. The mayor and the LAPD were very sensitive about public perception. Since Sunday is a slow news day, we were probably being broadcast live as "breaking news."

Beavers would be skillful with the press: cool,

professional, and soft-spoken. As always, he wore a suit and tie, with a crisp white shirt. Tall and fit, with white hair and a mustache, he looked so good, my teeth ached.

Sonia whispered, "Martha, your boyfriend's here."

"My ex-boyfriend," I mumbled. *Like I didn't notice him all on my own?*

Beavers scanned the crowd. He spotted Crusher and then looked back at me. "Why am I not surprised?"

He turned his back to us and spoke to the sergeant. "What do we have here, Mike?"

I couldn't hear what they were saying, but a couple of times Beavers looked over his shoulder at me.

Finally he turned around and walked over, his face a mask. "Talk."

CHAPTER 26

I worked my hands together and licked my lips. My voice cracked with nerves. Beavers and I were now face-to-face for the first time since the morning he threw his key to my house on the hall table.

"We brought over fifty blankets and fifty packages of hygiene items to distribute to the homeless who live here. We drove all those supplies down into the reserve with Yossi's truck. We didn't do anything illegal. We were just helping people."

The leaves of a nearby bush rustled and a familiar voice said, "Don't shoot. Don't shoot." Hilda emerged slowly from hiding, along with the smelly old vet with the wild beard and an African-American youth too young for facial hair. The vet clutched a bag of toiletries, which he desperately needed, and the boy hugged the green Windmill quilt to his chest.

Hilda looked at Beavers. "She's telling the truth. See for yourself." The two homeless males held up their packages for the cops to see.

Beavers twitched his nose. "What's that smell?" He looked down at my shoes, which were covered in an oily brown substance. The corner of his mouth turned up for a nanosecond. "No good deed goes unpunished."

Birdie walked up to us. "Hello, Arlo dear."

Lucy followed.

Beavers maintained his professional demeanor in front of the other cops. "Mrs. Watson, Mrs. Mondello. Nice to see you again."

Oh, sure. He can be nice to my best friends. After all, they haven't done anything to piss him off.

Birdie lowered her voice and leaned toward him, forcing Beavers to bend down. "Confidentially, this is ridiculous. Much ado about nothing. Now my knees are really hurting and I have to sit down. I'd like to go home, if you don't mind, dear."

Beavers straightened up and spoke briefly to the sergeant. Then he announced to the rest of us, "You're free to leave. Next time you plan something like this, let the authorities know beforehand. You'll save everyone a lot of trouble." He turned abruptly to walk away.

I cleared my throat. "Arlo." He turned back, face sober, hands on his hips. Cops and bikers streamed past us toward the road above. Birdie and Lucy sat in the truck with Sonia, waiting for Crusher to drive them up the hill.

Crusher came over and stood next to me. "You okay, babe?"

Beavers glared at him.

"I'm fine, Yossi. I need a word with Arlo. I'll be up soon."

When we were alone, I asked, "How's Arthur?"

"Still recovering at the hospital." He turned to leave.

"Someone from the Army Corps of Engineers called the police on us, didn't they?"

He turned and faced me again. "You know I can't answer."

I wanted to tell him everything I suspected about Beaumont School and the corps, even though Ed's attorney wanted to sit on the information for a while longer. I hoped to steer the police away from Ed and to prevent his arrest. I also hoped Beavers would see we were on the same side and soften his attitude toward me. How could I get him to take a closer look?

"Well, you might want to ask yourself why the Army Corps of Engineers—specifically Lawanda Price—would call for police intervention in an obviously peaceful activity."

"Why would I bother?"

He didn't deny the caller was Price.

"The homeless problem has been a part of the basin for years. Why did the corps choose today to call for a police invasion into the reserve? Is there someone they're trying to scare out of the area?"

"Who, for instance?"

"Oh, I don't know. Like maybe a couple of witnesses to a murder they'd like the police *not* to solve?"

Beavers took a deep breath. "So that's why you're

really here. You're trying to find the homeless witnesses I told you about, aren't you?"

"I resent that! Can't I just be doing a simple good deed?"

"Not when you're here with Levy and all his biker friends. Did you think I wouldn't realize you're meddling in police business again?"

Well, that's snarky!

I was all huffy until I remembered Uncle Isaac also called me a "meddler," only in Yiddish. He called me a *kuchleffel*. He also suggested I didn't trust Beavers to do his job.

Didn't I? The thing was, I did trust Beavers. Since Aiken wasn't ready for us to share our information with the police, I counted on Beavers to understand what I could only hint at.

I couldn't come right out and tell Beavers about Martin's affair with Diane Davis because of my promise to the Beaumont groundskeeper. Beavers would want to know where the information came from, and I'd have to tell him. I needed to point Beavers toward a possible criminal conspiracy between Beaumont and the corps, a conspiracy that might have resulted in Dax Martin's murder. If Beavers followed the trail, he might get to the affair on his own.

"What if the homeless witnesses could identify the killer? What if the killer then reveals something not kosher involving the baseball stadium, which connects to Dax Martin and the Beaumont School and even the headmaster and the Army Corps of Engineers?"

Beavers waved a sweeping hand around the wildlife reserve. "Let me give you some friendly advice, Martha. Get out of this crap hole and go home. Your fun is over for the day."

My patience ran out and I was on my last nerve ending, but I bit my tongue. I wasn't ready to be dismissed. "I know I'm right, Arlo. Lawanda Price and Barbara Hardisty from the corps are up to their ears in this. Why won't you at least consider what I'm telling you?"

"You and I've been down this road before. I know you're smart, and I know you have this weird knack for educated guesses, which turn out to be right. Unless you and your new boyfriend over there have some real information, I'm outta here."

That does it! Now I'm officially pissed off.

"Listen, you self-righteous prig. You couldn't be more wrong about me. Not that I care anymore, which I don't. Yossi Levy is *not* my boyfriend! But you know what? He'd like to be. You're not the only fish in the sea. Maybe I'll consider climbing on the back of his bike and sliding into his bitch seat!"

It started in the corner of his mouth. Small at first, because I knew he was trying to control it. Then it crept into his eyes and burst out of his nose.

Arlo Beavers was laughing! "'Bitch seat'?"

Fury nearly blinded me as I followed everyone else out of the reserve. With his long legs, Beavers easily climbed past me, chuckling on the path to

the road above. I don't remember walking back up.
I was so mad. Tears of humiliation blurred my
vision; and I could have slogged through an entire
stinking landfill, for all I knew or cared.

The television reporter waited for us at the top of
the access road. "Hi, I'm Heather Park from ABC
news." She asked Beavers's name, then shoved a
microphone in his face and turned to the camera.

"We're here at the Sepulveda Basin Wildlife Reserve in Encino, talking to Detective Arlo Beavers,
of the LAPD. Detective Beavers, what can you tell us
about the gang activity today?"

Beavers still had a smile on his face. "There was
no gang activity here today."

Heather Park leaned forward aggressively. "Well,
then, why was the riot squad here? The people of
Los Angeles deserve to know what's going on in
their own backyard."

Beavers leveled a look at her, refusing to rise to
the bait. "I'm glad you asked. We responded to an
urgent call for help and sent a dozen officers here
to handle a report of violent gang activity. The call
turned out to be a false report, which will end up
costing the taxpayers thousands of dollars."

"Was this another incidence of 'swatting'?" She
referred to a recent spate of prank calls to 911
resulting in the deployment of SWAT teams to loca-
tions where no crime was being committed.

"Filing a false report is a crime. We're now focused
on finding the person responsible." Beavers flicked
his eyes in my direction.

So he did listen to me! Beavers would check out what I told him about the Army Corps of Engineers. I felt hugely relieved and a little less angry.

Crusher's truck backed up out of the reserve and turned onto the road with a loud rumble. The interviewer raised her voice to be heard over the noise. "What did go on down there today, Detective?"

Beavers pointed to where I waited for Lucy and Birdie. "This lady can answer the rest of your questions." Then he strode toward his silver Camry.

The interviewer approached and asked my name. "We're talking to a Marsha Rose."

"*Martha.* It's Martha Rose."

She ignored me. "Marsha, can you tell me what went on down there today?"

I mentioned the West San Fernando Valley Quilt Guild and my Encino neighborhood. "Even though there's a heat wave right now, we're concerned about what the homeless people will do in the winter when the weather turns cold and rainy. We gave away over fifty quilts and blankets today. We also distributed toiletries and hygiene products donated by concerned neighbors."

The dull expression in her eyes said this wasn't the kind of story she had hoped for. "Such a good deed to do on a Sunday morning. Thank you, Marsha. Now back to the studios."

She hurried away.

"It's Martha. Martha Rose." Then I untied my shoes and placed them on the side of the road.

Lucy walked over. "Birdie's not riding back with us."

"Why not?"

She pointed over to where the Harleys were parked. Birdie giggled while Carl carefully adjusted a black helmet over her long white braid.

CHAPTER 27

As soon as I got home, I looked for the message light on my phone, hoping to hear from Simon Aiken, but nobody had called. I really needed to tell him what I overheard in the park between Lawanda Price and Barbara Hardisty.

In all the enthusiasm about helping the homeless, I'd forgotten about Charlissa's Weight Watchers meeting this morning. One week had passed since I joined, and I was due for a weigh-in. I'd either have to find another meeting tomorrow or skip this week. I sighed. After my encounter with Beavers, I really didn't care much about anything.

I scrubbed my feet with rubbing alcohol before stepping into the shower. My walking shoes sat forever abandoned on the side of Burbank Boulevard, near the access road to the wildlife reserve. I only wore them three times, and all three times nasty things had soiled them. It was a sign: Clearly, a walking career wasn't in the cards for me. I'd have to figure out something else to do for exercise. Maybe when this was all over, I'd ask Ed about Yoga.

Hot water and shampoo suds rolled down my body as I let myself cry. I didn't think I had any more tears left, but there they were, mixing with lilac-scented soap and Pantene. How could Beavers ever think I could be sleeping with another man? Then when I threatened to actually do it, why did he suddenly laugh? I refused to think about it.

I stepped out of the shower and reached for a towel. The homeless Latino man revealed Javier and Graciela were staying with someone at the Heart of Zion Church in Van Nuys. Even though the time was after two on a Sunday afternoon, I wanted to see if the church would still be open. Maybe I'd find Javier and Graciela, or at least someone who knew where they were. I quickly got dressed.

Lucy and Birdie were waiting for me at Ed's house, where everyone went for ribs and beer. To take his mind off his troubles, Ed offered to feed us when we got back from our mission at the wildlife reserve. Since I didn't eat pork, Ed was also barbequing some chicken. I briefly wondered if Crusher would opt for the chicken too. After all, he said his bandana was a religious head covering.

I hated to miss out on the party, but we had no time to waste; the witnesses could be on the move. If I didn't go to the church right away, I might lose my only opportunity to talk to them. I looked up the church address on Google and hurried down the street to Ed's.

I looked around for Aiken, but he wasn't there. Ed stood over a smoking barbeque in the backyard while people sipped drinks and laughed. Birdie listened intently to Carl, and Crusher stared at me like a trapped animal while Sonia chattered at him. For a fleeting moment, he reminded me of a big, lost teddy bear—I wanted to give him a hug.

Lucy walked toward me, holding a can of diet soda. "Hi, hon. Feel any better?" She knew seeing Beavers again rattled me.

"I'm so over him."

She looked at me sideways. "No, you're not."

"I don't want to talk about it. At least not here."

I walked over to the dining table and picked up a chicken breast and wrapped it in a paper napkin to eat in the car. I also grabbed a frosty can of diet cola. "Listen, Lucy, I can't stay. I got a lead on the witnesses and have to go over to this church in Van Nuys. I came to see if you wanted to come with me."

"Sure. Let's get Birdie."

Carl hunkered toward Birdie with an animated expression. ". . . and we only missed running into the sucker by an inch. Man, that was a good ride."

Birdie smiled at him. "You were so brave, dear. I'm sure the driver will never forget such a close call."

Carl beamed.

I gave them a little wave of greeting. "Sorry to interrupt, Birdie. Lucy and I are going to run an errand and want to know if you'll come with us."

"All right, as long as I don't have to walk. My knees are shot from standing all morning. Where are we going?"

"To church."

We drove in Lucy's vintage black Caddy. Lucy's husband, Ray, was a successful auto mechanic, who had a string of shops and a wide collection of loyal customers. He loved to restore old cars, and this one purred like a panther in love. I sat in the creamy leather backseat and read directions out loud between hungry bites of savory chicken.

The storefront church was situated in a strip mall on Vanowen Street, surrounded by three-story apartment buildings with FOR RENT signs in Spanish. Next to the church sat a convenience store, a *panadería,* and a liquor store.

Although the overwhelming majority of Latinos were Catholic, various Protestant denominations had made inroads in Latin America. Consequently, many immigrants brought their Protestant traditions with them and small, independent Christian churches emerged in the Latino community of Los Angeles.

We parked on the street and walked toward the sign saying IGLESIA CORAZÓN DE SIÓN. Music flowed from within—singing accompanied by the sound of guitars, drums, and a trumpet. I looked at my friends. "I didn't expect there'd be an actual service going on."

Birdie lowered her voice as we neared the door. "So many little churches are like families. They spend all day Sunday together. They worship in the morning, and then they eat lunch together and have fellowship in the afternoon. Some of them

have evening services or Bible studies to top off
the day."

"I'm impressed with such commitment."

"It's a tight little community, dear. So tight, they
may not be willing to hand over your witnesses.
You'll have to be careful how you approach them."

The windows and glass door of the storefront
were covered with beige privacy drapes. Lucy pulled
open the door and we immediately stepped into a
small white room, with around fifty dark-haired
men, women, and children sitting in folding chairs
facing a six-inch raised platform at the end. Two tall
oscillating fans swept the crowded room, working
hard against the heat.

The wall behind the platform featured a hand-
painted mural. Christ stood on a hill in a light
blue robe with a spiky yellow halo behind his
head. His arms were raised in blessing over a
crowd of people and animals. Parked discreetly
behind the Savior, on a side road, was a red truck
with SANDOVAL CONSTRUCTION lettered on the side.
Maybe Mr. Sandoval donated the money for the
mural.

A middle-aged man, with nut-colored skin,
sweated in an electric-blue suit and stood behind
the lectern at the side of the platform. He sang and
clapped along with his flock to the music of four
musicians. Happy voices sang in Spanish, and I
caught the words *"Diós," "gracias,"* and *"bendición"*
("God," "thanks," and "blessing"). Three men who
sat in the back row quietly stood and gave us
their seats.

When the singing ended, the pastor gestured to the back of the room and boomed out, "*Bienvenidos. You are welcome in the name of the Lord.*"

All heads turned and one hundred eyes focused on the three Anglo ladies sitting and smiling self-consciously. Birdie waved her hand. "Thank you so much. We feel most welcome."

Everyone clapped as the pastor gestured for us to stand. I regretted I hadn't thought to wear something dressier than just my clean jeans. Then again, I hadn't expected to walk into a religious celebration.

As we stood to be acknowledged, I leaned over to Birdie and whispered, "What exactly is going on?"

"Anglo visitors are uncommon, dear, especially in such a small Spanish church. I think they just want us to feel at home." Her eyes teased. "Smile big, or they may try to convert you."

We sat and the singing continued for the next ten minutes. Little children craned their necks to get a good look at us. I scanned the room. Were any of the couples the one we were looking for? Finally the singing ended and the pastor began to speak in Spanish. I understood about 30 percent of the words, but I couldn't string them together into anything meaningful.

Lucy leaned her bright orange head of hair in my direction and whispered, "What's he saying?"

I shrugged. "I don't really understand. Something about Jesus."

Lucy just looked at me. "*Duh.*"

Were Javier and Graciela in this group? When I

ruled out those mothers with children, a dozen couples still remained. Which one were they?

The service ended at around four and the pastor made his way to the back of the room to shake the hands of his flock as they left the storefront. I imagined they were all going home to prepare dinner.

Finally he turned to us with a smile and big question marks in his eyes. His English was only slightly accented. "I am Pastor Luis Sandoval."

Oh. That explains the red truck.

"Did you ladies enjoy the service?"

I spoke up. "We certainly did."

"Even though you don't speak Espanish?" His voice was unmistakably wary.

"We very much enjoyed the music," answered Birdie.

He looked at me; a sharp intelligence sparked his eyes. "You aren't dressed for church. Ladies of your generation normally wear their good clothes to church. My guess is you didn't expect to encounter people actually worshipping. When you did, you decided to stay, anyway, because you really came here seeking information of some kind. How am I doing?"

Lucy and Birdie looked at me as I took a tiny step forward. This man was astute. "You're right so far, Pastor."

"How can I help you, señora?"

I didn't waste time. "Six days ago, I discovered the body of a man who was murdered, not too far from my house. One of my neighbors is being blamed, even though he is innocent. The police have already questioned him once and they may arrest him soon. I want to prove he couldn't have done it."

"How does that involve my church?"

"A homeless couple was camping nearby on the riverbank. I found out their names are Javier and Graciela Acevedo."

Luis Sandoval's eyes went dark. I was in the right place.

"Somebody told me the couple is staying with someone from this church until they can find a ride out to Mountain View. I need to speak to them before they go. If the Acevedos saw the killer, they can tell the police it wasn't my friend. They might even be able to identify the real killer."

"If these people do exist, señora, their lives would be in danger. They wouldn't be safe talking to the police. Even if they could be protected from the killer, once they were exposed, they couldn't be protected from immigration. If they were deported back to their country, they'd be executed. They're political refugees."

"I've got a lawyer who could help them for free. What if this lawyer could get someone in the US Attorney's Office to grant them political asylum? If the Acevedos were given refugee status, they wouldn't have to return to their country."

"That would be a wonderful thing. Such a thing would guarantee their safety in a very important way. In that case, señora, they most certainly would be able to tell the police what they saw. They might be able to identify the killer."

"So they did see the killing?"

He said nothing.

"Can I just speak to them?"

"I think people in their position would first need assurance they wouldn't be deported."

"Can you at least keep them in the area while I work on their legal status?"

"If such people exist, señora, they might be persuaded to stay for a few more days."

I gave him a piece of paper with my name and telephone number on it. "Please call me before you let them go anywhere."

He looked at the paper and put it in his pocket. "Mrs. Rose, would you know anything about what happened in the Sepulveda Basin today? Some of my people live down there. One thought he recognized you from this morning."

So he already knew we'd been asking around for the Acevedos.

"Yes, Pastor Sandoval. We organized the event to try to help some of the people who have to live in those awful conditions. The need is so great. Twice as many people showed up as we planned for. I don't think we were able to make much of a dent in their suffering."

His voice softened and he looked at the three of us. "*Diós las bendiga.* May God bless you."

Then he reached over and took my hand in both of his. Kindness replaced the wariness in his eyes. "Please understand my first priority is to help and protect my people. If I can, I'll also try to help your friend."

"I believe you, Pastor Sandoval. I just hope you can keep Javier and Graciela—if they exist—from running away."

CHAPTER 28

Lucy dropped me off at my house and I waved good-bye as she and Birdie drove away. All the motorcycles were gone from Ed's house and the street was quiet. Bumper head-butted my ankles as soon as I walked in the door. I reached down to scratch him behind the ears and he purred in ecstasy. One good thing about animals—their love was uncomplicated.

I thought about Arthur's uncomplicated love and loyalty the night he got stabbed while trying to defend me. I decided to pay him a visit at the animal hospital to say thank you. It might be my only chance, since I'd probably never see him again once he went home with Beavers.

I drove to the Boulevard and entered the parking lot next to the hospital. Just as I passed the entrance, Beavers and Kerry Andreason, Arthur's veterinarian, came out the front door together. I quietly pulled into a parking space at the end of a row of cars so I could watch them without being seen.

"Little Miss Scrawny" wasn't wearing her lab coat. As a matter of fact, she wore a sexy hot-pink minidress that showed way too much cleavage. She grabbed Beavers's arm as they walked toward his car, swinging her perky little ponytail and hanging on to him.

He opened the passenger door; and before she slid in, he leaned over and gave her a quick kiss, right on the mouth. Her laughter tinkled like bells before he closed her door. I wanted to run right over there and stick all ten fingers in her eyes. Then, smiling broadly, he walked rapidly over to the driver's side and got in. I think they kissed again before he started the car, but I couldn't really see.

They drove right by my car to exit the lot, and I was terrified he'd see me, so I ducked down in the seat, heart in my throat, and stayed there for a good thirty seconds until I was certain they were gone.

I didn't know which one to be angry at the most. That scrawny vet wasted no time getting her claws into Beavers, but then who could blame her? He was quite a catch. However, it had been less than a week since Beavers had broken up with me. Here he was kissing someone else already.

So I was right not to trust him in the first place, and this proved it. At the first sign of trouble in our relationship, he broke up with me. Then he laughed at me. Now he was kissing another woman.

I decided not to stick around. All the way home, I told myself I was lucky to have seen them together.

I would just put Arlo out of my life, the way he shut me out of his. I wouldn't think about him anymore. I wouldn't miss him anymore. I wouldn't waste any more tears on him. At least I'd try not to.

My body felt achy and sore from all the exertion of the trip to the wildlife reserve in the morning, the shock and heartbreak of seeing Beavers, and the tension of tracking down Javier and Graciela at the Heart of Zion Church. I opened my prescription bottle, shook out a Soma for muscle pain, and cleaned up the mess in the kitchen from the morning. A lone apple fritter sat in the box from Western Donuts. I'd only eaten a piece of barbequed chicken since the morning, so I brewed a cup of Taylor's Scottish Breakfast Tea and ate the donut while waiting for the muscle relaxer to work.

Why hadn't Aiken called me back? He really should know about Lawanda Price and Barbara Hardisty. Now I also needed his legal help for the fugitives Javier and Graciela. The church pastor hinted they actually witnessed Dax Martin's murder. If we couldn't prevent them from being deported, they'd disappear in the next couple of days and we'd never find them.

I called Aiken's cell phone, which sent me straight to voice mail again. "Simon, this is Martha. Please call me as soon as you get this message. I've found our witnesses, but I can't question them without your help. I also want to tell you about a conversation I overheard between those Army Corps of Engineers people, Lawanda Price and Barbara Hardisty. I'm sure bribery and blackmail were involved in the Beaumont deal. You need to know all the details before you talk to the US Attorney's Office tomorrow. I don't care what the time is, just call me back."

I was still hungry, so I nuked the leftover brisket in the microwave and sautéed zucchini slices in olive oil and salt.

About two hours later, Beavers called. My hands started shaking as I remembered how he kissed Kerry Andreason just a couple of hours ago. I was tempted to hang up.

He got straight to the point. "I've been thinking about what you said this morning. Kaplan still has the lead on this case, but I want you to tell me what you know."

Oh, so now he's willing to listen. I knew he'd be smart enough to get my hint about something huge going on between the Army Corps of Engineers and the Beaumont School. After the way he dismissed me this morning and betrayed me this evening, I wasn't in the mood to cooperate.

"You want to know what I know? I know you're a stubborn cop full of pride who thinks he's been cheated on, which he has not. So you behaved like a wounded puppy. No, strike that. Your wounded dog behaved much better than you. You're self-righteous and unforgiving and were mean to me today. I also know you're completely untrustworthy. That's what I know."

Beavers's voice was taut. "The murder. Tell me what you know about the murder. You were being deliberately cagey this morning, but you clearly know something you wanted me to look at. Stop playing games and talk."

I wanted to tell him everything, but I couldn't risk sabotaging Aiken's defense strategy for Ed. If the cops tried to go after Javier and Graciela, Pastor Luis Sandoval would help them disappear.

"I'd take a real close look at the Beaumont School baseball stadium project. I'd want to know which government agencies were involved—both local and federal. I'd follow the money trail to see where the funds came from to build the stadium and where they went. I'd take a close look at the personal lives and finances of all the people involved, including the murder victim. That's what I'd do. But then, if I did, I'd just be meddling in police business."

"Do you have specifics?"

"You said so yourself. I have a weird knack for educated guesses that turn out to be right."

"What about the homeless witnesses? I know you better than to believe you went in the wildlife reserve just to distribute quilts."

I would be so insulted . . . if he wasn't so right.

"I don't know where they are." Not exactly a lie, but less than forthcoming.

Then I took a deep breath, knowing I was about to open up a tender subject. I still felt terrible about putting his dog in harm's way, but I also wanted to see if he'd admit to dating that vet. "When is Arthur coming home?"

Beavers grudgingly answered me. "He's walking,

and Kerry says he's making a remarkable recovery. He'll be able to come home tomorrow."

He's not even trying to hide he's on a first-name basis with the blond vet. However, just hearing him use her familiar name sent pangs into my heart. I tried to avoid reacting, but tears immediately sprang to my eyes and I swallowed hard.

"I'm so glad to hear he's going to be okay."

Beavers's silence lasted so long that I thought he'd hung up. Then he said in a quiet voice, "So you and Levy—"

"Never happened." Then I thought about his kissing the vet and added, "At least not yet."

"I thought—"

"Yeah, I know what you thought. The trouble is, instead of asking me about it, you walked away and treated me very badly. Apparently, it hasn't taken you long to get on with your life. Frankly, I'm glad I saw this side of you before falling even more deeply in love."

Oh, my God! Did I just use the L-word? Where did that come from?

Beavers was silent again for a long time. "Martha, we should talk about this."

"*Now* you want to talk? I'm going to have to think about having any further conversation with you. There's a lot going on in my life right now, and I don't have the bandwidth to deal with your crap at the moment."

Someone knocked.

"I've got to go. There's someone at my door."

I looked through the peephole. Simon Aiken

stood there; his new diamond still sparkled in his ear. I let him in and he sat in a cushy chair in my living room while I settled on the cream-colored sofa.

"You got my message?"

Aiken nodded. "Yes. You sounded urgent, so I came over right away. What have you found out?"

I told him about a conspiracy involving payoffs and possible blackmail between the Beaumont School and the Army Corps of Engineers, Hardisty's new Jaguar, and Price's demand for hush money.

"Simon, you really need to get the baseball stadium documents from the corps. Dax Martin may have known enough to get him killed. If so, his murderer might be anyone involved in that deal who wanted to silence him."

I also told him I was pretty sure Price was the one watching us from the Sepulveda Dam service road and called the police with the false report of gang activity. "She was probably afraid we'd find the witnesses to the murder, especially if they could lead us back to the corps."

"Good work, Martha. I'll contact my friend in the US Attorney's Office first thing tomorrow. Tell me about locating the homeless witnesses today."

I told Aiken about my conversation with Pastor Luis Sandoval and his determination to protect the couple from deportation to their country, where they'd meet certain death. "If you can talk to your friend at the US Attorney's Office about getting them political asylum, they will probably be willing to step forward and tell us what they saw. They might even be able to identify the killer. We only have a couple of days to do it. Otherwise, they'll leave Los Angeles and disappear. We'd never find them."

The whole time we talked, Simon held his cell phone in both hands, texting notes with his thumbs. He looked up from the small screen. "It'll be a tough sell, but I'll get right on it. The problem is time. The US Attorney's Office is pressuring the DA to arrest Ed. Based on what you've just discovered, I guess the US Attorney's Office is getting heat from their sister agency, the Army Corps of Engineers. With all these Feds involved, they'd like nothing better than to wrap up the case fast in order to prevent any scandal with the engineers over this Beaumont thing."

What chance will a little guy like Ed have in fighting the whole US government?

I looked anxiously at Aiken. "What are we going to do?"

He rubbed his eyes and sighed. "I'm trying to contact the DA to work out something."

"There's one more thing I've got to warn you about. You know a detective came into the wildlife reserve this morning? Well, he's also working on Dax Martin's murder. Until recently, he was my boyfriend."

"Have you told him anything?"

"Not really. He's been asking me what I know and I've managed to give him only vague answers. If I'm officially questioned, I'll be compelled to answer truthfully. I can't claim attorney-client privilege."

He thought for a moment. "You told me Pastor Sandoval spoke in hypotheticals, right?"

"Yeah. He never said he actually knew Javier or Graciela or where to find them. He said things like 'if they exist' and 'people like that.'"

"Then you should be okay. You really have nothing specific to tell the police."

I walked Aiken to the door. He bent over and gave me a filial peck on the cheek. "I'll see you at Ed's house tomorrow night."

I closed the door behind him and headed for bed. All I wanted to do was give my aching body a chance to lie comfortably on my memory foam mattress. I longed to fall asleep early and forget about Dax Martin, the Beaumont School, Lawanda Price, the riot police, and Pastor Luis Sandoval.

I especially didn't want to think about Arlo Beavers and the fact that, even though I saw him kissing someone else, I'd told him I loved him. What had gotten into me? Right now, all I needed was the uncomplicated affection of my orange cat curled up next to me on the Ohio Star quilt covering my bed.

CHAPTER 29

I slept like the dead on Sunday night and woke up early Monday morning. My body still ached and my head pounded with a migraine. I suffered a fibromyalgia hangover from too much stress and activity the day before.

I struggled out of bed and reached for my pain medications. Bumper rubbed against my ankles and begged for breakfast. I learned a lesson from my uncle Isaac when I was a little girl. I had found a stray kitten and he said, "You have a big responsibility now. Your *ketzel* is relying on you to look after her. Torah says you must first take care of your animals even before you take care of yourself. Always remember that."

And I did. I stumbled into the kitchen and poured some kibble in a dish and changed Bumper's water before starting a strong pot of coffee for myself.

While my cat crunched loudly on his star-shaped kibble, I poured myself a cup of dark Italian roast.

The extra caffeine in the coffee worked with my meds, and my headache slowly receded, but I felt fuzzy-headed and weak. The best way to get past a fibro flare-up was to spend the day resting. So, for the second day in a row, I'd have to postpone going to a Weight Watcher's meeting. I fetched my Dresden Plate quilt from my sewing room, settled in my most comfortable easy chair, and put up my feet. My mind wandered in quiet meditation as I focused on guiding the one-inch needle through the fabric, making rows of small, even stitches.

My phone rang at eleven. My back and legs were stiff as I rose from my chair. "Hello?"

"Wonder Woman, this is Hilda. Something horrible has happened!"

"What? Are you okay?"

"Yeah, but you gotta do something. They've torn up the wildlife reserve."

"They did *what*?"

"A construction crew showed up early this morning. All the people who lived down there were given ten minutes to get their things and leave. Ten minutes wasn't enough time and a lot of people were forced to leave their tents and other belongings behind. The people who weren't even there this morning will come back to find they have nothing left."

"How can that be? The reserve is a federally protected wildlife habitat. No one can come in and destroy it. A construction crew you said? Not the army?"

"Yeah. Men with chain saws cut down the trees

and big yellow bulldozers plowed the ground. They dumped all the tents and trees and brush into the lake and filled it over with dirt. The earth has been scraped clean. Plants, trees, lake—it's all gone. There's nothing left."

"And nobody from the army was there?"

"I did see someone in one of those camouflage outfits sitting in an army jeep watching the whole thing from the service road."

"Can you describe them?"

"I only saw red hair."

Lawanda Price! She didn't have the authority to order such flagrant destruction of protected land, but Barbara Hardisty, the woman who approved the Beaumont Stadium, did.

I could think of only one reason she'd do it. Hardisty must have gotten nervous when she found out we went into the reserve yesterday. She wasn't going to take any chances someone might find witnesses to Dax Martin's murder. So she made a preemptive strike and drove out all the homeless who lived in the basin.

This woman was a heartless monster. Where would those displaced people go now?

"How could you tell a privately owned construction company destroyed the wildlife reserve?"

"The name painted on the door of the truck was 'Valley Allstar Construction.'"

Holy crap. Valley Allstar is the same company that built the Beaumont Stadium.

"Where are you now?"

"I'm calling from Rafi's place. He let me use his phone."

"Stay where you are. I'm coming to get you."

I threw on a short-sleeved T-shirt and a pair of jeans. The waistline wasn't uncomfortably tight anymore, just snug. Did I lose some weight this past week? I was tempted to jump on the scale, but I decided not to take the time. I slipped into my pink Crocs and grabbed my keys.

Four hours had passed since I took my medication, and I felt clear-headed enough to drive. I drove south to the Boulevard and located a parking space in front of Rafi's Falafel.

Hilda sat inside with a glass of cold water. Her fingers drummed anxiously on the table.

Rafi frowned at me. "Who do such a thing? It's not enough these people have no house? Where is government? Where is *haganah,* the protection? Where they go now?"

I sat and shook my head sadly. "I don't know, Rafi. We tried to help yesterday by giving them blankets and other personal items. Our mitzvah may have actually triggered what happened today. I think someone was afraid we might be down there asking questions, so they forced everyone to disappear."

Rafi lowered his voice. "I don't know what you involved in, but you must be careful. If they get rid of people who can *answer* questions, maybe they try to get rid of people who *ask* questions."

Actually, that thought had crossed my mind—although I didn't sense any immediate personal danger. I was determined to unravel the tangled threads connecting the Beaumont School, the Army Corps of Engineers, Valley Allstar Construction, and the brutal murder of Dax Martin. And for what they destroyed this morning, I wanted badly to hurt them all.

Who knew? If we could blow the conspiracy wide open, maybe we could even compel the engineers not only to rebuild the reserve but to also tear down the offending baseball stadium while they were at it. They might be shamed into restoring the land to the public green space it was meant to be.

"I want to go to the wildlife reserve. Will you go with me, Hilda?"

"What for? It's done. I'm sick, I'm mad, and I'm ready to give up."

"Because I need to see for myself."

I parked my car on the shoulder of Burbank Boulevard, right where I parked the day before. My abandoned athletic shoes were gone. Hilda and I didn't have to walk down the access road to see the devastation. All the brush was gone, and we could clearly look down at the reserve from Burbank. The heavy construction equipment was gone and the dust had settled. Only the scorched earth was left.

Hilda and I walked down the access road to the bottom. More than eighty acres were scraped down to the bare dirt. Trees that once sheltered birds, animals, and human beings were now just low stumps with jagged edges. I walked over to a mound of topsoil where the lake once was. The corner of the half-buried green-and-white Windmill quilt stuck out of the dirt like a dead hand, shredded beyond repair. What would the young boy do now for warmth this coming winter?

Silence hung heavily where only yesterday I listened to the trilling of birds. All I heard now was the sound of cars whooshing down the nearby freeway and the harsh cawing of several crows circling overhead. My heart broke.

"I'd sure like to know what your uncle Isaac has to say about this," Hilda said quietly. "If there's a God, He wasn't much use this morning, was He?"

"I don't know what Uncle Isaac would say. I'm not going to let them get away with this!" My head was roiling with anger as we walked back up the hill toward Burbank Boulevard. When we reached the top, an army jeep was parked behind my Corolla.

Lawanda Price leaned against the door of the jeep, arms folded across her chest. She leveled a hard look at my face. "I saw you on television last night. Did you enjoy your fifteen seconds of fame?"

It took all my self-control not to slug her. "What you did here today—destroying this place and driving those poor people away—was criminal. I'm going to make it my business to see you pay for this."

Price was surprisingly unruffled. She pointed to my pink rubber shoes, her voice eerily calm. "I remember you from the park the other day. I know who you are, Martha Rose."

"So you know my name. So what?"

She stood straight and smiled slightly. "I also

know where you live." Something in her eyes blew a chill through my body.

Price turned her malicious gaze toward Hilda. Then, without another word, she climbed in her jeep and drove off. Hilda grabbed my upper arm and swung me around; her eyes were wide with fear. "Did you hear that? She threatened you!"

I still shook a little. "It didn't escape my notice."

Hilda wrung her hands. "Neither one of us is safe. I know how to disappear, but you have to hide, Martha. She's coming after you."

Four months before, I'd been in a similar situation and hid out at my friend Lucy's house for a few days. I didn't want to make a habit of pissing people off and then running away to Lucy's for protection. I'd have to figure out a way to handle this situation differently.

"Hilda, I'm worried about you. Come back to my house."

She threw her hands in the air. "Are you nuts? She knows where you live. Your house is the last place I want to stay."

"Well, at least come back with me until we can figure out a safer place for you. Your community is scattered. You're too vulnerable to be outside on your own."

"Everyone's vulnerable. Now they need my help more than ever. Don't worry about me, Wonder Woman. I have a superpower of my own. I know how to become invisible."

I suddenly felt bereft at the thought of losing touch with Hilda. "How will I find you again?"

"I've still got your phone number. I'll keep in touch." Then she teased, "And I know where you live." Neither one of us laughed.

I dropped Hilda back at Rafi's place and drove home. Something hung from the handle of my front door. A scrap of the green-and-white Windmill quilt was tied to the doorknob. A message. Lawanda Price wasn't kidding. She really did know where I lived.

Okay, now I was officially scared.

CHAPTER 30

The fragment of quilt had been cut with a knife. As soon as I got inside the house, I set the alarm and threw the dead bolt.

I instinctively wanted to call the police, but if I asked for police protection, I'd have to tell Beavers the rest of what I knew. I wasn't ready to do that just yet. First, I needed to find out how close Aiken was to getting political asylum for Javier and Graciela. Once our witnesses were secure, they could emerge from hiding and clear Ed. Then I could tell Beavers every rotten detail I suspected about Beaumont and the Army Corps of Engineers.

The clock read one in the afternoon, and I was starving. Fear made me hungry. Anxiety made me hungry. So did sadness, anger, boredom, excitement, and happiness. I pulled two sweet corn and cheese tamales from the freezer and stuck them in the microwave for five minutes.

The light blinked on my phone, alerting me to new voice mail. My daughter, Quincy, left the first message. "Hi, Mom. I may be getting a new job as the West Coast reporter for NPR. I might even be based in Los Angeles. How cool would that be? Call me back."

Quincy lived and worked in Boston. I missed my only daughter and worried about her being so far away. This message was the first really happy news since the day I discovered Dax Martin's body. I tried returning her call, but only got her voice mail. "Hey, honey. Sorry I missed you. This is great news. You know I'm thrilled at the thought of your living in LA again. Call me when you can talk. Love you."

Pastor Sandoval left the second message. "Hello, Mrs. Rose. I don't know if you heard what happened in the Sepulveda Basin this morning, but I've got a big crisis on my hands. My church is filled with homeless refugees who're destitute and scared. The couple we talked about is convinced what happened was a warning to them. They plan to drive north tonight. I won't stop them, but I did persuade them to talk to you before they leave. Please call me at this number."

No! If Javier and Graciela leave town, there'll be no one to give Ed an alibi. No one to identify the real killer. The DA will arrest Ed and charge him with murder.

Sandoval answered on the second ring. A din of upset voices filled the background. He must be in the storefront with many of the displaced people. I pictured Christ in the mural stretching his arms out over the crowd. "Pastor Sandoval, I'm sick about what happened this morning. I just came back from surveying the damage."

"The people we talked about, they're leaving after dark. If you show up here at nine tonight, I'll arrange for them to speak to you just before they go. You must come alone. I'll be here to translate and ensure their safety."

"What if we can get them political asylum and put them in protective custody? I have an attorney working on safe haven right now."

"Mrs. Rose, the United States government destroyed their homes this morning. Do you think the same government will protect them?"

How could I argue? Powerful people were connected to the Beaumont School, and the school was in bed with the army. They might even be in bed with the US Attorney's Office. Maybe Sandoval was right. Maybe the witnesses wouldn't be safe in protective custody in Los Angeles. Maybe they would be better off escaping north.

"You may be right, Mr. Sandoval. I appreciate your help. I'll meet you at your church at nine."

Next I called Ed Pappas. Five minutes later, Ed showed up at my door, with a brown leather computer bag slung over his shoulder. Light brown hair hung in his eyes and deep concern creased his features. He placed the bag on my coffee table, reached in, and pulled out his laptop and a gun.

"I've called Crusher. He's arranging for one of us to be with you twenty-four/seven. I'll be here until he closes the shop. Then he's coming over. This gun goes wherever you go. What happened?"

I told him about visiting the Sepulveda Basin in the morning with Hilda after Valley Allstar

Construction destroyed the area and drove out all the people living there. I filled him in on the conversation I overheard between Lawanda Price and her boss, Barbara Hardisty, a few days ago. Then I told him about the confrontation with Price and her threat of "I know where you live." I showed him the piece of mutilated quilt I found tied to my front door.

He clenched his fists. "I wish I'd never let you get involved in this."

I removed the tamales from the microwave and put them on a plate. They'd gone from frozen to hot and back to cold again. Ed refused the offer of food. "I've eaten. You go ahead."

I handed Ed my cell phone, picked up a fork, and tucked into the first tamale. "Ed, can you show me how to take photos and use this as a tape recorder?"

He laughed. "I assume you're not heavy into communication devices."

"Ummff," I answered, nodding with a mouthful of food.

He walked me through the remarkably easy steps and I took his photo. "Now I can look at your handsome face whenever I want," I teased.

We sat in the living room for the next couple of hours; Ed worked on his laptop while I picked up the Dresden Plate quilt and resumed quilting.

Tires squealed outside and I looked up. Two squad cars stopped in front of Ed's house; an unmarked car blocked the street. Detective Kaplan,

Beavers's younger partner, got out with his gun drawn.

"Crap! Ed, go hide in my bedroom. The cops are at your house."

He got up and walked toward the window to look. "What the—"

"Stop! They'll see you through the window. Go quickly." I pointed down the hall. "My bedroom's in the back of the house. They won't be able to see you back there. Close the drapes."

I sat in the chair and watched. When the police determined Ed wasn't home, they got back in their cars. Kaplan looked around, spotted my house, and swaggered toward my door. He knew where I lived, all right. Four months ago, he'd arrested me right on this very spot. I had no choice but to open the door when he knocked, but I didn't let him come in.

"What do you want now?" I demanded.

"Pappas. He's not at home. Do you know where he is?"

"Yes. He's in a cheap motel making love to your mother."

Kaplan's dark eyes snapped. He looked past me into my living room and caught sight of Ed's gun on my coffee table.

He pointed his finger accusingly. "Whose gun is that?"

"Mine. For protection."

"I think you're hiding Pappas. I'm coming in." He took a step forward.

I held out my arm. "Not without probable cause,

you're not. Get a warrant, Kaplan. Better yet, get a clue." I slammed the door in his face.

I quickly called Beavers. "Arlo, your smarmy little partner, Kaplan, was just at my front door, and he wanted to search my house without a warrant. He had some crazy idea Ed Pappas is here." I looked up. Ed stepped out of my bedroom into the hallway. I put my finger to my lips.

"Why would he think that?"

I cleared my throat. "He may have seen a gun on my coffee table."

Silence. Beavers was probably remembering the time four months ago when I borrowed a gun from Lucy to protect myself against a killer. Finally he said, *"Again?* You think someone's after you again?"

"Did you hear about what happened in the wildlife reserve this morning?"

"Yeah."

"Do you remember what I said about someone in the engineer corps not wanting the police to find the witnesses to Dax Martin's murder?"

"Yeah, but destroying the wildlife reserve seems like an extreme measure to make a couple of witnesses disappear. So, who's after you this time?" There was a certain mocking tone in his voice.

"Lawanda Price threatened me this morning."

"How did she threaten you?"

"She said, 'I know where you live.'"

"That's it?" He clearly wasn't convinced I was in trouble.

"Then she tied a cloth to my front door."

"A cloth? Sounds downright menacing."

I ignored the sarcasm. "Listen, I know stuff about her and her boss, Barbara Hardisty—criminal stuff that may be connected to Dax Martin's murder. I'll be happy to tell you everything after I tie up a few loose ends this afternoon, but you have to get Kaplan off my back."

"Why should I believe you?"

"Because I've been right before. Just give me twenty-four hours."

"Kaplan seems to have a special animosity toward you. Do you know what that's all about?"

"No idea. I've always been nice to him."

Beavers grunted. "If you really are in danger, go to your friend's house. Don't rely on a gun."

"I've got bodyguards."

His voice lowered a notch. "Levy."

"Let's not go there, Arlo. Let's wait to have that conversation when we both have the time."

"You mean when we both have the *bandwidth*?" He threw my expression back at me from our conversation yesterday.

"Arlo, Kaplan was going to arrest Ed."

"Correct. The DA's ready to prosecute Ed Pappas for the murder of Dax Martin."

"Why? The evidence is circumstantial."

"There's pressure from the US Attorney's Office to wrap up the investigation."

"And you buy that?"

"Not necessarily. Mostly because of what you just told me, but if you know where Ed Pappas is, you should have him surrender with his attorney." Beavers never asked me if Ed was actually at my house or if I knew where he was. He knew me too well. Beavers trusted me to do the right thing. It was a sign he might be thawing—too bad it was too late.

I hung up the phone.

"Is it safe to come out?"

"Let me close the drapes in the living room first."

We sat at the kitchen table, drinking wine. I told Ed about my conversation with Beavers. "The good news is he no longer believes you're a suspect, but he says you need to call your attorney and surrender yourself voluntarily. Arlo Beavers is a smart detective. He'll get to the truth, especially if we give him all we know."

Ed rubbed his forehead. "We should ask Simon, especially since I'm about to be arrested."

Ed called Simon Aiken and told him about the cops coming to arrest him. Then he handed the phone to me. "Simon wants to talk to you."

"Hey, Martha. You don't want to be arrested for harboring a fugitive. I'll be there at five-thirty to pick up Ed and surrender him to the police. Dana just called to alert the DA, so the cops shouldn't be bothering you again, even though they have a warrant. If they do show up, just let Ed go quietly. Make sure they see you recording the arrest on your cell phone. That should keep things peaceful." Aiken referred to the LAPD's reputation for shooting suspects at the slightest provocation.

"Okay. Simon, did you hear what happened at the wildlife reserve this morning?"

"No."

I filled him in on the devastation of the area by

Valley Allstar Construction, the confrontation with Lawanda Price, and her threat. "Simon, I'm not sure working with the Feds to get refugee status for Javier and Graciela is the safest thing to do right now. The Army Corps of Engineers took extreme measures to get rid of and intimidate any possible witnesses today when they destroyed the homeless community. Detective Beavers confirmed the DA is being pressured by the US Attorney's Office to prosecute Ed and wrap up the investigation."

Aiken swore. "You're right. Since the US Attorney's Office is working to protect the engineer corps, we can't let them get their hands on those witnesses."

I told him about Pastor Sandoval's call. "I've got a brief opportunity to speak to Javier and Graciela tonight before they leave Los Angeles. I'm going to show them Ed's picture and then I'm going to record what they say. That's probably as much as we'll ever get from them."

"It won't be good enough in court."

"Trust me. It'll be good enough for Arlo Beavers."

CHAPTER 31

Simon Aiken and Crusher converged on my house at the same time later in the afternoon. Aiken wore a navy blue suit; his engagement diamond sparkled in his ear. "Martha, you're going to interview the witnesses tonight at nine?"

I nodded.

"Good. Hopefully, they saw enough to rule out Ed as the killer. If they do rule him out, we should be able to get him back home tomorrow."

Ed reached in his pocket for his house key, which he placed on my coffee table next to his computer and his gun. "Hold on to these for me?"

"Of course." A lump filled my throat.

Aiken clapped a hand on Ed's shoulder. "You ready, dude?"

Ed nodded.

"Then let's do this."

I rushed to Ed and threw my arms around him. "Don't worry. I'm going to do everything I can to help get you out of this. Detective Beavers doesn't think you're guilty either. He'll find the real killer."

Ed Pappas held on to the hug for a long time. He whispered into my ear, "You're my Jewish mom, Martha." Then he kissed my cheek and looked at Crusher. "Take care of her, bro."

Crusher nodded and they did that dancing-hand thing guys do.

Ed squared his shoulders. "I'm ready, man."

Twenty minutes after they left, the doorbell rang. Detective Kaplan and the four uniforms behind him accounted for five firearms in five hands. He flashed a warrant. "I know he's here, Ms. Rose. Step aside so we can bring him in." Clearly, no one thought to tell Kaplan that Ed was turning himself in to the police at six.

I stepped back in disbelief and did as I was told. When Kaplan saw Crusher, he barked, "Hands on your head, Levy!" Insidious fingers of a migraine slowly squeezed my forehead. Could this day get any worse?

Crusher looked at me, rolled his eyes, and complied. He'd discreetly slipped Ed's gun out of sight. One of the uniforms trained his gun on us while the others rushed through my house and searched every room.

I heard them, one by one, yelling, "Clear."

Kaplan reappeared with a scowl on his face, demanding, "Where'd he go?"

"You must have missed the memo, Detective. Ed Pappas just turned himself in to the police with his attorney. If you want to find him, you'll have to go back to the station."

Kaplan's face turned red and he pulled out his cell phone. After a brief conversation, he said to the uniforms, "Pappas is in custody."

As they walked out the front door, I said to Kaplan, "How's your mother?"

He slammed the door and my head started pounding.

Crusher took Ed's gun out of the computer case. "Technically, as an ex-con, I'm not allowed to touch this." He picked up the gun, made sure a round was chambered, and slipped it back into the computer case.

I rubbed my forehead and went straight for my meds, washing them down with a glass of water from the faucet in the kitchen.

Crusher looked at the brown plastic prescription bottle in my hand. "What're those for?"

"Headache. Bad."

He stepped close to me and gently kneaded my neck and shoulders. I slumped into the comfort of his large hands working the hard knots in my muscles. In his deep voice, he quietly murmured, "You've had a bad day, babe. I could make it a lot better."

I looked at him. A picture of Kerry Andreason in a hot-pink minidress shaking her tail flashed through my mind, and I was tempted, but not for long. I said the first thing I thought that might discourage Crusher. "I'm in love with Arlo Beavers."

Crusher was nobody's fool. He must have sensed my relationship with Beavers had completely tanked. He brushed back one of my curls and his eyes searched my face. "How's that working out for you?"

It wasn't working out, of course, and we both knew it. Arlo laughed at me yesterday and then kissed that flirty blonde, Kerry Andreason. Later in the day, when I said the L-word, he told me we needed to talk about it. He probably wanted to tell me it was too late. Then this afternoon, he didn't even mention talking at all. He just told me to go to Lucy's house if I thought I was in danger. I turned away—anger and hurt burning in my cheeks.

"You need to get some rest, babe. Go lie down. I'll wake you when it's time to go. No one can hurt you while I'm here."

The rumble of his voice was surprisingly reassuring. I walked to my bedroom and climbed under my Ohio Star quilt; Bumper joined me on top of the bed. I closed my eyes and gave myself over to oblivion.

Two hours later, someone gently rubbed my back and shoulders, waking me from a deep sleep. Crusher sat on the side of my bed, causing me to roll toward the big dent he made in the mattress. "It's eight-thirty, babe. How's your headache?"

I opened my eyes and smiled. "Gone. Thanks, Yossi." I gestured toward the door. "Just give me a couple of minutes."

"Dang. Our first time in bed together and it was so brief."

I got up, splashed cold water on my face, and eventually made my way to the living room, where he waited.

Crusher tucked Ed's gun inside his leather vest and made sure no one lurked outside the house. Then he hurried me into his truck and we took off for Van Nuys.

We arrived at the church five minutes early. Pastor Sandoval waited inside. He looked at Crusher and stood. "Mrs. Rose, I asked you to come alone."

"I'm sorry, Pastor Sandoval, but I've been threatened too. This is Yossi Levy. He's my friend and bodyguard. He was the one who drove supplies to the homeless on Sunday."

Sandoval relaxed and offered his hand. "They told me 'un gigante rojo' came to give them blankets, but I thought they were exaggerating. Now I'm looking at the red giant with my own eyes."

I looked around in panic when I realized the three of us were alone. "Where are all the people? Are we too late?"

"No. I managed to find temporary shelter for most of the homeless with church families or in shelters. The Acevedos are still in the safe house. I'm going to drive you to where they're staying."

Crusher stepped forward. "I'll drive my car. We'll follow you."

Sandoval pressed his lips together. "You said someone might be after you. If they followed you here, they'll follow you to the safe house. I can't let that happen. There's a back entrance to this building. We'll slip out the door and walk to the next street, where my car is waiting."

Crusher nodded and pulled out the gun as we followed Pastor Sandoval out the back door into a dark alley. We ducked between two apartment buildings, weaving our way through a line of foul-smelling plastic garbage cans to the street beyond. A dark blue Chevy sedan was parked at the curb. Crusher sat up front with Sandoval and hid the gun again. We drove two blocks down the street with the headlights off and turned north. Just before we merged into the cross traffic on Sherman Way, Sandoval turned on the lights.

He drove evasively, with one eye in the rearview mirror. We turned up and down streets, doubled back, then ended up at a small house on Saticoy Street, near White Oak Avenue.

Crusher put his hand on Sandoval's shoulder. "You handled that like a pro. Where'd you learn those tactics?"

Sandoval smiled. "We're only a small stopover in an underground railroad, Mr. Levy. With the help of God, we save innocent lives."

A minute later we were in the tiny living room of a California bungalow built in the 1940s. A striped Mexican blanket hung over the back of the old blue sofa, and every flat surface in the room was covered with school pictures of four children progressing through the years. The remnants of a spicy dinner remained in the air, and my stomach juices churned in hunger.

Sandoval shook hands with a man I recognized as the one who gave up his seat for me on Sunday afternoon. The wife's long black hair was pinned back into a bun and she wore an apron with a bib over a simple flowered housedress. The man turned to his wife and nodded. "*Bueno,* Ana."

Ana disappeared down a narrow hallway and came back followed cautiously by a young man and woman: Javier and Graciela Acevedo. At last I'd found the people who witnessed Dax Martin's murder. People who could clear Ed Pappas.

They were small in stature, with the distinctive nut-colored skin of the *Indio*. Javier was about twenty years old, and I guessed Graciela was still in her teens. She looked to be about six months pregnant. When they saw Crusher, they instinctively clung to each other, glancing frequently at Pastor Sandoval for reassurance. Crusher took one step back in a gesture of peace.

I asked Sandoval if they knew why we were here, and he said they did. I pulled out my cell phone. "I want to record what they say. Is it okay?"

He conferred with the couple, turned back to me, and nodded. "They don't want you to take their pictures. Just ask your questions and I'll translate."

"*Buenas noches.*" I smiled. "You know why I'm here. All I need to know from you is, did you see the murder of the man across the river from your camp?"

Sandoval spoke in Spanish and then turned back to me. "They did see the murder. They are very upset and afraid."

"Can you tell me what happened?"

"They said two men walked in back of the ball field to the river's edge. At first, they seemed to be friendly, and the victim laughed. Then suddenly the killer pulled out a baseball bat he carried behind him and hit the second one in the head. The man went down and the killer hit him a few more times."

"Can they describe the killer?"

"They were too far away to get a look at his face in the dark. Plus, he wore a baseball cap."

I pressed a button on my cell phone and pulled up Ed's picture. "Is this the man you saw?"

Javier and Graciela studied the picture for a long time. Finally they shook their heads and shrugged.

"They can't tell for sure, because of the darkness. It could have been him."

Could have been him?

"Can they remember any details about him? Color of hair, build, how tall?"

"They say he was as tall as the victim and thought he had light hair under the baseball cap. The night was cool and he wore a sweatshirt, but they could see he was slim."

Crap! This doesn't look good for Ed.

Both he and Dax Martin were around six feet tall. Ed was slim and his hair was light brown. Their testimony wouldn't help. In fact, it would only make Ed look *more* guilty.

"Is there anything else they can tell me? Anything at all they might have noticed?"

Both Javier and Graciela thought for a moment. Finally Graciela spoke.

Sandoval looked at me. "She thinks the man in the cap had a funny voice."

"Can she be more specific?"

Graciela just shrugged again and I knew I had gotten all the information they possessed.

Okay. Maybe Ed resembled the killer, but so did thousands of men. Plus, Ed's voice was normal, which ruled him out as far as I was concerned. Was Martin killed by an angry school parent because his kid didn't have enough time on the field? If so, that would give a whole new meaning to the word *hardball*.

What about Jefferson Davis? I'd never actually seen him. Was he tall? Slim? Did he have gray hair? Gray hair would look light under a baseball cap. Time to get a good look at the headmaster of Beaumont.

I thanked the couple for the information and wished them Godspeed.

Sandoval drove us back to the truck. "Did you get what you needed?"

"Yes and no, Pastor. I know my friend didn't commit this murder, but except for the voice thing, he fits their description of the killer. The good thing is, we now have more details than we had before."

Back at the church, we thanked him for his help. As we walked toward Crusher's truck, he called after us, *"Diós guarde."*

On the drive home, I suddenly remembered what the groundskeeper had said. Dax Martin had argued with one of the parents who wore a baseball cap and had a stutter. Was that what Graciela meant by a "funny voice"? It was too late to ask her.

We stopped at a drive-through and brought our

dinner home. Crusher unwrapped the food at the kitchen table while I set up my laptop and pulled up the Beaumont School website. A smiling head shot of a handsome, older man displayed. Unfortunately, I couldn't tell how tall Jefferson Davis was, but his silver hair did qualify him as a suspect. I showed the picture to Crusher and closed the computer. "I'm starving."

I attacked my burger with enthusiasm. Crusher looked up from his second double-double. "I'm spending part of the night with you."

I remembered his offer to "make it better" from earlier in the evening. No way was I going to let anything happen between us. "What do you have in mind, exactly?"

He raised one eyebrow. "I'm your bodyguard, babe. Remember? I'll camp out on the sofa until the next guy comes to relieve me at two in the morning."

Heat warmed my cheeks and I ducked my head so, hopefully, he wouldn't see my embarrassment. "Let me get you a pillow and bedding."

"I won't be needing those. I plan to stay awake and alert. You, however, should go to sleep. Go on. You'll be safe with me."

I looked up at the gentle giant before me with—what had he said on Shabbat?—hidden depths. What did I actually know about him? Nothing. Yet I knew I could trust him.

"Good night, Yossi." I turned and walked down the hall.

How did this happen? I'd lived alone successfully for years, happily doing without any man in my life. Now there were two. The one I thought I loved made me very sad, because I was sure I'd lost him; while the other kept reminding me he was more than willing to step in the breach.

Heaven help me, what was I going to do? Thank goodness tomorrow was quilty Tuesday. I hoped Lucy and Birdie would help me figure things out.

CHAPTER 32

When I woke at eight, Carl was sitting in my kitchen. "The guy who was supposed to take over from Crusher last night couldn't make it, so the big dude crashed on your sofa. He filled me in on everything when I got here at six."

"Want a cheese-and-egg-white omelet?"

"Cool. Very healthy."

I grated cheese and chopped onions, mushrooms, green peppers, and tomatoes. Twenty minutes later, I topped two steaming hot omelets with slices of fresh avocado and salsa and served them with buttered toast and coffee.

So much work and the food was gone in thirty seconds. That's why I hated to cook.

As we left the house, Sonia hurried across the street. "Hi. Did you hear about the Army Corps of Engineers destroying the wildlife reserve the day after we were there? What's going on?"

She didn't wait for an answer. "I saw the cops at Ed's house yesterday. Then I saw Yossi's truck. I noticed he stayed quite late." Her words hung in the air like dirty laundry.

"We can't really stop to talk now, Sonia. Ed's been arrested and I've been threatened by someone in the engineer corps. Yossi stayed as my bodyguard *only*." I emphasized the last word and gave her a meaningful look. She seemed to relax.

"Because you were part of the giveaway on Sunday, you might even be in danger. You'll probably be okay, but just be careful."

Sonia's eyes lit up. "I know exactly what to do. I'll ask Ron Wilson and the Eyes of Encino to activate the EAP."

"What in the world is *that*?"

"Enemy attack plan. It's an armed patrol with spotters. Ron will post people on roofs at night to serve as lookouts. Then if anyone comes after us, they'll radio HQ, which is Ron's living room. Ron will then direct the armed patrol to the scene. He knows all about combat stuff. He was in the army special forces."

"Yeah, but that was more than fifty years ago. Haven't military tactics changed since then?"

"Don't worry. Desperate times call for desperate measures!" Sonia power walked back to her house.

We waited until ten; then Carl drove my car to Birdie's house for our weekly quilting bee. I pointed to the bulge under his black leather vest. "Are you carrying Ed's gun?"

He looked at me and gave me a half smile. "I prefer my own piece."

"Do you have a license to carry?"

I got the other half of the smile. "Gotta do what a man's gotta do."

First of all, as far as I was concerned, Carl was barely old enough to be a man. Second of all, I wasn't happy he was breaking the law. I had the urge to send him to his room.

"Carl, shouldn't you be at school or something today?"

He laughed. "Dude! How old do you think I am? I've got a degree in computer science from Caltech."

My mouth dropped open. Caltech rivaled MIT as the top science university in the nation. You had to practically be a genius to get in.

He laughed again. "I work with Ed, man. He's a big deal in fraud detection and prevention software. You didn't know that?"

"No."

"Well, the sooner he gets out of jail, the sooner we can start working on our project again. We've got a gig right now with the SEC."

I was speechless for the rest of the short ride to Birdie's place.

Birdie gave a little shout of joy when she saw Carl. He scooped her up off the floor in a bear hug and gently swung her around, being careful not to bump her slight body. She laughed as he set her back on her feet.

"This is a big surprise. Why are you here today, dear? I'm guessing it's not about quilting."

Lucy wore red capris and sandals, a red-and-white striped blouse and red button earrings. She pointed at Carl, but she looked at me. "It's always something with you. What now?"

"They arrested Ed last night, and I was threatened yesterday by the United States Army!" I filled them in on the events at the wildlife reserve and the threat from Lawanda Price.

"Yossi arranged for me to have bodyguards around the clock. Carl's my guard today."

Lucy scowled. "Are we safe? Do you think they might come after you *here*?"

Carl gave her a boyish grin. "Don't worry. I made sure we weren't followed."

Birdie's face glowed. "Well, you just sit right down and I'll bring you a nice piece of cake."

He chose a chair facing the door and the front windows and absently patted his vest. A minute later, Birdie gave him a plate with a double slice of applesauce cake and a big glass of milk.

Carl grinned. "Dude!"

I pulled out the Dresden Plate quilt from my tote bag and laid out my sewing supplies on the broad arm of my favorite green chenille chair. Soon Birdie came back in the room with smaller slices of cake for Lucy and me and cups of coffee.

I tightened the quilt in the hoop and threaded my one-inch needle with glazed cotton thread. I knotted one end, took a stitch, and popped the knot through the top fabric, hiding it in the batting inside. With a thimble on the hand that was on top of the quilt, I pushed the needle, guiding it with the fingertips of the hand that was underneath the quilt. In a slow and steady up-and-down, the point of the needle bit through the weave until I'd loaded the shaft with several stitches. Then I pulled the thread through all three layers and repeated the process. In this way, I began stitching a circle inside the center of the plate.

Carl swallowed the last of his glass of milk. "Tell us about last night."

"Pastor Sandoval called me yesterday, and I finally talked to the witnesses last night before they left Los Angeles."

Lucy stopped sewing. "What did you turn up?"

"Nothing that would help, I'm afraid. Their description of the killer was too vague and could have been a hundred people, including Ed. They did have a few specifics. Tall, slim, baseball cap, light hair, and a funny voice."

Birdie looked at me over her glasses and nodded. "You're right, dear. The description does sound like your neighbor Ed, except for the part about the voice. Do you know what she meant by that?"

"I'm not sure."

Lucy said, "So, after all our efforts, the interview was a dead end?"

I ended off my thread and cut a new piece off the spool. "Not entirely. I remembered something the groundskeeper Miguel said about Martin having a fight with one of the fathers of his ballplayers. Miguel described the man as always wearing a baseball cap and speaking with a stutter. Graciela could have been referring to that when she mentioned a 'funny voice.' We need to check him out."

Birdie looked befuddled. "Why in the world would a father want to beat a coach to death?"

Carl snorted. "You've never been to a Little League game, have you?"

I continued. "I also found a photo of Jefferson Davis online last night. He's slender and has light hair. I just need to find out how tall he is and listen to his voice."

"How do you propose to do that?" asked Lucy.

Birdie stood. "I know!" She returned with a newspaper. "Look here. I read in today's obituary page there's going to be a memorial service for Dax Martin at the baseball stadium on Thursday. Maybe Jefferson Davis will make a speech and you can listen to his voice."

I took the paper. "Can I keep this?"

"Of course. Just leave me the crossword and jumble. Now tell me, what does Arlo think about all this?"

"He doesn't exactly know I located the witnesses and talked to them. He won't like it when he finds out. Imagine how furious he'll be when he discovers I also let them leave town without giving him a chance to interview them."

"I think you need to call him, dear."

"Last time we spoke, I told Arlo about the bigger picture with the Beaumont School and the Army Corps of Engineers. He agreed Ed didn't look guilty. I don't want Arlo to change his mind back again because he's mad at me."

Lucy asked, "Does Arlo know you were threatened by the United States Army?"

"Yes. He said if I thought I was in danger, I should go stay with you and Ray."

She looked stunned. "That's all he said?"

I pressed my lips together and nodded.

"Well, you know you can always stay with us." What Lucy didn't say was if Beavers still cared about me, he would have been more proactive about keeping me safe. The fact he passed me off on my friends seemed to indicate Beavers and I were done. Her eyes told me she was pissed off and disappointed.

If she only knew!

The recent ups and downs of romance in my life were new territory for me. I wanted to talk to my friends in the worst way about it. I wanted to talk about how devastated I was Beavers had already moved on to someone else and how he had proven I was right not to trust him—or any man for that matter.

I also wanted to get some advice about how to handle the situation with Crusher. Obviously, pushing him toward my neighbor Sonia wasn't working. Unlike Beavers, Crusher was actively protecting me, but he also indicated he wanted more than friendship. I needed to pour out my confusion and ask Lucy and Birdie to help me figure out what to do.

However, I couldn't have a conversation in front of Carl, so I kept silent. I'd have to deal on my own for a while longer. At least that was territory I knew.

Because of the August heat, Birdie served a cold gazpacho for lunch made with fresh veggies from her garden. She also served thick slices of warm homemade bread with butter melting on top. She positively beamed each time she refilled Carl's bowl. By the end of the meal, the pot stood empty and the whole loaf had vanished. All that work!

At two, Carl's cell phone rang. The handsome young biker/computer scientist in the black leather vest had been winding balls of royal blue yarn for Birdie's next knitting project. He stood and walked away from us. "Yeah? Okay. Right. Now? Right."

He walked over to me. "Dana just called. She finally got hold of a directory for the Beaumont School."

"Is Barbara Hardisty a parent?"

CHAPTER 33

The law offices of Aiken, Teeters & Proulx were on the fifth floor of a high-rise in Woodland Hills, near the Marriott hotel. The waiting room was paneled in dark mahogany, with splashes of colorful abstract art on the walls. A Remington bronze bronco and rider stood encased atop a locked glass pedestal in a place of honor near the reception desk.

Carl and I sat in two luxury leather chairs on one side of a glass coffee table covered with an assortment of magazines, a fresh flower arrangement with proteas, and a wire sculpture of a Harley-Davidson. A large Turkish carpet covered the dark hardwood floors.

Dana didn't keep us waiting long. "Hi, come with me." She smiled, tucking her long, dark hair behind her ear with her left hand. Her engagement diamond sparkled on her finger.

We followed her down the hall to a door with a brushed-nickel nameplate: DANA FREMONT, PARALEGAL. Her small office boasted one window overlooking the parking lot of the Westfield Plaza shopping mall. Carl and I sat in two plain office chairs while Dana took a seat at a desk full of papers, files, and a large computer monitor.

"How's Ed doing?" I asked.

"He won't be arraigned until tomorrow. If the judge agrees to release him, bail won't be a problem, but the DA is going to argue for remand."

That was distressing news. If Ed was denied bail, no telling how long he'd have to stay in jail before he went to trial. With a backlog of cases in the LA legal system, Ed might not see the light of day for months. Possibly more than a year.

We needed to find answers fast.

Dana handed me a large booklet with the Beaumont School logo on the glossy maroon-and-gold cover. "Go ahead. Take a look."

I quickly turned to *H* and found not one, but two Hardisty children: Jason and Emily. Their parents were listed as Lowell and Barbara Hardisty. *Bingo!* There it was, the connection we were looking for between the Army Corps of Engineers and the Joshua Beaumont School. Whatever illegal stuff went on, Barbara Hardisty was right in the thick of it. She occupied the perfect position to clear the path for the stadium to be built.

The Hardistys lived in Sherman Oaks, near Laurel Canyon—a good neighborhood, but not a millionaire's enclave. Yet she drove a luxury car and spent nearly one hundred thousand dollars a year in tuition at the Beaumont School for her two children. Her lifestyle couldn't have come from her

salary with the engineer corps. Did it come from
bribes? From her husband? I had to find out more
about Lowell Hardisty.

Just how involved was Barbara Hardisty in Dax
Martin's murder? She was certainly the architect of
the destruction of the wildlife reserve. What better
way to get rid of any possible witnesses? Did she act
on her own, or was she carrying out instructions
from someone at Beaumont? During the conversation I overheard in the park, Lawanda Price demanded money. Hardisty replied, "People who get
in *their* way," and "I'll talk to *them*."

I looked up from the directory. "Dana, what do
we know about Hardisty's husband, Lowell? Has
anyone taken a look at him?"

She pointed her finger at the booklet in my
hands. "Not yet. We just got this copy an hour ago."

I waved the directory in the air. "Do you mind if
I take this home? I want to see what else I can discover about Lowell Hardisty."

"Not at all. I'm so swamped I could use the extra
help."

Back at my home, I fired up my laptop. "You're
the computer expert, Carl. What's the fastest way to
find out about Lowell Hardisty?"

"What exactly are you looking for?"

"I want to see what he looks like. Either rule him
in or out as a suspect based on the witnesses' description. I also want to look at his financials. How

can this couple afford to send their kids to the most expensive private school in the country?"

"If I had my computer here, I could use the proprietary software Ed and I developed to search for the information. Using your computer will limit the extent of our search."

"Would the software be on Ed's computer?"

"Well, yeah, but—"

"We're in luck, then. Ed left his computer with me." I smiled at him.

Carl grinned in turn. "Dude!"

I fetched Ed's laptop from the living room. Carl typed furiously, pulling up screen after screen until he found what he was looking for. The word "Hermes" stood in bold black letters on a blue background. Beneath the logo was a box asking for a password.

"Here we are. We named our fraud-detection software after the Greek god of communication, trade, commerce, and thievery."

"Cute. What's the password?"

"Madoff."

I groaned. Because of his titanic acts of fraud, Bernie Madoff singlehandedly reinforced centuries of anti-Semitic prejudice. Now his name—his Jewish name—would forever be synonymous with the biggest swindle in history. I cringed every time I thought about him.

"What does the program do, exactly?" I asked.

Carl kept typing. "First, we're going to see what kind of businesses, bank accounts, and other financial records there are in his name. This program allows us a global look. If he stashed money outside the country, we'll find it."

He sat back while the computer executed a slow search. "Your Internet connection sucks, dude. This may take a while."

The time was nearly four in the afternoon. I pulled out a bottle of Pinot Grigio from the refrigerator.

Carl held up his hand. "None for me. I'm on duty. Crusher would have my bal . . . my neck if he thought I was compromised in any way. I will have a cup of coffee, if you don't mind."

By the time the coffee had brewed, text and numbers had shown up on Ed's computer screen.

"Wow!" said Carl. "Take a look at this."

I handed Carl a steaming cup of coffee and sat beside him, holding my wine in my favorite red Moroccan tea glass, with the gold curlicues. "Tell me what I'm looking at."

"This is Lowell Hardisty's financial history. His company lost money for about three years in a row. The man had no other source of income, and his business accounts were overdrawn. There were pending lawsuits from creditors, including former employees. The dude was bankrupt. Then two years ago, he got a huge infusion of cash, putting him back into business. He paid off his creditors and hired employees again."

"What's the name of his company?"

Carl looked at me triumphantly. "Valley Allstar Construction."

I put down my glass of wine. "No way!"

"Way."

"Can this program spell out exactly where the cash infusion came from?"

Carl clicked a few more keys. "The cash came from SFV Associates."

Jefferson Davis's company. Now we had proof positive of a conspiracy between the Beaumont School and the Army Corps of Engineers. The Beaumont School needed a site for their million-dollar baseball stadium. Barbara Hardisty needed money to save her husband's company and finagled an entrée into the exclusive and expensive private school for her children while she was at it.

Even more egregious was the conflict of interest in the devastation of the wildlife reserve. Lowell Hardisty's company was the contractor on that deal too.

"Carl, is there anything there showing us if any funds went to Valley Allstar Construction before or after yesterday's destruction in the Sepulveda Basin?"

"Just a minute. Holy crap! One million dollars was transferred on Monday to Valley Allstar's account from the United States Treasury."

"How did Barbara Hardisty funnel one million dollars of federal money into her husband's business without anyone else noticing? I mean, we're not talking petty cash here. Even though the army is notorious for wasting taxpayer money, I doubt Hardisty has access to a million-dollar slush fund."

"There's some kind of number on the originating federal account. Maybe it will tell us something about the pot of money it came from. Could be an earmark. I'll keep digging."

I still didn't know what Lowell Hardisty looked like. I Googled his name and up popped a two-year-old image from a newspaper article about breaking ground for the Joshua Beaumont School baseball stadium. A line of smiling people wearing hard hats stood on a mound of dirt.

The caption underneath identified the man holding the shovel as Jefferson Davis. Lowell Hardisty stood at his left and Dax Martin at his right. They were all around the same height. Dax Martin was soft around the middle, but both Davis and Hardisty looked fit. I already knew Davis's silver hair potentially matched the description given by the witnesses. Unfortunately, I couldn't say the same for Hardisty. His hair was hidden by the hard hat.

Carl pulled out his cell phone. "Simon needs to hear about all this."

At six o'clock, someone knocked on the door. I started to get up, but Carl unbuttoned his vest and gestured for me to stay at the table. He looked through the peephole and then visibly relaxed.

"*Awww.* Are those for me?" Carl pointed to a bunch of flowers Crusher held.

Crusher ignored him and walked to where I sat in the kitchen. He looked freshly showered; under his black vest, he was wearing a blue button-down shirt, which made his eyes look like summer in the Caribbean. The sleeves were rolled up enough to reveal his muscled forearms covered in freckles and red hair. Instead of a do-rag, he wore a dark blue crocheted *kippah* on his head. For the first time, I saw his hair, which was red shot with gray and cut very short, and his beard was freshly trimmed. He cleaned up nicely. Except for his modern clothes, he looked like many of the observant Jews walking the streets of Los Angeles. Yet, he clearly did not live a totally observant life. This six-foot-six biker, with a weightlifter's build, was an enigma. Sonia was right: Crusher was one hunk of a man.

He handed me a mixed bouquet of fragrant ginger, stock, roses, and Boston ferns. "I thought after yesterday you could use these."

I closed my eyes, buried my face in the fragrant petals, and took a deep breath. "How thoughtful, Yossi. Thanks." When I opened my eyes and looked at him, he had a tender but slightly hungry look in his eyes.

Uh-oh.

CHAPTER 34

I felt so disoriented by Crusher's transformation, I didn't realize Carl had left until the door closed softly behind him.

"You look nice, Yossi. Special occasion?"

"Well, I figure if we're going to spend the night together . . ."

I laughed a little too brightly and busied myself finding a vase for the flowers. "You mean, you'll be sitting watch in the living room like before."

He didn't respond. I could feel his eyes following me around the kitchen as I fluttered peripatetically from cupboard to cupboard.

Vase. Vase. Find a vase.

I finally remembered I kept them in an upper cabinet and stretched unsuccessfully to reach the top shelf.

Yossi ambled over, plucked the crystal vase as easily as a ripe peach from a tree, and handed it to me with a bemused twinkle in his eye.

I quickly turned my back to him and turned on

the faucet, filled the vase with water, and shoved the flowers in. My hands shook as I jittered the vase over to the apricot-colored countertop and set it down. I wiped my wet hands on the sides of my jeans.

Dear God, why doesn't he say something?

"So, how was your day?" I asked lamely.

He opened his mouth to speak, and then the doorbell rang. He walked over, bent down to look through the peephole, muttered something, and opened the door. A severely upset Arlo Beavers stood, clenching and unclenching his hand, as he glared at Crusher.

Double uh-oh.

Beavers strode over to where I stood. He glanced at the flowers and the muscles rippled in his jaw. Then he focused on me. "You've been in touch with the witnesses to Dax Martin's murder!"

This wasn't a question; it was an accusation.

I looked at the man I had thought I was in love with: dark eyes a woman could drown in, and a really pissed-off expression.

"What makes you so sure?"

"Someone in the US Attorney's Office tipped us off about a request by Simon Aiken to expedite a couple's petition for political asylum in exchange for testimony in a criminal case."

I made a grand gesture with my arm. "Oh, sure. So you assumed the refugees were the witnesses we've all been looking for and I've been in touch with them?"

Beavers sizzled with some interior lightning.

"Your twenty-four hours are up. I want everything you know, and I want it now. You can start by telling me how you found the witnesses and where they are. I'm assuming since you haven't come to me with that particular information, the results of your inquiry didn't turn out well for Ed Pappas."

I had to give him credit: Beavers was good, but he wasn't good enough to see behind his back. While we were talking, Crusher quietly removed Ed's gun from inside his vest and slipped it under a sofa pillow. An ex-con could be thrown in jail just for touching a gun—let alone carrying one.

I walked over to the coffeepot and filled the carafe with water. Clearly my bravado hadn't worked. "Oh, all right. A promise is a promise. You might as well sit. It's a long story."

Beavers stood watching me, and Crusher stood watching Beavers.

"Oh, for pity's sake! Will the two of you just grow up and sit down?"

Beavers turned abruptly and headed for the sofa. He sat and shifted his weight against the pillow where the gun lay hidden. Crusher sat as far away as possible.

A few minutes later, I brought out three mugs of coffee on the tray painted with tole roses. "Okay. Here's what I know."

I told Beavers about Javier and Graciela Acevedo. "Unfortunately, you're right. Their testimony doesn't definitively clear Ed Pappas, but they did give us some details to go on. The killer was tall and slim, had light hair, wore a baseball cap, and had a funny voice. With their permission, I taped our conversation. Listen to this." I fetched my cell phone from my purse and played the recording for Beavers.

"Where are they now?" he asked at the end.

"I don't know. I caught them just as they were leaving town."

"What about Aiken's attempt to get them asylum?"

Beavers once told me about how the government seized the lands that had been owned by his tribe along the Siletz River in Oregon.

"Would *you* trust the government to protect you after they destroyed your home?" I questioned with that in mind.

He looked at me for a beat, long enough to tell me he knew what I was referring to.

"What else have you found out?"

I looked at Crusher. If I told Beavers everything I knew, I might be sabotaging Aiken's defense strategy for Ed. On the other hand, if I kept back information, I could be getting myself into serious trouble. Beavers still might have some compunction left about throwing me in jail. Kaplan, however, wasn't my biggest fan, so he'd feel no such hesitation in doing it.

Crusher could tell I was in a spot. He nodded slightly for me to continue. The exchange didn't escape Beaver's notice as he looked from one of us to the other, but he said nothing.

I told him about Jefferson Davis's deal between the Beaumont School and his company, SFV Associates, to develop the baseball stadium. I told him SFV Associates then subcontracted with Valley Allstar Construction to do the actual building. They somehow did all of this without city permits.

Then I told him about Barbara Hardisty's connection to the US Army Corps of Engineers, Valley Allstar Construction, and the Beaumont School. I also mentioned Valley Allstar was recently paid by funds from the United States Treasury to destroy the wildlife habitat in the Sepulveda Basin yesterday. "Barbara Hardisty must have arranged that too."

Crusher looked surprised. "When did you make the connection?"

"Today. I just haven't had the chance to tell Simon yet."

Beavers looked fiercely at Crusher. "Shut up, Levy. I'm asking the questions right now." Then he turned to me again. "How did you discover all this?"

I took a sip of coffee, deciding if I really could be compelled to reveal my sources at this point in the police investigation. Was Ed and Carl's software even legal? No use getting anyone else in trouble. "I have people."

Beavers put down his mug. "Martha—"

"Can't you be satisfied with all the information I'm giving you? Where I get my information is not important. If you want my sources, you'll have to invoke the Patriot Act and torture me—which you seem to be very good at doing already."

He leaned back in his seat and sighed. "Is there anything else?"

"Plenty." I told him about Lawanda Price wanting a piece of the action and what Hardisty said about anyone getting in *their* way and also talking to *them*.

I turned up the palms of my hands. "Don't you see? Because of a known history of violence against Martin, Ed Pappas was set up by 'them'—Davis, the Hardistys, and whoever else was involved in the illegal stadium deal. Martin's murder could have been connected to the conspiracy and conflict of interest in building the stadium."

I finally seemed to be making sense to Beavers. "Why else would they send Lawanda Price to terrorize me? I was getting too close to finding the witnesses. Obviously, someone involved in this whole conspiracy is worried about being identified as Dax Martin's killer."

Beavers looked at Crusher. "What is your role in all this?"

"I take the threat against Martha very seriously. I'm here to protect her from *anyone* who would hurt her." He leaned toward Beavers and said softly, "Anyone."

Beavers stood, turned toward the sofa, pulled the gun out from under the pillow, and laid it on the coffee table. "You know what happens to an ex-con caught with a firearm?"

How did he do that? He must have felt the gun when he was leaning on the pillow. Does he know Crusher put it there, or is he just guessing?

Beavers must have read my mind. "Windows on ovens. Reflections."

So he did see Crusher hide the gun!

I reached for the pistol. It felt cold and heavy in my hand. "I borrowed this from Ed to protect myself. Go ahead and check. This gun is registered to Ed Pappas."

Beavers looked at Crusher. "Uh-huh."

He could have arrested Crusher, but he didn't. He had just given Crusher a pass. I thought I knew why. Beavers finally understood I was in real danger and needed protection. Could it be he still cared, after all?

I put down the firearm, stood, and touched Beavers's arm with my fingertips. He stiffened ever so slightly. "So, what do you think, Arlo? Don't you agree there's plenty of evidence to indicate someone else killed Dax Martin?"

"You still haven't given me a motive."

"What about blackmail? Have you looked into Dax Martin's finances? Maybe he got greedy, or maybe he threatened to expose the corruption?"

"Maybe."

I tried to think of how to tell Beavers about Diane Davis and the other things Miguel had divulged about Coach Martin—without revealing the groundskeeper source.

"Look. I heard Martin was cocky. Maybe he crossed a line with someone else's wife, someone high up in the school hierarchy. Maybe Martin was beaten to death in a fit of jealous rage. You should look into that."

Beavers crossed his arms. "Go on."

"Also, Martin was a bully who liked to throw his weight around. Maybe he pissed off one of the parents. You know how pushy parents can be when it comes to their kids playing ball. Maybe there's a father who fits the description of the killer. You could look for someone who wears a baseball cap, has light hair, and speaks with a funny voice—like a stutterer, for example."

"Those both sound pretty specific. And you know this how?"

"As I said, Arlo, I've got people."

"What about names? Your people give you any names?"

"It won't take much digging to find that out."

Beavers shook his head. "This is vintage Martha Rose. Clever but devious. Always holding something back."

Look who's talking! What about your blond veterinarian with the perky tail?

Crusher walked to my side. "Hey, man. Show some respect for the lady. She stuck her neck out and did your detective job for you."

Beavers leveled his gaze. "What makes you think I don't already know everything she's told me?"

Crusher sneered, "Because, man, she was the one who found the witnesses while you just dicked around."

Beavers studied the crystal vase filled with flowers on my kitchen counter. He looked at me with eyes both sad and hard. "Enjoy your evening."

Then he left.

I stared at the closed front door, torn between wanting to yell and cry.

Crusher put his arm around my shoulders. *"Putz!"*

I leaned into this huge man and let angry tears spill from my eyes. He stroked my head as I buried my face in his chest and left dark, wet patches on his blue shirt. Then he picked me up in his arms and carried me toward the bedroom. I wrapped my arms around his neck for balance, and he rumbled an approval from somewhere deep in his chest. Nobody had ever been strong enough to carry me before. I felt delicate and cherished.

He placed me gently on my bed and lay down next to me, bending over to kiss my wet cheeks. I still held on to him. He kissed my eyelids. "This is my promise to you, *neshamah*. I will never make you cry." He called me by a word in Hebrew meaning more than just "honey" or "babe." He'd called me his "soul."

Then he brushed my mouth with a soft kiss, which turned wet and urgent. His hands and fingers read the curves of my body, and I shifted my weight so he could unhook my bra. If this was a mistake—and I'm pretty sure it was—I'd think about it tomorrow. For now, I closed my eyes and gave myself over to the comfort of Yossi's generous lovemaking.

CHAPTER 35

Once our passion was spent, Yossi Levy held me in his arms for the rest of the night. I woke up early in the morning to the sound of his soft snoring. I lay on my side with Yossi curled up behind me, forming a huge carapace, his heavy arm draped over my shoulders. Dawn would be breaking soon and then what? Was I ready for this? Was Beavers now a thing of the past?

Oh, my God, what have I done?

I quietly slipped out of bed and hurried into the bathroom. The sky turned from black to gray through the frosted glass of the window. Last night with Yossi was pure magic; but as day broke, I was terrified I'd just made the worst mistake of my life. I was pretty sure if there existed somewhere a hand-basket labeled DESTINATION: HELL, I'd just earned a reserved seat.

I turned on the shower and stepped in. *What'll Uncle Isaac think? He really liked Beavers. Oh, my God. What will I say to Sonia?*

Later, in the kitchen, I stirred a large heap of diced potatoes and onions in sizzling hot olive oil while Crusher showered and made a couple of phone calls. Then he came up behind me and kissed my neck, tickling my skin with his beard. "It's all settled. I'm staying here with you for as long as you need."

All of a sudden, the room got very small; I couldn't find enough air to breathe. I turned to face him. "No, Yossi. You staying here is a bad idea. I think we may have just made a huge mistake. A spectacular mistake."

He smiled indulgently. "Babe, it was spectacular." He lightly stroked my cleavage with his fingertip and my whole body vibrated. "You didn't like it?"

I turned back to the stove and spoke to the potatoes, stirring as fast as the words tumbled out. "Of course I liked it! A lot! But that's the whole point. Now my life is more complicated than ever. I've got to figure things out. You've gotta let me have some space here."

"This doesn't have to be complicated."

What had my uncle Isaac told me? *"It doesn't have to be complicated, faigele. Love and trust. They should be simple."*

Right. He hadn't just gone from dating a straight-arrow cop to spending the night making glorious love to a six-foot-six mountain of muscle—a mysterious ex-con/biker/lover/dude in a *kippah*.

And what about food? Feeding Crusher would require me to stir vats of food all day long, and I hated to cook. No, this could never work.

We ate a huge breakfast, starved after our marathon workout. How many calories had I burned? Then I brushed away the thought as unworthy.

At one point, he was staring at me with those hungry eyes. I quickly looked back at my plate. My head told me I should never again be intimate with Yossi Levy. I also knew that if he touched me, my body would volunteer a resounding *You betcha!*

"You cooked—I'll clean." He'd just slathered his fourth piece of whole grain toast in butter and jam.

As we cleared the table, the doorbell rang. Yossi motioned for me to stay where I was. He picked up the gun and slipped it inside his vest. He wore clean clothes he'd fetched from an overnight bag in his truck: black T-shirt, jeans, and a blue bandana. Yossi bent down to look through the peephole. He turned toward me and all the color drained out of his face. My heart started to race.

Beavers? Kaplan? Army Special Forces?

He muttered a four-letter word and opened the door.

Sonia!

She smiled at him; he looked over at me; I mouthed, *"OMG!"*

"Did you see her last night?" She took a tiny step toward him.

"See what?" He took a step backward, bare foot landing heavily on the wooden floor. His boots were still under my bed.

She looked at me. "The army jeep, of course.

She drove by your house several times yesterday evening."

Crusher and I looked at each other. Army jeeps were the last thing on our minds last night.

He scratched his head. "Uh, I guess I missed that."

Sonia frowned. "I thought you were supposed to be guarding Martha. Where were you? I saw your truck here all night."

Neither one of us said a word and the silence deepened.

Then her mouth fell open and her eyes got wide.

I tried to smile, but my face felt all rubbery and fake.

Then she noticed Crusher's bare feet. "Oh, I get it."

I felt like a traitor. "Sonia, I—"

Her shoulders slumped and she held up her hand. "Never mind. I just thought you were on my side. I thought we were friends." She turned to leave.

"We are friends. I'd never deliberately hurt you, honestly. It's just that, well, things changed."

"Obviously." She stared at Crusher's bare feet.

Crusher finally found his voice. "You're a nice lady, Sonia, but I've always liked Martha. I'm sorry if I gave you a different idea."

Sonia sighed. "No, you didn't." Then she glared at me. "What about your cop boyfriend? What about him?"

"We're not together anymore."

She thought for a moment. "So . . . does that mean he's free now?"

I swallowed. I hesitated to mention that Beavers was probably spending all his free time in the arms of a lady vet.

I walked up to Sonia and took her hand. "Look, I've just made some fresh coffee. Why don't we sit down—I want to hear about the jeep."

She gave Crusher's feet one last disapproving glance and followed me into the kitchen. We took our mugs to the table, where the sugar and cream still sat from breakfast.

"Last night at eight, the EAP spotter observed a redheaded woman driving an army jeep."

Lawanda Price.

Crusher scratched the back of his neck. "What does EAP mean?"

"The neighborhood patrol put in place our enemy attack plan when we found out someone was after Martha."

I asked, "So you mean you actually placed a spotter on someone's rooftop?"

"Yup. Ron and Yuki Wilson's teenage grandson, Parker, hid on Ed's roof with a pair of binoculars and a walkie-talkie. It's a primo spot because the overhanging mulberry branches made a perfect blind for him to sit in. Anyway, he logged four passes in front of your house between eight and nine p.m. He said she drove slowly, almost as if she wanted to be seen."

I was pretty sure Barbara Hardisty sent Lawanda Price to frighten me. Too bad for them. Instead of being scared, I was probably in the throes of a *petite mort* with Yossi at the time of the drive-by. My cheeks heated red at the memory. "What happened?"

"Ron grabbed his pistol and drove over in his Buick. Tony came separately on his scooter."

I was confused. "No disrespect, but what could Tony do from his scooter?"

"He brought a big camera and deliberately positioned himself in your driveway so she would see him taking her photo. It worked. She left and never came back."

Crusher raised his eyebrows. "So you drove off an enemy attack? Cool."

I was glad to see Sonia soften a little with his praise. Hopefully, she would come to accept a new reality that didn't include Crusher.

"What are you going to do now?" she asked.

I took a sip of coffee. "I'm not sure yet. Tomorrow is Dax Martin's memorial service at the baseball stadium. Maybe something will turn up there."

Sonia stood and looked from Crusher to me. *"Mazal tov."*

I jumped up and hugged her. "We're still friends, right?"

She nodded and went back to her house.

"Yossi, I'm thinking maybe I overreacted to Lawanda Price's threat. From what Sonia just told us, Price only wants to scare me. Maybe I don't need a twenty-four-hour guard. I think I'll be safe enough alone. Why don't you go back to your shop? After all, you have a business to run."

Not to mention, I need some breathing room.

"You ain't getting rid of me that easily, babe. Don't worry. I've got the shop covered. Wherever you are, I'm there, too, until the killer is caught." He gave me a meaningful look. "And long afterward."

I started pacing. Partly from anger about being stalked, but mostly from panic at his "long afterward" remark. "Well, I just can't sit around doing nothing. I'm thinking the best defense is an offense. I'm going to the Army Corps of Engineers office downtown and confront Barbara Hardisty. Once she knows I've already told the police everything I know about her corruption, she'll no longer have a reason to try to intimidate me." I turned to Crusher. "Are you in?"

He slipped on his socks and boots. Then he stood with the keys to his truck. "Babe, you've got enough stones to make you an honorary guy."

"Is that supposed to be a compliment?"

Crusher laughed. "Actually, I like you much better as a woman." His voice softened and he stepped in close. "My woman."

You betcha! sang my body.

I put on a mental hair shirt. "Let's get out of here."

CHAPTER 36

The Army Corps of Engineers was on the eleventh floor of a high-rise on Wilshire Boulevard between the 110 Freeway and Figueroa Street in downtown Los Angeles. Crusher hid his gun in the truck so he wouldn't get tagged going through the body scanner on the first floor.

We stepped off the elevator into a large beige room and met a pleasant-looking African-American woman sitting at a steel desk.

"I'm here to see Barbara Hardisty."

She smiled. "Do you have an appointment?"

"No, but if you tell her Martha Rose is here from Valley Allstar Construction, I'm sure she'll make the time to see me."

She gave me a puzzled look and made the call to Hardisty. After a minute, she put down the phone. "Follow me, please."

We walked past a dozen prefab tan steel cubicles populated by civil servants; worker bees nurturing the bloated hive of government. Crusher's boots landed heavily on the gray vinyl floor tiles, inviting curious stares.

The receptionist stopped at a bank of executive offices in the back and knocked on the third door in.

A woman's voice commanded, "Come!"

Barbara Hardisty sat in front of a window behind a cheap government-issued desk covered with fake wood veneer. Tall tan file cabinets lined the walls on either side, and two office chairs of the stacking variety faced the desk. Her brown hair was styled in an asymmetrical bob, hanging approximately to her shoulders. She scowled and didn't offer us a seat.

"You're the woman with those hideous pink shoes, aren't you?"

"Yes, but I'm also known as the woman who just informed the police of your connection to an illegal conspiracy between SFV Associates—specifically Jefferson Davis, Valley Allstar Construction—specifically Lowell Hardisty, and the Joshua Beaumont School—specifically the baseball stadium."

Crusher stood next to me, filling the space like a silent monolith.

Hardisty's calculating eyes darted back and forth between us. "I've got no idea what you're talking about. That transaction was completely legal. You people have been whining about the stadium for years. Get over it."

"How about this? I'm also known as the woman who told the police you paid Allstar Construction—

specifically Lowell Hardisty—with a million dollars of government money to destroy a federally protected wildlife reserve."

She crossed her arms. "I don't know where you're getting your information, lady, but I've done nothing illegal. The LAPD wanted that hellhole cleaned up. Believe me, there are people who'll vouch for me all the way up to the highest levels in this city and beyond."

All the way to hell, I'm guessing.

"You sent Lawanda Price to try to intimidate me. In case you don't know, along with conspiracy, fraud, bribery, and embezzlement, stalking is a serious crime. I have a photo of Price in the act last night. Time to call off your dogs."

Hardisty shuffled some papers on her desk. "You're just a hysterical nobody who wants to feel important. Why don't you go back to your quilting bee?"

It irked me Hardisty knew about the quilts because her spy, Price, watched us give them away to the homeless.

I put my hands on the back of a chair and leaned forward. "I've got two words for you—Dax Martin."

She looked up warily. "What about him?"

"Why was he killed? Did he know too much? Was he trying to blackmail one of you? Did he get greedy, like you?"

Hardisty busied herself rolling up a topographical map. "I don't know who killed the poor man, and I don't know why. I had nothing to do with his death."

"Oh no? When the police come after you, let's see which one of your high-level friends is going to risk an indictment in order to protect you. The higher up your so-called friends are, the more they'll have to lose if they do."

I swept my hand toward the bank of dull file cabinets. "Take a look around. Is this the office of someone who's valuable? You'll be thrown under the bus so fast—you won't know how you got there."

Hardisty's face reddened. "Get out of my office."

I couldn't help myself. I thought about my friend Hilda, the Acevedos, and all those poor, displaced homeless people. "You destroyed one of the few places homeless people could find refuge in this city. Jason and Emily, your kids. Where will they find refuge when both of their parents are in jail? I doubt the Beaumont School will still want them around. Don't worry. They won't be homeless. The state will split them up and place them in foster care. Good luck to them with that."

Barbara Hardisty stood behind her desk and shrieked, "Get out! Get out of my office now!"

I narrowed my eyes. "Grab a parachute, lady, because you're going down!"

Hardisty tried to hide her shaking hands.

* * *

Crusher and I waited until the elevator doors closed and we were alone before we bumped fists.

"Maybe I said too much. Do you think I said too much?"

Crusher shook his head and laughed. "What'd I say before? Stones of steel."

We arrived at the first floor and Detective Kaplan flashed a badge on his way through security, followed by a couple of uniforms. Beavers must have checked out my evidence and clued in his partner, because Kaplan appeared to be coming after Hardisty.

I might have been able to hide myself among the people in the lobby, but Crusher was impossible to miss. Kaplan did a double take and then barreled his way toward us.

"What are *you* doing here?"

Crusher crossed his arms. "It's a free country."

Kaplan looked at me. "If I find out you've interfered in police business—again—I won't hesitate to throw you in jail—again. I don't care who you've been sleeping with."

Is it that obvious Crusher and I had sex last night? Then I realized Kaplan was referring to Arlo Beavers. Kaplan didn't know Beavers and I weren't together anymore.

I lowered my voice and spoke confidentially. "Detective Kaplan, we just spoke to Barbara Hardisty and she says she has friends in high places in this city. Are you sure you've got enough authority to go after her?"

Predictably, Kaplan planted his thumb in his chest.

"Of course I've got authority. I don't care whose friend she is. I'm taking her in for questioning."

"Wow. Okay, then. Good luck, and I mean it."

Kaplan smirked and swaggered toward the elevators.

Crusher muttered, *"Putz."*

Back in the truck, we hopped on the 110 Freeway north and transitioned to the 134 west to Encino. My confrontation with Hardisty left me elated, which meant I was also hungry. I checked the digital clock on the dashboard, relieved to find it was lunchtime.

"I'm starved. How about some lunch?"

Crusher let his eyes slide down my body and grinned. "I know what I want for lunch."

You betcha!

I struggled for control. "How about a falafel instead?"

Hilda wasn't in her usual spot near Rafi's on the Boulevard, nor was she inside. I hadn't heard from her since Monday and wondered if she was okay.

"She take recycle this morning like always, but then she leave, *chik-chok*." Rafi slapped his palms together. He pointed to a padded banquette seat running the length of one wall. "I let her sleep there."

He looked at Crusher and half-smiled. "You not from Health Department? You do not shut me down?"

"Oh, sorry, Rafi. This is my friend Yossi Levy."

Rafi grinned and stuck out his hand. "Levy? *Atah medaber Ivrit?*" ("You speak Hebrew?")

Crusher took his hand and smiled. *"Ketzat."* A little.

Was Crusher just being modest? After all, he quoted Torah, chapter and verse, during Shabbat dinner last week. There was so much I didn't know about Yossi Levy, but what I did know I found intriguing and attractive. Unfortunately, I wasn't ready to let go of Arlo Beavers.

After lunch, Crusher drove back to my house. "You can just drop me off, Yossi. I don't need a bodyguard anymore. All of Hardisty's financial secrets are out, so she has nothing left to hide there. If she's protecting the killer, the police will find out. Either way, I'm the least of her worries. With Hardisty in custody, I doubt I'll see Lawanda Price again."

He cut off the engine and turned to me. "You're forgetting one thing, babe. The killer. The tall guy in the baseball cap with the funny voice—he's still out there."

"Why should I be worried?"

"Maybe he'll want revenge for blowing the whole fraud-and-conspiracy thing wide open."

"I don't think so. My money's still on Jefferson Davis. He had a double reason to want Dax Martin dead—one, for having an affair with his wife and two, for blackmail. The first motive we know for sure. The second one we're just guessing at. Either way, Davis has no reason to come after me."

Crusher appeared to agree I was probably safe. It was also clear how much he wanted to get me in bed again.

"Are you sure? I just don't feel right leaving you alone."

"I'm positive, Yossi. What happened between us last night was out-of-this-world, but it might never happen again. You have to give me a chance to figure things out on my own."

"Is this still about Beavers?"

"That's one part, yes."

He reached over and took my hand. "The other part?"

I smiled at the only man in the world who could make me feel like a size four. "You called me *neshama*."

Crusher, aka Yossi Levy, closed his eyes and pressed his lips into the palm of my hand.

I got out of the truck and walked to the door without looking back. As soon I was inside the house, his engine started up and he drove away. I slumped against the door and breathed a sigh of relief mixed with a most sincere regret.

CHAPTER 37

Simon Aiken answered on the third ring. "Yeah."

"Simon, I want you to know, last night I was officially questioned by Detective Beavers. I had to tell him everything."

"I know. Crusher called me this morning. He said you did fine. He even said you protected your sources. Nobody could ask for more, Martha. Is he there?"

"No, I'm by myself." I told Simon about my little talk with Barbara Hardisty. "On our way out, we ran into Detective Kaplan. He showed up to take her in. What's happening with Ed?"

"The DA still seems determined to go forward. I'm prepping for the preliminary hearing. With all this new information we've uncovered, along with a dearth of evidence against Ed, I'm presenting a motion for dismissal."

"What about the pressure from the US Attorney's Office to prosecute?"

"They'll probably back down. They'll have their

hands full defending the Army Corps of Engineers. The press has really jumped on the destruction of the wildlife reserve. We just learned the funds transferred to Valley Allstar Construction were misappropriated. They were federal relocation dollars specifically earmarked to help the homeless move from publicly owned lands to low-cost housing. Both Barbara and Lowell Hardisty are now in custody. Hopefully, the police will find out if they were also involved in Dax Martin's murder."

"I hope the Hardistys get what they deserve. What about the conspiracy to get the Beaumont Stadium built?"

"That's going to be a little tougher to prove, since the corruption involves so many sitting officials, but someone at the *Times* is working on it. Eventually the public will know about the scandal."

"So, does Ed still have to stay in jail?"

"Yes, at least until the hearing or until the real killer is found."

I bristled at the unfairness. "Dax Martin's memorial service is tomorrow at the baseball stadium. I'm sure Jefferson Davis will be speaking. I know he fits the physical description of the killer. I'm going over to check him out. I want to hear his voice."

"Be careful, Martha. They know who you are. Take Crusher with you."

"He's too easy to spot. I want to walk unnoticed through the crowd."

"Don't go alone."

"I'll take my friends with me. Nobody will pay attention to three old ladies."

The smile came through Simon's voice. "Maybe your friends fit that description, but I know one big dude who definitely doesn't put you in the same category."

I was glad he couldn't see me blush.

I called my best friend next. "Lucy, are you busy? I need to talk."

"Just reading a cozy mystery, hon. Come on over."

Fifteen minutes later, I sat in my friend's living room, holding a frosty glass of iced tea. The aroma of roasting meat, garlic, and oregano came from the kitchen.

Lucy wore a shade of green today that complemented her orange hair: a grass-green denim jumper, with big pockets, over a short-sleeved white T-shirt. Apple jade circled her wrist and punctured her earlobes. I was amused she owned matching green open-toed flats. She reminded me of a carrot in Mr. McGregor's garden.

"What's up, hon'? You look like something big is on your mind. Arlo?"

Bless Lucy. She reads me like a book.

"Yes and no. On Sunday, after you dropped me off, I went to visit Arthur in the veterinary hospital. When I got there, Arlo was leaving the hospital with Arthur's pretty young doctor. She was wearing a sexy little dress."

"No! What did you say?"

"They didn't see me. I managed to park far enough away so I could watch them. He kissed her, Lucy. Then they drove off together."

"I'm so sorry, hon. That must really hurt."

I rubbed my forehead. "Yeah. I was right not to trust him. He didn't take very long to find someone else, once he broke up with me."

She came over to hug me. "I'm sorry. You seemed so good together. Can you try to talk to him?"

"I already have, sort of. At one point, I admitted to Arlo I'd fallen in love with him. He said we should talk about it, but I know what he wants to say. He wants to dump me for that sexy blonde. Then last night, he came over to question me while Yossi was there. He was really hostile."

"Do you suppose Arlo's reaction had something to do with seeing that particular man in your house again? Why don't you call him and suggest the two of you meet alone? Maybe you can patch things up."

I took a deep breath. "The thing is, after Arlo left, I kind of slept with Yossi . . . a little bit."

Lucy's eyes popped out of her head. "You did *what*?"

"I never meant to. I was so pissed and sad, and Yossi was incredibly sweet. It just happened. The problem is, Yossi's already making noises about sticking around after this thing is over."

"Dang it, Martha, I can't leave you alone for five seconds. What do you even know about this man?"

"Well, he's a businessman, kind of like Ray, only he repairs Harleys, not cars."

Lucy tilted her head. "He's also an ex-con. Did you ever find out why he went to prison?"

"Not yet. That doesn't prove anything. Arlo called him an 'outlaw,' but they don't seem to have ever arrested him. Whatever he did in the past, he seems to be straight now."

"What else do you know?"

"He's a leader in the Valley Eagles motorcycle *club*—not *gang*. He's a loyal friend. He's a lot deeper than you'd suspect. He's smart, knows Torah, and speaks some Hebrew. He's really scary to look at, because he's so big and tough, but he can be very gentle." I gazed in the distance, remembering all the different ways he'd been gentle with me the night before.

"You're smiling, girlfriend."

I looked at my friend. "Oh, Lucy, it was so good. I think I'm going to hell."

Lucy put down her glass of tea and leaned forward. "You have a decision to make, Martha Rose, and soon. If you want Arlo, you have to go after him and try to mend fences before it's too late."

"And wait until the next time he gets angry and leaves me for someone else? I can't live like that."

She dismissed my concern with a wave of her hand. "I don't believe Arlo is so manipulative. Maybe there's another explanation for this lady vet. I think Arlo really loves you. He's probably hurting as much as you are right now."

"He didn't look like he was hurting on Sunday evening."

"Well, Yossi Levy said he wants to stick around. Are you ready to make such a commitment after only one night together?"

I tossed my hands up in a helpless gesture. "I

honestly don't know what I want right now. Life was simpler when I was alone. Maybe that's the answer. Forget about both of them."

Lucy sighed. "Yes, your life was a whole lot simpler, but your life was also lonelier."

I took a long sip of tea. "I actually came over here for a second reason. Will you come with me to Dax Martin's memorial service tomorrow?"

"Why?"

"I want to look for the killer."

I brought Lucy up to date, including my blow-by-blow encounter with Barbara Hardisty this morning and the news both she and her husband were under arrest. "Everyone agrees I'm no longer in danger, but poor Ed's still in jail and there's a killer yet to find. Jefferson Davis is at the top of my list, and he'll be at the service tomorrow. We might also come across the parent who stutters. Maybe if we poke around, we'll get lucky. Nobody will notice a couple of old ladies in the crowd."

"How about Birdie?"

"Sure, if her knees can take some walking. The service starts at ten. Be at my house at nine-thirty. As soon as the stadium starts to fill up, we'll make our move and mix in with the grieving throng."

By the time I got home around six, I was exhausted. Bumper greeted me at the door with a reproving look. His kibble bowl was empty. The exhilaration of the previous night with Crusher and the adrenaline of confronting Hardisty had finally worn off, and I was ready to collapse.

I fed the cat, changed my sheets, and climbed into a fresh pair of cotton pajamas with little blue flowers printed in an allover pattern. Then I returned to the living room with a turkey sandwich, snuggled on the sofa with my blue-and-white quilt, and turned on *Jeopardy!*.

"I'll take 'Americana' for six hundred, Alex."

"'Ohio Star and Hole in the Barn Door.'"

The *Jeopardy!* theme song plunked in the background as the camera zoomed into the blank faces of the contestants.

"What are quilt block patterns!" I yelled at the screen. Nobody heard me.

"Oh, sorry. The correct question is 'What are quilts?'"

Bumper jumped up on my lap and settled in, purring.

I bent over and scratched his ears. "Aren't we smart?"

The doorbell rang.

I pressed the Mute button on the remote control and got up to answer the door. I hoped Crusher wasn't coming back for seconds. I didn't know if I'd be able to resist.

Arlo Beavers stood outside. Heart pounding, I hurried to put on my blue chenille bathrobe before I opened the door.

He wore his off-duty clothes—snug jeans with cowboy boots and a white cowboy shirt with snaps down the front. He asked warily, "Are you alone?"

My neck pulsed. "Yes."

"Can we talk?"

I stared at him in panic.

His voice softened a little. "Please?"

Stepping aside, I let him in, inhaling his heart-breakingly sexy cologne as he passed. I returned to the sofa, pulled the quilt up to my chin, and waited nervously for him to speak. His face was unreadable and gave me no clue about what he had on his mind. One thing was obvious, though, this wasn't going to be an easy conversation.

Beavers sat on the edge of a chair, leaned forward, and looked at the floor, rubbing his hands together as if searching for the right words. Then he looked back at me.

I braced myself for the worst.

"Martha, I'm sorry."

Here it comes. He's officially dumping me.

"I've been acting like an ass. I was wrong, and I'm so sorry."

Surprise jolted my whole body, and my brain froze. This was the last thing I expected to hear from him.

I said nothing.

"I mean, I was angry about my dog getting hurt, sure. But when I cooled down, I realized if I'd listened to you in the beginning, maybe you wouldn't have felt compelled to go out there on your own to help your friend."

Whoa! This is definitely not what I expected to hear.

Beavers searched my face for a response, but I just looked at him. I still didn't know what to say.

"Look, Martha. When I kept seeing you with Levy, I admit I was jealous. I should have trusted you more. I should have known you were only trying to help Ed Pappas. I was an idiot to think you would ever sleep with a guy like that."

Oh, my God. Oh, my God. Oh, my God.

"Then last night, when I saw him here again, I kicked myself. I realized he was only here because you needed protection. That's why I didn't confiscate the gun. I failed you. I shouldn't have trusted your safety to a thug. I should have been the one protecting you."

I was dizzy from hyperventilating. *If only the earth would open up and swallow me. If only the world would end. Please, God . . .*

The corners of his mouth turned up. "You're one-of-a-kind, Martha Rose. You're not only the smartest woman I know, you're gutsy. Kaplan told me about how you challenged Barbara Hardisty this morning." His eyes got all soft and sexy. "Please say you'll forgive me. I've been a total jerk. I miss you, honey."

He called me "honey"!

"I love you and I don't want to risk losing you. I want us to move in together."

Tiny black dots danced before my eyes and the room spun around.

CHAPTER 38

I came to with Beavers's anxious voice coming from somewhere above me. "Martha! Honey! Wake up!"

I opened my eyes and looked up into his anxious face. *Wheel of Fortune* whirled soundlessly on the television behind him.

"Water, please," I croaked, struggling to sit up again.

He helped me sit back up, touched my face, and then grabbed me in a desperate embrace. "You passed out for a few seconds." He kissed the top of my head. "Are you okay?"

A few days ago, I would have given anything to be back in these arms, where I thought I'd been safe. Then I flashed again on him kissing the vet with the perky ponytail. I pulled back. "Please, Arlo, can I have some water?"

Vanna turned over five *E*'s before he returned with a tall glass hastily drawn from the tap. He sat next to me, but I shook my head and gestured toward the chair. He moved with a reluctant frown, back to where he'd been sitting before.

"Arlo, I appreciate your apology. Obviously, I wasn't expecting it. In fact, I was certain you were serious about ending our relationship the night Arthur was injured."

"I was just angry."

I held up my finger. "Please let me finish. I've already apologized for causing Arthur's injury. You know I'm sick about that, but you've put me through a lot of heartache since then. You've made me cry and you even laughed at me on Sunday."

"I was only amused you even knew what a 'bitch seat' was. You were so cute when you said it."

"Maybe I wasn't aiming to be 'cute.' Maybe I wanted you to understand how badly I was hurting."

He chewed on the corner of his mouth. "Okay."

"Then I saw you with Arthur's vet."

He looked up sharply. "What? When?"

"Does it matter? Do you deny you're sleeping with Dr. Andreason?"

"It isn't like that. I made a brief mistake and went out with her a couple of times, but I never slept with her. I'd never do that to you. You're the one I want to be with."

Great. Now I get to be the hussy.

"Well, how do I know the next time you get pissed off, you won't just up and leave again?"

He put his hand over his heart like he was a Boy Scout saluting the flag. "Because I'm making a pledge. I'll never abandon you again. If there's a problem, we'll work it out."

I thought about the vow Yossi made last night. "Can you promise you'll never make me cry?"

"Who could make a promise like that? Things happen. Who can control how another person will react?"

I took a slow, deep breath. *Here goes.* "You're right, Arlo. Who knows how a person will react? As a matter of fact, your leaving and taking up with another woman triggered one surprising reaction in me. Now I don't know if either of us will be able to move past it."

His body tensed. "What are you talking about?"

I held his gaze and tried not to blink. "I'm talking about Yossi Levy."

He looked confused for a second and then the room filled with ozone as lightning struck. He stood and reached the sofa in two strides. I was being lifted to my feet by my shoulders. The glass of water fell from my hand to the floor.

Hands firmly clamped to my shoulders, Beavers thrust his face in front of mine. "What are you saying, Martha? Are you saying you slept with Levy?" His face was as serious as I'd ever seen it.

I put my hands on his chest and gently pushed him back. "It happened only after I saw you with that woman."

He suddenly let go of my shoulders and shook his head, hands on his hips. "Oh, God, what did we do?" His anger subsided and his voice was throaty. "Did you really mean it the other day when you said you'd fallen in love with me? That was the first time you ever used the word 'love.'"

"Yes."

"What about Levy?" He searched my face. "Are you in love with him too?"

The past twenty-four hours were arguably the most intense twenty-four hours of my life, and my head was about to explode. "To be perfectly honest, I don't know what I feel right now."

Head wagging, Arlo turned to leave. "I can't live with that."

Didn't I say almost exactly the same thing to Lucy?

"So, is this you walking out on me again?"

He stopped and turned around. "No, this is me going home to try to figure out how we screwed up a good thing. I'm back if you want me, but only if I can have all of you. I won't share you."

As tired as I was, sleep eluded me for half the night. I was glad I didn't have to worry about keeping secrets. Each man knew about the other, but now I had to work out what to do next, and my mind seesawed for hours.

In the morning, Bumper jumped on my body a couple of times, landing with all four paws on my shoulders to jar me awake. I must have clenched my jaws all night long because my face was sore.

I got up, fed the cat, fed myself, and got dressed. My usual jeans were too casual for a memorial service, so I slipped on a peach linen summer dress and brown sandals. Lucy and Birdie showed up at nine-thirty, just as I draped a large printed cotton scarf over my bare arms.

A pair of yellow-gold baseballs the size of a dime dangled conspicuously from Lucy's ears, left over from her days as a Little League mom.

Birdie had wound her long white braid around the crown of her head. She'd abandoned her usual denim overalls, T-shirt, and Birkenstocks for an elastic-waisted pantsuit made out of lavender polyester. She turned around on her brown orthopedic shoes, demurely showing off her ghastly outfit.

I looked at her. "Really?"

She smiled wickedly. "I'm in disguise, dear. Isn't this perfect? Nobody will notice or remember me in this forgettable outfit. I'll be like a maiden aunt at a wedding party."

Lucy pointed to the rug next to the sofa. "Do you know you have a big wet spot there?"

I stared at the dark patch left like a giant teardrop from last night. "Yes. I dropped a glass of water." I wanted to tell my friend about Beavers's visit and the emotional ambush he brought with him last night. I wanted to hear her say I'd done the right thing when I confessed I'd slept with Crusher. Now wasn't the time. We needed to focus on the task at hand.

Birdie smiled and sat in one of the chairs. "What exactly is the plan, dear? What are we supposed to be looking for?"

I opened my computer and found the photo of Jefferson Davis on the Beaumont School website. "He's my number one suspect. I'm sure he'll be speaking today, and I want to hear if he has a funny voice."

"Okay, dear, but you can do that all by yourself. What can we do to help?"

"I need you to be extra eyes and ears. Try to mingle in the crowd and listen for any gossip. We still don't know for sure if Davis is our guy. If you find anyone else who fits the witnesses' description of the killer, try to get close enough to listen in on their conversation. If they have a distinctive speech pattern, try to get a name."

Birdie held on to Lucy's arm as we walked in back of my house to join the stream of mourners making their way from the parking lot to the Joshua Beaumont Stadium.

We were off to find a killer.

CHAPTER 39

Charter buses disgorged hundreds of students in their maroon blazers with the gold school crest on the pocket, accompanied by faculty wearing photo identity cards around their necks. Parents and dignitaries arrived in luxury sedans, SUVs, and even a couple of limousines. Miguel and the other Beaumont maintenance staff, wearing maroon shirts and khaki pants, directed traffic in the parking lot. Security staff barred a couple of news crews from entering the area.

Birdie, Lucy, and I agreed to split up and meet back at my house after the memorial service. I approached Miguel, who recognized me immediately and looked worried. "Good morning, Mrs. Martha." He pointed an SUV down the row of cars.

"Hello, Miguel." I lowered my voice. "I want you to know I've kept your secret. The police don't know where I got my information about Coach Martin."

"Thank you, Mrs. Martha. I was worried."

"The police arrested my friend, so I'm trying harder than ever to clear his name. I wonder if you could help me one more time."

He looked away and moved his arms in circles, pointing the oncoming cars to vacant slots.

"Okay. If I can."

"The father you told me about, the one who argued with the coach and speaks with a stutter. What color hair does he have? How tall is he? Is he fat or thin?"

Miguel paused momentarily and closed his eyes. "He's tall, not fat. He always wears the *marisco* baseball hat, but underneath his hair is black. Excuse me, Mrs. Martha." He turned and guided a red Volvo down the row.

I took the hint. "Okay, Miguel, thanks again for your help."

So cross another suspect off the list.

If the stuttering father had dark hair, he couldn't have been the killer. Who was left? Davis, Lowell Hardisty, or someone unknown? The Hardistys were taken into custody yesterday. I wished I could find out from Beavers how much they were involved in the murder, but I didn't know how much he'd be willing to talk to me after last night.

I joined the stream of people walking toward the baseball field. The school orchestra played "You'll Never Walk Alone" on the sidelines near the visitors' dugout as mourners made their way to the seats. In addition to the metal bleachers, precise rows of white folding chairs marched across the brilliant green grass of the baseball field.

A wooden lectern stood at home plate. On one side, a six-foot-long screen of fresh white flowers created a backdrop for a poster-sized photo of Coach Martin. On the other side stood a jumbo television monitor. Wires from a microphone, loudspeakers, and the monitor snaked backward from the lectern toward a table holding an elaborate electronic console with toggle switches and sliders.

A very pregnant woman dressed in black sat with three small children in the front row of the reserved seats facing home plate. The rows immediately in back of her were filled with Beaumont ballplayers dressed in clean maroon-and-gold baseball caps, jerseys, knee socks, spotless white pants, and shiny black cleats. Four assistant coaches sat at the ends of the rows. One was tall and slender, with sandy hair. Was Dax Martin's killer an assistant looking to get the job as head coach? I raised my cell phone and took his picture.

Lucy and Birdie made their way to the white chairs, looking like a couple of sad grandmas. Birdie must have spotted the assistant coach, too, because she headed his way and spoke to him. He rose to his feet, said something and politely directed her to a row of empty seats. I couldn't wait to find out from Birdie if the man had a "funny voice."

I found a seat at the end of the bleachers, where I could easily get up without disturbing anyone if I needed to leave. From my end perch, I continued to scan the crowd. Out of maybe two hundred men in the stadium, a couple dozen could have fit the physical description of the killer. No way could we listen to every one of them speak to determine who had an odd voice or a speech impediment.

Then I saw them. Jefferson Davis, handsome and impeccable in gray pinstripes and a maroon silk tie, with a gold school crest, traveled toward the front row of reserved seats. He clutched Diane's upper arm possessively, strictly managing their pace to avoid conversations with the crowd.

Diane's blond hair, which was pulled back in a severe bun, was topped by a tiny black hat that had a whisper of a veil and was perched at a ridiculous angle. Her black suit skirt, tailored to perfection, ended just above the knees of her elegant, long legs. Diamond drop earrings swung from her earlobes and a diamond cuff dazzled on her right wrist.

They passed in front of me on their way to the front row. "Hello, Diane."

She looked my way with a blank expression, obviously not recognizing me.

I mouthed "Martha Rose" and she frowned, apparently still searching her mental contact list.

They reached the front row of white chairs, and Jefferson marched Diane to the end farthest away from Mrs. Martin, sat her down, and whispered something into her ear. Diane nodded dully and stared straight ahead. Then Jefferson stood, assumed a serious but amiable expression, and made his way to the lectern, shaking hands with the widow and dignitaries in the reserved seats.

I couldn't take my eyes off Diane. She looked so miserable and docile, utterly controlled by her domineering husband. I feared for her safety once again. If Davis killed Martin in a jealous rage, he'd be capable of killing Diane. Right now, she looked trapped and afraid. My heart went out to her. Was there nobody in her life who could help her escape?

Someone walked up behind me and spoke quietly in my ear: "I knew you'd be here."

I tensed and turned my head to whisper back to Beavers, "I assume we're here for the same reason?"

He just grunted. "When it comes to my job, we never have the same reason."

I was tempted to open my mouth and defend myself. After all, we were both seeking to find truth and justice in the end. Our overarching goals were the same. Only our methods differed. I could sometimes get there quicker because I wasn't a cop. Could I help it if people were more likely to open up to someone they perceived to be less threatening—like a sweet little quilty lady?

However, my logic broke down when I remembered four months ago a killer came after me because when I arrived at the truth, I stopped being a sweet little quilty lady and became a threat. I closed my mouth.

"Why are you here?"

"To take Davis in for questioning."

"What about the Hardistys?"

"The DA and the US Attorney's Office are looking at them for a number of things, but they both have solid alibis for the murder."

"Wow. So that means we're here for the same

reason, after all. You want to hear Davis speak, too, don't you? If he has an odd voice, you think he could be the one."

"No comment."

Jefferson Davis slowly made his way to the lectern and waited for the orchestra to stop playing a bad rendition of the Byrds' "Turn, Turn, Turn."

I waited anxiously for him to speak. The next moment would reveal if I'd been on track and if I was correct in pursuing the theory Jefferson Davis was the killer. Davis was involved in a very shady deal when the Beaumont School built this stadium, almost certainly involving bribes and possible blackmail. Now, if his voice was "funny," I'd be sure Davis was the one who killed the man who had an affair with his wife.

"Welcome," his amplified voice commanded silence. "Thank you all for coming to this service to honor our fallen coach, Dax Martin."

Jefferson Davis pronounced it "MAHtin" in confident tones with a clear, crisp, upper-class British accent.

Yesss! A thick foreign accent qualifies as a funny voice, right? Forget about anyone else. Jefferson Davis has to be our guy!

I looked over toward Beavers with a big smile that was totally inappropriate for the occasion, but he was already gone. I searched around briefly for him, while Davis continued his welcoming remarks.

When I looked back up at the lectern, Kaplan and Beavers were already edging into place, preparing to apprehend Jefferson Davis. Out of respect for the dead man's family, Beavers would wait until the service was over before making an arrest. I was flooded by an overwhelming urge to kiss him.

Then I thought about Diane Davis. Even though she might feel some sense of relief at being delivered from the clutches of her controlling husband, how humiliating would this be for her to watch him being led away in handcuffs? I got up and did some maneuvering of my own, walking around the sea of white chairs to a position not far from Diane. I would offer her a quick escape to my house when the time came.

The service droned on. Tributes were spoken by the articulate and the awkward. A video and photo montage of the coach with his team and his family played on the jumbo television monitor. The very pregnant Mrs. Martin dabbed her eyes with a handkerchief and attempted to control her three active little boys throughout the proceedings. What must this young widow be thinking? Even though her husband proved to be unfaithful while she carried his child, did she still love him? Did she miss him?

A trustee of the Joshua Beaumont School announced the establishment of a Dax Martin baseball scholarship. The Martins' family priest offered a closing prayer, and then the service ended.

Jefferson wasn't handcuffed in front of the crowd. Beavers and Kaplan merely escorted him off the field as if in a very private conversation. The crowd moved without alarm or question toward the parking lot to get in their cars and buses and leave.

Diane looked confused, then alarmed, when she

saw her husband being forced discreetly toward an unmarked car parked at the edge of the field. Her hand flew to her mouth and I quickly walked over to her.

"Diane." I laid my hand on her arm. "It's Martha Rose. Do you remember me? I live in that house over there. You visited me right after Dax Martin died."

She turned to look at me, eyes wide with horror, blinking rapidly against the tears.

"The police have just arrested your husband. If you want to get away from all these people right now, you can come with me to my house and I'll try to explain what's going on." She nodded and followed me in a daze as I guided her toward a side gate just behind the maroon-and-gold building.

In less than five minutes, I unlocked my front door and led a shaken Diane Davis over to the sofa. "Just sit here while I bring you a glass of water."

I drew two glasses of ice water and sat down next to her. "I'm so sorry about your husband, Diane. This must be quite a shock for you."

She sipped, then gulped the cold water down.

I asked softly, "Do you know why the police took your husband today?"

"N-no. Do you?"

"It's too long a story to tell right now. Let's just say I've been involved in the investigation of your friend Dax's murder from the beginning. I'm sorry to say the police have evidence linking your husband to some questionable business activities. Those activities may have led to his involvement in the killing."

Diane shook her head decisively and put down her glass of water. "No! You're wrong." Then she frowned at me. "How come you know so much about this? Are you a cop?"

"No, but my neighbor was arrested for the murder, even though he's innocent."

"You mean the guy down the street who hit Dax? The house where they found the bloody baseball bat?"

"Yes. I've been working with his attorney to clear his name. I'm sorry to say, in the course of our investigation, we found some pretty incriminating evidence against your husband, which we have turned over to the police."

Diane frowned. "You're wrong! My husband didn't kill Dax Martin. No, no, no. You're wrong."

The poor girl's reaction struck me as being pretty typical for an abused and controlled wife. She automatically defended her husband, even though it was against her best interest. Maybe when the reality of his crimes set in, Diane Davis would come to accept and even welcome the fact she would have nothing further to fear when Jefferson Davis was convicted and sent away for life. She'd be free.

She twirled the diamond cuff around her right wrist with her left hand and asked the air, "What am I going to do?"

"Is there someone you can call to take you home? Someone who can be with you, like your parents?"

She looked at me like I'd suggested she buy her clothes at Target. "My parents? Why would I call them? Jeff's going to need a lawyer. I've got to get him a lawyer."

She seemed to recover from the shock and stood up decisively. "Since you know so much, do you know where they've taken him?"

"Probably to the West Valley Police Station on Vanowen Street, near Reseda Boulevard."

She took a set of car keys out of the small silver handbag she carried and put on a pair of sunglasses. "Fine. I'm going there now."

She walked toward the VIP section of the mostly empty Beaumont Stadium parking lot and climbed into the driver's side of a silver Mercedes sedan.

Something she said set off an alert in the back of my brain, but I didn't know what it was. Maybe it would come to me later.

CHAPTER 40

Birdie hobbled through my front door, hanging on Lucy's arm. "My word! I had to stop back there and sit for a while because my knees started acting up. Otherwise we'd have been here sooner, dear."

She sat down with a sigh on the sofa. "And I'm afraid we were only able to talk to one person fitting the description of the killer. A baseball coach."

"Yeah, I saw you guys approach him. What did he sound like?"

Birdie shrugged. "Ordinary. His voice was normal. By the way, who was the woman we saw coming from your house just now?"

"Diane Davis. Arlo and Detective Kaplan took her husband in right after the service. They did it so smoothly, I don't think anyone noticed. Did you?"

Lucy came back from the kitchen with two more glasses of water and handed one to Birdie. "No. We were sitting too far back."

"Well," I said, "my hunch was right. You can

forget about any other suspects. Davis has got to be the killer. I mean, he fits the whole description. He's tall, slender, light hair, and thick British accent—what Graciela called a 'funny voice.' He certainly had no shortage of motives."

Birdie dug through her purse, removed one of her blue anti-inflammatory tablets from a tin pillbox, and took a gulp of water. "Why was Diane Davis here?"

"When Arlo moved in to make the arrest, I made my way over to her. Poor thing didn't know what was about to happen, so I offered her a fast escape from any prying eyes or unkind remarks. It's a good thing I was there. She froze like a rabbit when she saw her husband being led away. I took her through a side gate and back here to the house."

"What did she say?" asked Lucy.

"Diane jumped to his defense, just like you'd expect someone to do who was in the thrall of a control freak. She denied he could be a killer. Then she said she intended to get him a lawyer, asked where he was being held, and left."

Birdie absently massaged her knees with wrinkled hands and fingers enlarged at the joints. "The poor child."

"Yeah. I don't know why, but when I suggested she call her parents, she completely rejected the idea. Almost as if she didn't want their support."

"Or couldn't count on it," said Lucy. "You can never tell what really goes on inside families, can you? Remember Claire Terry."

Lucy referred to the young woman we found

murdered four months ago and the family secrets she kept. "You're right. You can never tell, for sure."

Birdie stopped rubbing her knees. "If Arlo has just arrested Jefferson Davis as the killer, does this mean your friend Ed can now come home?"

"I certainly hope so." I took a deep breath. "Arlo came over last night and apologized for being such a jerk. He said he loves me and wants me to move in with him."

Lucy's jaw dropped about three feet toward the ground. "Just like that? What changed his mind?"

"I'm not sure. Maybe it had something to do with my telling him the other day I'd fallen in love with him. Maybe it was the fact he saw another man moving in on his territory. He called himself an 'idiot' for thinking I'd ever sleep with Yossi."

Lucy choked on a drink of water. "Oh, Lord, girlfriend. You didn't tell him, did you?"

Birdie spoke up. "Tell him what? Has something been going on I don't know about yet?"

I told Birdie about Yossi and me. "He's very special."

She smiled. "I don't doubt it, dear, but it's such a shame. I really like Arlo. He's very special too."

And there in a nutshell is my dilemma.

Lucy held up her hand. "Okay, okay. So, last night?"

"I told him about Yossi. I'm not ashamed of what happened, and I'm not sorry. Besides, telling him was the fair thing to do."

Lucy rolled her eyes. "These things never turn out well."

"You're right. Last night was no exception. Arlo gave me a kind of ultimatum. He still wants me, but only if he can have all of me. We're both taking a step back to consider our options."

Lucy asked, "Did you speak to him this morning at the memorial service?"

"Briefly. He said both Hardistys have solid alibis for the night of the murder."

We chatted a few more minutes and Lucy stood. "Well, girlfriend, time to go. Looks like you didn't need our help today, after all. Good luck with the other thing."

She hugged me; and as they walked to Lucy's Caddy, Birdie said, "It's a shame about Arlo, isn't it?"

I waited a couple of hours to give Beavers time to interrogate and process Jefferson Davis. Then I called him to ask about Ed.

"Beavers."

"Hi, Arlo. It's me. I called to find out when Ed is being released."

"I'm working on it."

"Have you charged Davis with the murder? I mean, he fits the witnesses' description to a tee."

"You know I can't discuss this with you. There are still a lot of question marks and loose ends even you, with all your people, don't know about."

"Did Diane Davis make it to the station? I told her where she could find her husband."

"And thanks for that. She ran into Kaplan. Turns out they know each other."

Of course! When Kaplan had questioned me right after I discovered Martin's body, he bragged about being an alumnus of Beaumont. Now that I thought about it, he and Diane were about the same age.

"Between their personal connection and the fact Kaplan also knew Jefferson Davis, he's been taken off the case and I'm back as lead."

"So . . . wait a minute. If Kaplan and Diane went to school together, he must have known Dax Martin also. Were they all classmates?"

Beavers didn't answer.

"Come on, Arlo. Why didn't Kaplan say anything about knowing the victim? When you went to arrest Davis, did you know Kaplan was his former student?"

The possible conspiracies in this case just kept growing.

"As I said, 'Sherlock,' Kaplan is no longer on this case. So unless you have any more information, I've no further comment." The phone went dead.

He hung up on me! But he did call me "Sherlock." Joking around is a good sign, right?

I immediately called Simon Aiken and repeated what Beavers just revealed about Detective Kaplan's connection to the case. "I know Arlo better than to think he'd be careless with information. I think he meant for me to tell you in order to help with Ed's release."

"I'm on my way to the DA's office as we speak. In view of the arrests yesterday and today, I'll try to get the charges against Ed dropped."

"Tell her about Detective Kaplan's connection to the prime suspect, his wife, and the victim. He could be construed as having a personal interest in the outcome of the case, which would look very bad for the police department. That could give her further incentive to drop the charges against Ed."

"On it. Talk to you later."

Hunger pangs gnawed at my stomach, and the clock read an hour past lunchtime. I scooped some cottage cheese into an ice-cream bowl and sliced a fresh, juicy peach on top. I chewed my last mouthful of "faux peach ice cream" when the phone rang.

"Hi, Mom!" Quincy and I finally connected. "Get my bedroom ready. I'm coming home."

"Oh, Quincy. Did you get the West Coast job with NPR? Are you moving back to Los Angeles?"

"Not exactly. NPR wants to do a story on the wildlife reserve in the Sepulveda Basin. A YouTube video of the destruction went viral. The Audubon Society, homeless advocates, and environmentalists from all over the country are up in arms against the Army Corps of Engineers. Since I'm from the area, they thought I'd be the perfect person to do the story. Plus, this'll be a kind of tryout for a permanent assignment there."

"Oh, honey, that's just great. Uncle Isaac will be thrilled when I tell him. When are you coming?"

"Sunday evening. Don't bother to meet me at the airport. I'm renting a car."

I hummed as I changed the sheets in the spare bedroom and cleaned up the bathroom. I didn't have much to do, as Hilda had already done a good job after her overnight almost a week ago. As I vacuumed the dust curls under the bed, it occurred to me Quincy's visit provided me with a perfect excuse to avoid any encounters with Beavers or Crusher. Having her in the house would give me plenty of space to think things through.

As long as she was around, my daughter would be my priority. I'd introduce her to Hilda and Pastor Sandoval so she'd get a real inside track on the plight of the homeless. Her story would be so good, NPR would beg her to take the West Coast assignment.

At about four o'clock, the phone rang again.

"Babe, just got a call from Aiken. Ed's being released."

"That's great news, Yossi."

"Listen. I can't stop thinking about you. I miss you. Let me come over and show you how much."

I was wrong. He didn't have to touch my body to get it to sing. Just thinking about making love to him made me want to join the "Hallelujah Chorus."

"I'm sorry, Yossi. I still need time."

"What about tomorrow night? We can have Shabbat dinner again with your uncle Isaac. I'll pick him up and take him home. Then afterward, you and I can fulfill a mitzvah."

The Sabbath is considered a time of joy and pleasure and is often alluded to as a bride. Crusher's comment referred to the rabbinical directive for a husband to make love to his wife on Friday night as a way to celebrate with joy the coming of the Sabbath bride.

"Yossi, first of all, that particular mitzvah only applies to married couples."

"We can fix that."

"What? No. What? No. Are you saying you want to get married?"

"I'm saying I want you to be my woman."

"For heaven's sake, Yossi. We've known each other for less than two weeks."

"So? Jacob loved Rachel as soon as he set eyes on her."

As Uncle Isaac would say, *Oy va voy!*

CHAPTER 41

Darkness had fallen on this late August night. Ed Pappas dropped by earlier to pick up his computer, house key, and gun; then he invited me to the Cantina, where everyone was going to celebrate his release. If I was around Crusher tonight, I might not be able to resist his charms, and I still had a lot more thinking to do about my love life. So I opted to stay home and enjoy a quiet evening.

Bumper meowed to be let out the back door. I might have worried about coyotes coming down from the hills looking for water in the river and easy meals from ground squirrels and wandering house pets, but Bumper never left my fenced-in backyard. So far, the coyotes respected the six-foot-high wooden boundary between my territory and theirs.

The weather had eased from ninety-five degrees in the daytime to a much more comfortable sixty-five degrees at night. I opened the door and we both stepped outside to enjoy the cool night air. A froggie chorus rose up from the river, mixed in with the high-pitched chittering of crickets in the field and the muted sound of a television audience clapping through somebody's open window. The neighborhood felt almost normal again. The murderer—Jefferson Davis—was in custody, and my daughter was due back home in another three days.

The rustling of the branches was so subtle that I didn't notice it at first. My heart began to race as a tall, slender silhouette stood up from where it had been crouching near a mock orange bush in the thick darkness. Surely, my mind played tricks on me. Surely, I was just overstimulated by my myopic determination to find the killer. As the figure slowly approached, my knees melted. This wasn't a trick of the mind. Someone was really there!

I backed up a couple of steps until I reached the door and pushed it open. The shape advanced rapidly toward me, forcing its way into the kitchen light. Illuminated before me stood the unhappy figure of Diane Davis.

She had changed out of her elegant black suit and diamonds into baggy gray sweatpants and a loose T-shirt. Her luxurious blond hair cascaded past her shoulders instead of being pulled back under that ridiculous little veiled number she had worn to the memorial service.

Strapped to her back was a small canvas backpack, and on her feet was a pair of white athletic shoes stained with spots of dark brown. Did she take my soiled shoes from the side of the road, where I had abandoned them on Sunday? No, she couldn't be wearing them; her feet were much larger than mine.

Her eyes were red from crying and her black mascara was smudged and smeared. She glared daggers at me and spoke through clenched teeth. "Thanks for saving me the trouble of breaking into your house."

Oh, my God! She came here to force her way into my house?

It couldn't be to take anything. After all, what could I possibly have she couldn't afford to buy ten times better? There was only one reason for Diane to break in. She meant to hurt me. I backed up a step and leaned on the counter to keep my knees from buckling.

"What do you want?"

Diane's voice was hard. "Jeff's in jail and it's all your fault."

So she was angry at me that her husband was in jail? She wasn't relieved to be free of that control freak? Did I get their relationship all wrong?

"Why is it my fault?"

"Noah told me how you kept poking around Dax's murder."

"Who's Noah?"

"Noah Kaplan."

"You mean Detective Kaplan? Is Noah his first name? I always wondered." My mind reeled in confusion. What was going on here?

Diane narrowed her eyes and growled, "I want Jeff back. If he's in jail, I'll be all alone, and who'll take care of me then, huh?"

*Well, all right, then. That settles it. Let's just suspend
every law of decency so someone can take care of Diane.
Clearly, she needs a caretaker, or meds, or something!*

"Aren't you afraid of your husband? After all, he
killed Dax Martin in a jealous rage."

Her eyebrows pushed together in surprise.
"What?"

"I know about your affair with your old boyfriend, Dax Martin, Diane. Don't deny it. Apparently, your husband also found out and killed him.
If Jefferson's capable of murder, he could harm
you too. Think about that."

She threw her head back and laughed a little too
harsh and a little too crazy. In that moment, I knew
the truth. How could I not have seen it sooner?

The woman standing before me resembled the
description of Dax Martin's killer. She was tall, slender, and had light hair. If she wore loose clothing
and pinned her hair up under a baseball cap, she
could look like a man in the dark. What would account for the funny voice Graciela heard?

Then I realized my mistake. Jefferson Davis's
British accent wouldn't be a flag for a non-English
speaker like Graciela; all English speakers would
sound the same to her. But a softer, high-pitched
feminine voice would sound incongruous, or
"funny," if she thought she was looking at a man.

What was Diane's motive? I swallowed.

"You killed Dax Martin, didn't you?"

Diane just glared at me. "Nobody leaves me."

And there it was. Motive. Martin and his wife
were recently overheard arguing about his affair

with Diane. Maybe he tried to end the affair. Diane obviously didn't take kindly to anyone leaving her. She must have arranged to meet Dax that night. If she caught him off guard, she certainly could have incapacitated him with the first blow and then beaten him to death. Dax Martin was killed in a jealous rage, all right. Diane's jealous rage, not her husband's.

I looked at the brown stains on her shoes. Blood? Back splatter from when she beat a man to death?

"You killed Dax because he wanted to end the affair and go back to his wife?"

"Noah was right about you."

"What did Noah Kaplan say about me?"

"He said you have cop envy. You only sleep with a cop because you want to be one. He pities the stupid bastard who sleeps with you."

I'd file that away for future disclosure: *Hey, Arlo, your partner tells other people you're a "stupid bastard."* I just hoped I had a future. I had to figure out a way to get out of the house and get help. I no longer had Ed's gun.

"How did you end up throwing the murder weapon into Ed Pappas's backyard?"

"I called Jeff. He came right over to the field. Jeff always knows what to do. He knew which house belonged to that Pappas guy, so he threw the bat over the fence. He said everyone would believe your friend killed Dax because they had a fight. Then he called the police the next morning to place an anonymous tip."

That was it—the thing she had said earlier in the

day that bothered me. She had known where Ed's house was and that the bloody baseball bat had been found in his backyard. However, the police had never publicly disclosed the exact nature of the murder weapon. Of course the killer would know.

Diane extracted a pair of gardening gloves from her backpack and put them on. "Your friend wasn't home tonight. He has a nice set of tools in his garage." Then she removed a hammer. "I'll bet his prints are all over this. When they find your body, they'll think he killed you. Then they'll release my Jeff."

Oh, my God. She means to kill me with Ed's hammer.

I needed to draw her outside. If we were outside, maybe someone could help me. Maybe there'd be a witness. Maybe she'd be afraid to be seen and leave. I turned and ran from the kitchen. I threw open the front door and ran outside, yelling as loud as I could, "Help! Help! She's going to kill me!"

I moved forward and managed to duck as Diane took the first sideways swing with the hammer. Instead of splitting open my skull, it clipped a gardenia plant growing in a pot on the porch. Diane's rage was now in high dudgeon for all to see. She obviously didn't care anymore about her plan to blame my murder on Ed. She just wanted to kill me.

She swore and raised the hammer over her head, preparing to create an opening in the top of my cranium.

"Help!" I yelled as I ran, praying her long arms couldn't reach me. I knew I could never outrun her, so I headed toward my car parked in the driveway, hoping to put it between the two of us.

I reached the far side of my Corolla just as the hammer came down on the windshield. It shattered with a resounding *crack!* The glass dissolved into thousands of shiny little pebbles.

"Bitch!" she screamed. "Get back here!"

Thwack! The hammer came down on the car, again and again, as she chased me.

"I hate you!"

In the frantic circuit around my vehicle, I desperately looked for something to defend myself with. Then I heard a loud "meow." Bumper had followed us out of the house and into the front yard.

Diane stopped and looked at me with wild eyes. By now, she was completely off the rails. Bumper meowed again. She turned away from me and looked down at my orange fluff ball. Her lip twisted into an ugly snarl. "I hate your cat. I'm going to kill your cat."

"No!" I shouted. I ran over and jumped on her back, wrapping my legs around her and putting my hands over her face so she couldn't see.

Diane tried to shake me off, but I was way too heavy. We both fell to the ground. I landed on my back and she landed on top of me. I tried to get up, but she turned over and sat on my chest. Her knees pinned my arms to the driveway. I couldn't breathe. I couldn't move.

A nasty smile curled her lips. She raised the hammer. "You're dead."

I closed my eyes and waited for the end. I pictured

the people who would be sad if I died. Quincy. Uncle Isaac. Lucy. Birdie. Beavers. Crusher.

Then I heard a loud *bonk!* It wasn't on my skull. I looked up.

Diane's eyes rolled back in her head just before she dropped the hammer and fell sideways.

"You okay?" wheezed Tony DiArco. He sat in his scooter next to me, holding a heavy green metal oxygen tank.

Sonia panted as she arrived and helped me out from under Diane's body, while Ron and Yuki's grandson, Parker, pulled out his cell phone and called 911.

I looked at the three of them. "How did you get here so fast?"

Sonia said, "The EAP. Don't you remember? When the spotter heard you screaming and saw you being chased out of your house, he called HQ. HQ called Tony, who was on patrol nearby. I heard the screaming and came out of my house. Looks like we got here just in time."

I'd forgotten all about the enemy attack plan. When I knew Barbara Hardisty was in custody and no longer a threat, I forgot to tell Sonia to cancel the EAP. Thank God! They must have been watching my house this whole time. If they hadn't been, I'd be as dead as Dax Martin right now.

CHAPTER 42

Detective Arlo Beavers insisted on riding with me in the ambulance to the hospital, even though I told him I was okay. The ER doctor sent me for a full-body scan because I'd fallen on my back. Aside from the nasty green marks blooming on my upper arms, where Diane had pinned me down with her knees, I had no other injuries. But I knew I was in for a bad fibro flare-up because of the trauma my body had just gone through.

The doctor gave me an injection of Dilaudid for the pain and sent me home with a prescription and an admonition to "take it easy for a couple of days."

Between the Dilaudid and the fatigue, I don't remember exactly how I got home and into bed. I vaguely remember Beavers wiping the drool from the side of my mouth. I think Sonia was there too, along with Alex Trebek, but I can't be sure.

I slept until ten the next morning. The first sensation I became aware of was my bladder warning me I had exactly ten seconds to get up and pee.

The second sensation was one of whiskers tickling my cheeks. I opened my eyes. Bumper's green eyes stared at me from two inches above my face.

When I rolled over to sit up, the third sensation hit me. Pain. My muscles and nerves were screaming, especially in my arms and back. I groaned like an eighty-year-old, pushed myself off the bed, and shuffled over to the bathroom, holding my right hip. The sound of the toilet flushing brought Lucy into my bedroom with a cup of coffee and a brand-new bottle of pills.

"Good morning, sunshine. From the looks of you, I'd say you're not doing so well." She thrust the bottle toward me. "Here. I sent Ray to get your prescription filled this morning."

"Thanks, Lucy. I don't remember much about last night. When did you get here?"

"Arlo called me from the hospital. I was waiting here when he brought you home. I put you in some clean pajamas and stayed the night in Quincy's room."

"What about Alex Trebek?"

"Huh?"

"Never mind." I looked at the label on the bottle. Inside were ten tablets of Dilaudid. I shook one out and swallowed it with the coffee. It must have been a lot milder than the injection, because I didn't slide directly into a coma. After about twenty minutes, I did go to a happy zone, way north of the pain. I mean, if the pain was located in Los Angeles, I was floating somewhere over the Yukon.

I put a bathrobe over pink pajamas printed with

frosted cupcakes and stumbled in a daze into the living room.

Lucy sat me down on the sofa. "Just stay here and I'll make you some breakfast."

I glanced out the window and over to the driveway. The windows in my car were shattered and every surface was disfigured by huge dents. "Lucy! My car!"

"Better your car than your head. Don't worry, hon. Ray is going to take care of everything." She came into the living room and closed the drapes so I wouldn't have to look at the results of Diane Davis's murderous temper tantrum.

At eleven o'clock, Ed Pappas showed up at my front door with a huge flower arrangement, along with a humongous box of See's chocolates. He hurried to the sofa, where I sat with a dopey smile. He bent down and gathered me in grateful arms.

"You almost got killed, Martha. I'm so sorry. And to think it happened because you wanted to find the real killer and clear me. You're awesome. I'm so glad you're okay. I don't know what else to say. 'Thanks' isn't enough."

I smiled at him. "You'd do the same for me, right?"

"You know I would." He leaned in closer and whispered, "Crusher wants to come and see you. He's right outside. I'm tellin' you, if you don't let him in, he's going to explode. He told me to ask you for something called *rachmunes* and let him in."

I giggled. Crusher had used the Yiddish word for "pity" and "compassion."

"Oh, it can't be that bad," I slurred.

Ed just looked at me. "I've never seen him like this."

I felt hugely magnanimous in my happy place. "Sure, why not."

Ed rushed to the front door and motioned with his hand. In two seconds, Crusher was inside. He held a bouquet of fragrant flowers in one hand and a large brown sack from the deli. "I brought you chicken soup with matzo balls and a loaf of deli rye."

He hastily set everything on the kitchen counter and returned to sit next to me on the sofa. I grinned stupidly at him and put my arms around his neck. "Thanks, Yossi."

The next thing I knew he was holding me and giving me a lovely, long kiss, which I was happy to return.

"Babe," he whispered, "you could have died."

Finally Lucy cleared her throat. "Okay, lover boy, put a sock in it. This woman's in no condition to give her consent. She's higher'n a kite."

Then she turned to Ed. "Take him back to your house and let him cool down. Hose him off if you have to."

Ed smirked and punched Crusher softly in the shoulder. "Come on, man. You can see for yourself she's okay. We'll come back another time."

Crusher gave Lucy one last pleading look, but she crossed her arms and jerked her thumb toward the front door.

As soon as they left, Lucy sat in a chair and

fanned herself with her hand. "Dang, girlfriend, I see what you mean. The man is just crazy about you."

I grinned from ear to ear. It was all good.

At four in the afternoon, I took my second dose of Dilaudid. Beavers showed up ten minutes later, carrying a dozen yellow roses and a pink box of pastries from Eva's European Bakery. I was already flying over Portland, Oregon, in my mind.

Beavers asked Lucy, "How is she?"

Lucy took the packages from his hands. "Why don't you ask her yourself?"

Beavers came over to the sofa and sat next to me. I gave him a loopy grin and put my arms around him. He gathered me in a tender embrace and gave me a long, gentle kiss, which said, *I miss you; I love you; I'm glad you're alive.*

Of course I kissed him back. The Dilaudid made me do it.

Lucy returned and sat on a chair directly across from us, apparently determined not to let anybody take advantage of my diminished capacity. She looked at Beavers. "Down, boy. What's the latest?"

"Thanks to Martha, the murder is solved. Diane Davis suffered a concussion, but she'll survive."

"What about Jefferson Davis?" I asked.

"He's being held as an accessory to murder. We've handed off the rest of the case to the fraud division. The DA is looking into the shady deal over the baseball stadium."

"What about Barbara Hardisty? Why did she want

to scare me away from finding the witnesses to Martin's murder?"

"Jefferson Davis called Detective Kaplan to find out how the investigation was going. Kaplan told his former headmaster the police were looking for two homeless witnesses. Davis was afraid the witnesses could identify his wife, Diane, as the killer, so he contacted Hardisty and told her to get rid of the homeless. When she found out you were sniffing around the wildlife reserve, she ordered Lawanda Price to scare you off. Then she hatched the plan to pay her husband with federal funds to bulldoze the area."

"Why would she agree to help Davis if she had nothing to do with the murder?"

Beavers shrugged. "She was up to her neck in conspiracy and fraud. If Davis was somehow involved in the murder and if he was caught, their corruption would be exposed. She had a stake in keeping Davis's secret because she had a lot to lose. Once we threatened to charge her as an accessory to murder, she gave us everything."

"Like how the stadium was allowed to be built in the first place?" I was approaching the Yukon once more.

"Yeah. Once Davis brokered a deal with Hardisty, he was instructed by certain trustees and big donors to set up a dummy company, SFV Associates. Money was then funneled through the company to pay off Hardisty by using Valley Allstar Construction. In addition, the Hardisty kids were given full scholarships to Beaumont, worth about one hundred thousand a year. The Hardisty boy was assured a place on the baseball team."

I yawned. "There has to be more to the story than that. What about permits, inspections, environmental impact reports—all the things the City of Los Angeles is supposed to oversee?"

"The councilman used his influence to bypass the permit process. It wasn't hard to do. The head of Building and Safety has a kid in Beaumont. There is the possibility, though, that because the stadium was built illegally, the school will be forced to tear it down and restore the land to open space. The fraud division is working on that right now. As far as we're concerned, Dax Martin's killer has been caught and our job is over."

Lucy said, "That would make a lot of people around this neighborhood awfully happy, wouldn't it, Martha?"

I thought about the people who were still homeless. "It's a beginning." Then I asked Beavers, "What was the deal with Noah Kaplan and Diane Davis?"

"Kaplan didn't do anything worse than leak information about the investigation. He had no clue he was dealing with the killer. He just thought he was talking to his old school friend. The captain gave him a warning and a lecture about poor judgment."

Through the fog enveloping my brain, I remembered something. "I think you should know your partner told Diane Davis you were a 'stupid bastard.'"

Arlo shrugged. "Was that before or after he was

pulled from the case for leaking information to the killer?"

I giggled. Happy place.

"The US Attorney's Office is all over the misappropriation of public funds and the mismanagement of public resources by the Army Corps of Engineers. The commanding officer of the Los Angeles office, Colonel Trane, has already been replaced. Between the City of Los Angeles and the Feds, there are enough crimes and malfeasance to keep the prosecutors busy for the next decade."

My eyes got heavier and Beavers's voice receded into the distance until it was only a droning sound and then nothing. I floated in sweet oblivion for the next few hours.

Lucy gently touched my shoulder, waking me at seven. "Come on, Martha. Time to eat some of that nice soup Yossi brought."

I opened my eyes and found the room filled with bouquets of flowers. I turned to Lucy in amazement. "Where'd these come from?"

She smiled. "Your friends and neighbors. I guess Sonia got the word out."

Good old Sonia. The ATT and CNN of our community.

I stretched my stiff body and walked into the kitchen, where a steaming matzo ball the size of New York sat in a bowl of savory chicken soup. When she opened the refrigerator to pull out the loaf of rye bread, the shelves were filled with covered casseroles. The countertops all around me were laden with plates of brownies, homemade cupcakes, and chocolate chip cookies.

I looked at her. "Really? These all arrived when I was sleeping?"

She smiled. "I had to put a sign on the door that said, 'Please knock softly. Do not ring bell.' People are grateful, Martha."

The following day, Saturday, Ed threw a party and asked Sonia to get the word out and invite all the neighbors. Two folding banquet tables stood under the mulberry tree in Ed's front yard topped with barbequed burgers and hot dogs. I insisted on donating all the food everyone had so generously given me.

People arrived with their folding chairs, tables, and umbrellas; the lawn and sidewalk in front of Ed's house and three of his nearest neighbors were filled with dozens of chatting adults and playful children. The teenagers sat in the primo spot on Ed's roof underneath the mulberry branches, while Parker told them the story of how his quick thinking saved my life.

Ed thanked everyone for showing up and gave a little speech about friendship, neighborhood, and community. He asked me if I wanted to say a few words.

Flanked by my friends Lucy and Birdie, I praised Tony, Sonia, and the Eyes of Encino. I thanked everyone for their flowers and food. Per Lucy's insistence, Crusher stayed his distance, although he watched my every move.

A cheer went up from the crowd when Simon Aiken announced his law firm would sue the Army Corps of Engineers and the Beaumont School pro bono to remove the baseball stadium and restore the wildlife reserve on behalf of the community.

Finally Crusher walked over to where Tony sat on his Chair-A-Go-Go to make him an honorary Valley Eagle. He presented Tony with a new battery for his scooter and a black leather vest with *VE* painted on the back in purple letters. Tony got the biggest cheer of all when he put on the vest and stuck out his scrawny arm to bump fists with all the other Eagles.

After another twenty minutes, I walked back to my house with Lucy and Birdie. My poor Corolla was gone from the driveway, and all the broken glass had been swept away. A loaner BMW from Lucy's husband, Ray, sat waiting for me to use.

Back inside, Birdie made a pot of tea while Lucy put fresh linens in Quincy's room, started a load of laundry, and packed up her things to go home.

"You sure you're going to be okay by yourself now? Those pain pills are rather strong."

"Yeah. The pain isn't so bad now. I'm done with the pills. Besides, I need to be functional. Tomorrow's Sunday and Quincy's coming home."

After they left, I carried one of the flower arrangements into Quincy's room. Then I ran my hand slowly over the bumpy texture of the Grandmother's Flower Garden Quilt on top of the bed.

My little girl was coming home for a visit after a long time away. While she was here, she'd get all my attention. The other thing—my Beavers/Crusher dilemma—would just have to wait for another day.

I hung some fresh towels in the bathroom and spotted the scale on the floor. Two weeks had passed since I joined Weight Watchers. After all the running around, skipped meals, and physical activity, my jeans felt a lot looser. I stepped on the scale and smiled when I saw the numbers. Tomorrow Charlissa would give me a gold star.

Sometime during the middle of the night, I awoke to the smell of smoke. We were in the height of the fire season in Southern California, and the mountains ringing the San Fernando Valley were covered in dry forest and chaparral, the perfect fuel for out-of-control brush fires. The Santa Ana winds coming from the northeast had been responsible for the recent heat wave and were notorious for fanning small brush fires into conflagrations that could burn for days, consuming thousands of acres. I was afraid the smoke meant one of those fires was close by.

As I got out of bed and put on my robe, the guttering of a motorcycle receded into the distance. I opened the front door and looked to the south for signs of fire: a pink light in the night sky or a corona of flames on a mountain ridge. Even though the smell of smoke was strong, I saw nothing unusual. The winds had died down and all of Encino seemed to be sleeping peacefully. So I turned around and went through the house to the back door to see if the fire was burning in the north.

As soon as I opened the back door, flickering light came from the direction of the baseball stadium. I rushed outside in my bare feet to get a better look. At the edge of the field, the maroon-and-gold two-story monstrosity—the place where Dax Martin was king, the place where he and Diane carried on their affair—was in flames. Fortunately, because the air was still, our houses were in no immediate danger from the fire spreading. Fire House Eighty-Three was just a few blocks away. If I called right away, it was possible they could save the building.

I walked back in my house, put on some water, and placed a bag of Taylor's Scottish Breakfast Tea in a cup. All was quiet as I waited for the water to boil. After about five minutes, I brewed the tea, stirred in some milk and sugar, and sat on the sofa to enjoy a slow, satisfying cup. Then I picked up the phone and dialed 911.

Please turn the page for a quilting tip
from Mary Marks!

CHOOSING A NEEDLE AND THREAD

You've pieced the top of your quilt and made a "sandwich" by laying it over a backing with a layer of batting (*wadding,* if you're British) in between. Now it's time to stitch the three layers together. What do you do?

First you choose the right needle. Needles come in different shapes and sizes. The shapes are determined by what you're going to use them for: embroidery, appliqué, basting, or quilting, to name a few. The sizes are numbered. (Note: the larger the number, the smaller the needle.)

"Betweens" are the preferred needle for quilting. A size twelve between is the shortest at one inch. I prefer to use the hybrid size eleven, which has the short length of the twelve but the bigger eye of the ten. (Larger eyes are easier to thread.)

Why choose the shortest needle? Small needles

make small stitches, and the mark of a skillful quilter is in her small, even stitches.

Now you're ready to choose the right thread. Avoid thread made with polyester. Polyester is a hard synthetic fiber that will eventually saw through the soft cotton fibers of your quilt. Choose an all-cotton thread instead.

Threads are also numbered; the smaller the number, the heavier the thread. Regular cotton sewing thread has a weight of fifty, and is more easily broken. For durable quilting stitches, I use a quilting weight thread, which is around thirty.

In the olden days, women used to run their thread through beeswax to prevent it from tangling while they stitched. The drawback of using beeswax is that it can deposit a yellow residue on your quilt. Nowadays some quilting thread comes already coated with a glacé finish, which accomplishes the same thing without leaving a residue.

In today's world, hand stitching has been largely replaced by quilting machines. But in times past, women used to compete with each other to be the best quilter, aiming at twenty stitches to the inch. I find that seven to ten stitches to the inch, evenly spaced, produce a stunning quilt.

With the right tools and lots of practice, you can produce a hand-quilted work of art that will be treasured for years to come.

Please turn the page for an exciting sneak peek of Mary Marks's next Quilting Mystery,

GONE BUT KNOT FORGOTTEN,

coming soon from Kensington Publishing!

CHAPTER 1

So far, the morning mail had only yielded credit card invitations, an interesting flyer for yoga classes and—now that I was a member of AARP—another postcard advertising the Neptune Society. I picked up a white number ten envelope, glanced at the unfamiliar return address, and almost tossed it in the junk pile, but something stopped me.

The envelope looked personal. First, it was addressed to Martha Rivka Rose, my full legal name. I never used my middle name, even on my checks, credit cards, or driver's license. Second, I realized the postmark was not one of those presorted things, a sure giveaway of a mass mailing. The law offices of Abernathy, Porter & Salinger of Los Angeles, California, had paid full price for the stamp.

I reached for the white plastic letter opener, a prize I received from the UCLA Department of Internal Medicine after having my first colonoscopy. The envelope tore neatly along the top fold, and I pulled out a one-page letter:

Dear Ms. Rose:

  We regret to inform you of the death of
Mrs. Harriet Gordon Oliver. You have been
named the executor of her estate. Please contact
me personally at your earliest convenience to
initiate the process of probating her will.

  Very truly yours,
  Deacon "Deke" Abernathy, Esq.

Harriet was dead? I hadn't heard from her in over twenty years. We had been best friends in high school, but we had lost touch when she moved to Rhode Island for an Ivy League education at Brown and I lived at home and attended UCLA. One of the last times I saw Harriet was at our fifteenth high school reunion in the late 1980s. She had moved back to Los Angeles with her husband, Nathan Oliver, a fellow Brown graduate, and I had married Aaron Rose, a local boy finishing his psychiatric residency at LA County Hospital.

Since Harriet and I lived in Brentwood, a tony part of the west side, we met a few times for lunch after that. Harriet and her East Coast husband collected wine and art; Aaron and I focused on raising our three-year-old daughter and paying the mortgage on our much smaller home. Eventually even the lunches stopped. By the time I divorced Aaron and relocated to a not-so-tony part of Encino in the San Fernando Valley, Harriet and I had long since lost touch.

Now she was gone at age fifty-five. What had taken her so soon? Why hadn't she made her husband executor? What about children? The more I thought about the letter, the more questions I had.

The telephone number Deacon Abernathy gave me must have been his cell phone because he answered it himself. "Deke here."

"Mr. Abernathy? My name is Martha Rose and I just received your letter about Harriet Oliver."

"Oh, right. Thanks for calling, Ms. Rose. We have some details to go over, including Mrs. Oliver's funeral instructions. How soon can you come to my office?"

"Wait a minute. Please slow down. When did Harriet die? How did she die?"

"I'm sorry. Got ahead of myself. Has it been a while since you spoke to Mrs. Oliver?"

"Decades, actually."

"That explains the problem we had in locating you. The last address she had for you was in Brentwood. Under the circumstances, I guess I'm not surprised."

"What do you mean, 'circumstances'? What's going on?"

"There's no delicate way to say this, Ms. Rose. Your friend Mrs. Oliver's body was discovered in her home about three weeks ago. The coroner estimated she had been dead for at least ten months."

I was glad I was already sitting down. My ears started ringing and a black circle closed out my peripheral vision. I saw horrible pictures of desiccated corpses and skulls with gaping jaws. "Ten months? Didn't she have family? What about her husband?"

"It's too complicated to explain over the phone.

The thing is, Mrs. Oliver hasn't been buried yet. We had to wait until we located the executor to make certain, ah, decisions. So you see, Ms. Rose, the sooner you get here, the sooner we can, ah, lay her to rest."

Poor Harriet. How was it that nobody missed her? She had been such a vibrant and pretty teen-ager with long black hair that she ironed straight every morning before school. During our sleep-overs, we would whisper about our plans for col-lege, our hopes for the future, and which girls at school were having sex. When she left for Brown, we hugged and cried and promised to write letters every day. But time and distance eventually slowed our friendship. With the exception of our brief re-union in Brentwood, we moved into completely separate lives.

I shuddered at the thought of her body lying un-attended for ten months. It really bothered me that nobody had missed her. Didn't the neighbors notice any bad odors? I agreed to meet the attorney at the Westwood office of Abernathy, Porter & Salinger later that afternoon.

After ending my conversation with Deacon Aber-nathy, I gave my shoulder-length gray curls a once-over with a wide-toothed comb. Then I stuffed my Jacob's Ladder quilt, my sewing kit, and an emer-gency package of M&M'S into my large red tote bag and headed for my best friend Lucy Mondello's house. Today was Tuesday, and I never missed our weekly quilting group. I drove in a daze, trying to make sense of the shocking news about Harriet's death. What a horrendous way to go—alone and evidently forgotten.

I drove across Ventura Boulevard and wound around a couple of side streets before pulling up in front of Lucy's house. The Boulevard was a natural dividing line between classes in Encino, one of the many small communities in the San Fernando Valley. Small homes, condos, and apartment buildings were located on the valley floor north of the boulevard. That's where I lived, in a tract of medium-priced midcentury homes. Houses south of the Boulevard—especially those built in the foothills of the Santa Monica Mountains—tended to be large, custom-built, and *très* expensive. Lucy lived somewhere in between: south of the Boulevard, but not in the hills; gracious home, but not a McMansion.

Lucy smiled and greeted me as I pushed open the front door. "Hey, girlfriend. You're a little late. Everything okay?"

I marveled at how perfectly put together my tall friend Lucy was. She was famous for always dressing with a theme. Today she wore canary-yellow twill slacks, a yellow-and-white long-sleeved T-shirt, and dangly citrine earrings. Her bright orange hair looked freshly colored; her eyebrows were perfectly drawn; her lips were painted a soft coral. Even at sixty-something, Lucy could have been a model. I, on the other hand, wore my usual size-sixteen stretch denim jeans and T-shirt straining under my ample bosom.

"I just had to deal with a last-minute phone call.

Give me a minute and I'll tell you all about it." I settled down in one of the cozy blue overstuffed chairs in Lucy's casual living room. Every few years, she changed the décor in her home as easily as she changed her daily outfits. This latest version evoked an elegant cabin located in some snowy resort: furniture upholstered in richly colored woolen fabrics, Navajo and cowhide rugs on wide-planked wooden floors, and a coffee table made of polished burled tree roots. Above the fireplace hung a reproduction of a mainly yellow Remington painting of longhorn cattle. The room literally screamed Wyoming, where both Lucy and her husband, Ray, were born and raised.

"Was it an upsetting call? You look a bit peaky, dear." That was Birdie Watson, Lucy's across-the-street neighbor and the third member of our little sewing circle.

I fitted my multicolored Jacob's Ladder quilt in a fourteen-inch wooden hoop. The Jacob's Ladder block featured lots of little squares and larger triangles of contrasting light and dark materials. The more fabrics, the more interesting the quilt, and this one had dozens of different cotton prints. I threaded a needle with red quilting thread and looked at my friends.

"I got a letter from an attorney in LA this morning asking me to call him." I told them about Harriet's death and my surprise at being named executor of her will after such a long estrangement. "The creepy thing is, she was dead for more than ten months before her body was discovered."

"How awful!" Birdie, naturally predisposed to worry about people, frowned and twisted the end of her long white braid. Birdie was in her seventies and looked like Mother Earth. She always wore the same thing: white T-shirt (short sleeves in summer, long sleeves in winter), denim overalls, and Birkenstock sandals (with socks) to accommodate her arthritic knees.

Lucy handed me a cup of coffee with milk. "You must have been close, for her to make you executor. Yet, I don't think I ever heard you mention her name before."

"We were best friends growing up." I told them how our teenage friendship didn't survive our adult lifestyles. "After I moved to Encino, my West LA friends forgot about me, including Harriet."

Lucy shook her head. "Well, obviously, she didn't forget about you. Do you know what happened to the husband?"

"I really don't know any details. I have to see the lawyer this afternoon in order to get poor Harriet buried. The lawyer said he'd explain everything then."

Birdie tilted her head. "So you've decided to go through with becoming the executor? Without knowing what's involved?"

How could I say this without sounding morbid? "Let's just say I want to do one last favor for an old friend."

And I'm curious.

Lucy narrowed her eyes. "Uh-oh. Please tell me you're not going to get involved in another one of *those* again."

Lucy's voice was more than a tad disapproving as she alluded to my recent penchant for discovering dead bodies and getting sucked into murder investigations. And both times the killers came after me.

"This is way different, Lucy. First of all, the attorney never said we were talking about murder here. Second of all, being the executor of someone's estate only involves signing papers and selling stuff. There's nothing to worry about. What could be more straightforward?"

My redheaded friend shivered slightly. "You know, Martha, I'm getting a strong feeling about this."

Lucy swore she had ESP and could tell when something bad was going to happen. In the past, I dismissed her feelings as some kind of displaced anxiety. But if I were completely honest, I'd have to admit that in the last several months her warnings turned out to be real. Still, the lawyer gave no indication that poor Harriet's death was anything more than tragically premature.

"Oh, for heaven's sake, Lucy. Don't you think I've learned my lesson? Don't you think I'd run straight to the police at the first sign of something suspicious?"

Without hesitating, Lucy and Birdie responded in unison, "No!"